THE MORTICIAN'S WIFE

LINDA COOKSON

ISBN: 154885865X
ISBN 13: 9781548858650
Library of Congress Control Number: 2017911074
CreateSpace Independent Publishing Platform
North Charleston, South Carolina

For Robert Craig

CHAPTER 1

The first time I saw him was at a funeral.

My grandmother's best friend, Patsy, had died. Normally, Grande went to funerals by herself, and believe me, she went to a lot. I was chauffeuring her that day because she swore she shouldn't be driving since she'd just had cataract surgery, which in my opinion was a lame excuse. I really think she simply needed someone to comfort her from the loss of her close friend. My mom was out of town, and Grande's other friends were, in her view, too judgmental toward Patsy, so she felt she needed me for support. And I didn't want her to go alone.

I rather liked Patsy (Mrs. Grover to me). She'd been my third-grade teacher, so we had a history all our own. The thing was, she'd been having an affair with a married man. Grande and I had discussed the situation several times, but she just seemed to take the approach that it wasn't her sin. She understood Patsy and Harvey's need for each other, whereas her other friends were offended by Patsy's lack of shame and her ease of speaking of her debauchery.

As I drove us to the mortuary, Grande's hands were knotted in her lap. She said, "They almost act as if Patsy should go straight to hell. That she's the only woman who's ever done something like this. I know for a fact that Birdie was promoted to office manager because she lifted her skirt for her boss. She told me so."

"Boy, what a hypocrite."

"She doesn't see it that way. Her boss wasn't married, and neither was she at the time."

She sighed and then looked straight ahead, making no further comment. I parked the car, and we entered the funeral home. The sickeningly sweet smell of flowers, the soft, mournful music, and, of course, the casket seemed to bear down on us. I glanced at Grande's pale face and was glad that I'd come with her. As we walked to our seats to sit with the family, I sheepishly waved to her judgmental friends as I trailed behind her.

The service was mediocre. The organist seemed to lose the tempo. The soloist was rather high and screechy, but I can't sing myself, so I shouldn't say a thing. I held Grande's hand and tried my best not to wince at the preacher's sermon. He made Mrs. Grover out to be Mother Teresa. Granted, she was a fine woman, a great teacher, but certainly no saint. Obviously, no one had told him about Harvey. Even Grande flinched a few times.

When it came time to view the body, we'd already been told to wait until after the service. Mrs. Grover's daughter had said Grande could have her own private viewing since she'd been unable to attend visitation night. We waited until the family was in the receiving line before going forward. I linked my arm with Grande's, for both moral and physical support.

Looking down at Mrs. Grover, I had to bite the inside of my cheek to keep from laughing. She'd never had eyebrows, or else they were so light they were unnoticeable. Either way, she'd always drawn them on. Now her brows were so high and dark she looked startled—as if surprised by her death or the fact that Harvey had come to her funeral with his wife in tow. No matter, I could barely hold myself together.

Grande simply stared, until I thought she'd gone to sleep or her cataracts had clouded back over. That was the moment he came to us. He took Grande's hand.

"I'm John, and I'm very sorry for your loss."

Grande finally looked up, but no words came out of her mouth. Then he looked at me. I couldn't open my mouth for fear I'd howl with mirth.

Bless his heart—he could see that I was going to make a fool of myself. He gently took my arm and led us out a side door. I broke down in fits of laughter. Even Grande seemed amused. Waving my hands in front of my face, I finally said, "Her eyebrows did me in."

"The makeup person got married and quit. My mother took over until the position is filled. Obviously, she doesn't have the touch."

Wiping my eyes, I said, "No, she doesn't. Her makeup was appalling."

I then looked at Grande. That's when it happened. We both broke down sobbing. Went into the ugly cry: our faces became red and blotchy, our eyes swollen and makeup smeared, our noses running like faucets.

John patted my grandmother and handed us a box of tissues. Once we had our cry, I blew my nose and looked at him to say thank you. That's when I really, truly saw him. He was divine. I swallowed several times while gawking at his amazing face. He was all the things a warm-blooded female could want. Broad shoulders. Gorgeous face. Amazing hair, thick and dark. Beautiful smile. Obviously, a kind, kind heart.

His suit was impeccable. Expensive and fitted to perfection. I wanted to lean into him. Lay my head on his shoulder. Smell his neck.

Thankfully, he was talking to Grande, so he didn't notice my ogle or the desire that was surely showing in my eyes. Now he was apologizing for the tacky makeup job. Grande looked at me inquisitively. I knew what she was thinking, so I shook my head. I wasn't going down that road. Not for one minute. As a cosmetologist myself, I was quite qualified for the job. I owned a salon and had my own makeup line: M. E. Cosmetic. M. E. were my initials—Macie Emerson.

Dead people were not on my agenda, though.

Grande, thankfully, didn't say anything. She and I managed to pull ourselves together and blew our noses again. John said his name for a second time, but I didn't tell him mine. I only wanted the hell out of there. I'd already made quite an ass of myself. And if I stayed any longer, who knew what I'd do or say to him.

That evening Grande called; she couldn't sleep. I had insomnia, too, so I was awake myself. She wanted to talk about Patsy's funeral and was concerned about her own funeral as well.

"Please promise me that you'll do my makeup. I can't bear the thought of lying in a casket looking like that. She looked quite ridiculous. Did John call you?"

"No. Why would he?"

"Because I saw the way he looked at you…at your legs, but your skirt was a little short."

"It was not."

Grande laughed. "There was something between you two."

"It was the whole funeral thing. He felt sorry for us and contrite about the horrific makeup job."

"Which brings me back to why I called. I don't want to spend all eternity with bad makeup."

Even though I knew better, I made the promise.

After Grande's call, I couldn't sleep. Couldn't stop thinking about everything that had happened. OK. Honestly, it was the man. John. I couldn't quit thinking about him. The way he'd treated Grande. His kindness. The way he looked in that dark suit with his tie knotted so perfectly at his throat. He was hot, and he was young. Probably only a few years older than me. I guessed him at maybe thirty. And I couldn't ignore the way he'd looked at me. He must've thought I was crazy with my roller-coaster emotions. Laughing my ass off, and then crying my eyes out. Shit, I blew my nose at least three times. How embarrassing. What was he doing working at a mortuary? I decided to Google the Harnon Funeral Home. Maybe he was mentioned on the web page.

The website was well done. Professional and somewhat elegant in a weird sort of way. I read the home page. Family owned. Had been in business for seventy-two years here in Warner Robins, Georgia. Started by Josiah Harnon (deceased). Taken over by his son, Jacob Harnon (deceased). Now owned by his son, John Harnon. Must be young John's dad. That explained a lot. He had been born into the business. I could live with that. He was probably only working there that day to help his parents out by pushing the casket into place and driving the hearse to the cemetery. He said there'd been some turnover. Shit happens.

Reading further, I learned that seven years ago Jacob had bought land and built the current mortuary on Covet Lane. The website showed pictures of the old building and the new building. I scrolled back to the picture of the old building. Obviously, the family living quarters were above the mortuary. That was something that always bothered me. In the past the mortician and his family had slept above the dead souls below. Talk about eerie. Goose bumps popped instantly on my arms, making me shiver. I scrolled down to look at pictures of Josiah, then Jacob, and then John's dad. But it wasn't John's dad. It was him.

Holy shit.

John was a mortician.

CHAPTER 2

I had two weddings to work on Saturday. The first was an early afternoon wedding, and the second an evening wedding. The first bride was on her second marriage. She talked shamefully about her first husband, and then she and her two bridesmaids gossiped (unkindly) about some mutual friends. I was never so glad as when that job was done.

For the second job, my team and I worked our butts off. We styled hair and applied makeup on fifteen women. Lucy, a cute, little Asian thing, was speedy. Valley was great at keeping nervous brides under control, although with her red hair and fiery attitude, you'd think just the opposite. Both had worked for me for four years. We had a system down pat.

I sold bride packages in several different price ranges. The second bride had picked the most expensive (the Bride's Dream), which included drinks and finger food…almost like a party before the wedding. We finished a little after five, cleaned up the shop, and drove to an upscale restaurant. Hungry and worn out, we inhaled our first drinks. Even though I paid my team generously and made a nice sum myself, we were starting to rethink the bride packages. I thought perhaps Lucy might want to take the brides over if I should decide to give it up, but I knew Valley would quit when I did.

Lucy surprised me though when she said she was sick of brides and all their neuroses. "Every woman wants a perfect wedding, but these women carry it too far. I wanted to slap that bride and her mother today."

I laughed. Maybe it was time for us to quit. All three of us were burned out.

Back home, Grande called to invite me to bunco the next week. I'd gone before and always enjoyed myself, but for some reason, I knew there was an ulterior motive this time. Usually when they invited me, it was a last-minute invitation because someone couldn't be there. This was too planned.

"Who can't make it?" I asked.

"Birdie."

I could ask a hundred questions, but why? "OK. I'll plan on being there."

Monday, I restocked product, prepared my station for the week, and handled the clerical part of my business. I owned the salon, but the other hairdressers rented their own stations. That kept me out of their business, and I wasn't responsible for keeping them busy. My booth rent was on the higher end, but my salon was in a high-traffic area. I knew I'd snagged a lucrative location.

As I restocked the makeup, I was more than happy with my sales for the last week. My makeup line was starting to take off, mainly by word of mouth. It wasn't overpriced, and it had a wide selection of color options. I wanted to focus all my attention just on the salon and my makeup line. I'd thought that the weddings would be a good way to promote my makeup, and I'd certainly been right about that. Even though brides were neurotic on their wedding days, they still noticed the blending wonders of this makeup.

Tuesday and Wednesday, I cut and colored hair all day, so I was ready for good wine, a little food, and juicy gossip. Supposedly, the bunco hostess was only to provide snacks, but I'd learned from previous times not to eat before I went. The snacks ended up being a small meal, and the drinks...well, it was more like a drunko party than bunco.

The age range was wide, but I was the youngest. Four of the women were in their thirties and forties; the rest were older. I liked every one of them. They got me liquored up and then ganged up against me. Wanted me to promise to do their makeup at their funerals. I glared at Grande;

she simply smiled. I'd promised her, but I certainly didn't want to promise any of them.

Cathy was the one who changed my mind. She had breast cancer; we all knew she probably wasn't going to make it through this time. When she took me aside and pleaded with me, I told her, "I don't really think I can do it. It's not something I'm cut out for."

"Touching a dead body?"

"Something like that."

She took my hand and laid it against her face. She closed her eyes and became very still. Then she looked at me. "It won't be any different than that. I don't want my children or my young granddaughter to see me dead and looking ridiculous."

For some reason this resonated with me. I swallowed several times and nodded. But deep down I knew I'd regret having agreed to this.

That Friday, Grande called to tell me that her neighbor had passed away. "That makes two. One more, and then I'll be done with funerals for a while."

Grande believed funerals came in threes. Because of that, it seemed as if they did for her.

"It's at the old mortuary across town. I hate that place, but he did a prearranged funeral several years ago, so he's stuck going there."

"I'm sure it'll be fine, Grande. He won't know the difference."

Two weeks later, the third person died. Grande called, almost relieved that it'd happened and the chain of three was over. Also, the funeral was at Harnon Funeral Home, which was on her side of town. She said, "The woman who cleans my house...it's her mother-in-law."

"Did you know her?"

"Nope. Never met her."

I wondered if that really counted as one of the three, but Grande was determined to attend the funeral, so it would.

Two days later she called to tell me about the funeral. "My God, Macie, this woman's makeup was terrible."

"I thought you'd never met her."

"I hadn't, but I knew she couldn't have looked that bad. Her makeup was pancake thick, and she looked like death."

I laughed.

"I saw that young man there again. He asked about you."

"He did?"

"I didn't tell him much of anything because I was ready to get out of there and meet your mom for lunch."

She didn't sound very sympathetic to her cleaning lady, but who was I to judge?

"He asked if you were seeing anyone. I told him you were and that Chance was extremely cute. Eye candy in every way. He asked if you were serious. I told him you weren't. You were just waiting for something better to come along. The end was imminent."

"Bloody hell, Grande."

"Well, that's the truth. I also told him I wasn't crazy about Chance at all."

"I thought you said you didn't tell him much."

"I didn't. I didn't tell him your name or anything about you. You know, Macie, he's very charming and quite a looker."

I couldn't disagree with any of that.

The next two weekends, I did nothing but weddings. All the brides had bought the Bride's Dream, which meant we worked while they all ate and drank. Because of my work schedule, Chance was feeling rejected even though we'd gotten together during the week. Wednesday, he came into the salon for a (free) haircut and asked about Friday night.

I said, "That'll probably work. I'll call you Friday afternoon; we'll see where we're at."

After he left, I wondered why we weren't more compatible. I knew it wasn't going to work for us, which was sad because he was so darn cute.

His eyes alone could make me do almost anything. His thick hair was the color of wheat but had the most fantastic copper highlights. I'd never seen more beautiful hair on a man. Our sex life was just ok; Chance was a rather lazy lover. Really, I think he was unsure of himself. Maybe I was too demanding. I knew what I wanted and wasn't afraid to ask for it.

Our biggest issue, though, was finances. I wasn't a bitch about money. I paid for our meals and evenings out as often as he did. I definitely made more than him, so I never expected him to pay for everything. But I wasn't a stupid ass either. On more than one occasion, I knew he used me. I paid to have his truck repaired (new transmission) when he was short of funds, and I'd paid for a trip to Vegas that he'd planned. He liked to brag to his friends about his "rich girlfriend." On one hand, he was proud of the fact; on the other, it was as if he felt threatened by it. I wasn't rich by any means, but I certainly had more disposable income than any of his buddies or their girlfriends.

Another problem we had was his jealousy. And honestly, I made him jealous quite often even though I'd never been unfaithful myself. When he confessed that he had, I already knew (gut instinct). I didn't take it personally, and that alone probably said a lot about our relationship. Since he was so insecure with me, with us, and especially with himself, he wanted to use his joystick to prove himself.

Friday afternoon, we made plans for dinner and a movie. Both of us knew it would be our last date. I wasn't giving, lending, or spending any more money on him. I guess he felt the same for me. I did plan on sleeping with him one more time, though. A good-bye, adios, so-long-amigo, farewell fuck.

I dressed in a black lace top with a zebra-print cami underneath and boyfriend jeans. The tops of my breasts were revealed quite nicely through the lace mesh. *Thank you, Mom and God, for these fantastic boobs.* Lucy had highlighted my hair two days ago, and Valley had given me a trim earlier that day, so it looked amazing as it brushed the tops of my shoulders.

Driving to the restaurant that he'd picked, which was rather expensive—as in we'd actually have a waitress and would need to leave a tip—I suggested we go dutch. He considered and then dropped his eyes to my cleavage. He licked his lower lip and said, "I'll pay. I want to end on a good note with you."

I laughed to myself because he was paying for something I'd already decided to give him for free. (Stupid man.)

Our meal was pleasant, and the movie was great. I liked action movies, and for once the actor was naked, whereas the actress kept her clothes on. Before leaving, we used the restrooms. He said he'd wait out front since it always took me longer.

I'd just started down the hall to return to him when I looked up and, much to my surprise, saw John standing there. As I walked up to him, his mouth dropped open. I said, "John."

He grabbed my arm as if he'd been looking for me forever. I again said his name, never taking my eyes from his lovely face or his ice-blue eyes.

"My God. It's you." He took a lock of my hair and rubbed it between his fingers. Then he touched my face. "I don't even know your name."

"Macie Emerson."

He slowly said my name. The way it rolled off his tongue and fell from his mouth was so moving that my eyes locked onto his full, generous lips, which were so kissable that I felt such a need inside me, a craving so strong that I thought I really would collapse. We stood staring at each other until he finally said, "Are you alone?"

"No. I'm on a date. We're breaking up tonight, though. This is just a parting-of-the-ways date."

"Where is he?"

"Out front waiting for me."

"Don't go to him."

I laughed. "Now, John."

"What are you doing tomorrow night?"

"I have to work."

"How about Sunday?"

"I have a date with the neighbor kids." An idea hit. "Do you Rollerblade?"

"Yeah. I'm not bad, either."

"Show up at my house Sunday around two with your Rollerblades. You can go with us."

He smiled. My lord. I could've died happy from that alone.

"What's your address?"

I fished in my purse for paper, but he handed me his business card. As I was handing it back, Chance appeared and said, "I wondered what the holdup was."

He looked from me to John. I turned to face Chance and, unseen by him, slipped my hand into John's. I introduced them; they nodded at each other like two Indian chiefs. Chance had no reason to be upset because we both knew that it was over, but he copped an attitude quite quickly. He grabbed my arm and said, "Let's go, Macie. I'm ready to get you home." His meaning was quite clear.

John leaned down and whispered in my ear, "Please don't sleep with him tonight."

Touched, I decided right then: Chance was dropping me off at the door. I guess his dinner deal wasn't a bargain for him after all.

Saturday's work was intense for Lucy, Valley, and me, but the wedding party was a joy to work with. The bride's grandmother took me aside and slipped me an envelope—a special tip, which I thought was truly sweet of her. But I might just let it be said that I'd done an amazing job on her hair. And her makeup—perfection.

When we finished at six, though, we were ready to be done.

The next day, I couldn't wait to see if John would show for our rather weird first date. The neighbor boys (two teenagers) were waiting for me when I walked out the door. Our skating together began innocently enough. Their mothers simply didn't want them out by themselves. Now that they were older, the mothers didn't care, but we'd formed a bond. I enjoyed their young antics, and I guess they liked the shape of my butt.

We were warming up and horsing around while waiting for a couple more of their friends to show when John pulled into my drive. I was curious to see what kind of car he drove but wasn't prepared for the Ferrari. My neighbor boys were speechless, and I was too.

Once John emerged from the car, it suddenly seemed quite simple compared to him. Dressed in long shorts and a tight T-shirt, he walked toward me and kissed me lightly on the forehead. I introduced him to JJ and Kurt. He shook their hands as they fired question after question about the car. (I realized my yellow Mazda Miata was no longer a big deal in their eyes.) He answered a few of their questions, then turned to me, and winked. Warmth spread all the way through me.

Three other teenagers showed up: two guys, one girl. I knew the girl and one of the guys. Again, the guys had to discuss the car; then we got on with our afternoon. I was an above-average skater, as was John. His body was muscled and cut, making me sweat more than normal.

As we were coming back to the house, he grabbed my hand and smiled at me. "Thanks for asking me today."

I slowed down until we had both stopped. I stared at him until he said, "Don't look at me like that. It only makes me want to kiss you. I don't want our first kiss to be in front of a bunch of horny teenage boys."

I laughed because, when I looked around, the guys were all watching us. Back at the house, JJ and Kurt invited him to join them again. It was obvious that I didn't even need to be there for the invitation to stand. I cocked an eyebrow at Kurt, but he grinned and shrugged his shoulders.

John and I removed our Rollerblades and were walking to the house when his phone went off. He looked at it and groaned. He answered, but the whole time his eyes were on me. He said yes a couple of times, and as he repeated an address, he looked at me with regret. After hanging up, he said, "I need to pick up a body. I'm sorry to end our first date this way. This isn't usual, but it isn't unusual either. I mean, we could go out twenty times and this wouldn't happen again, or it could happen the next time we're together."

"I understand." And I really did. I'd already decided I wanted to date John. And with that decision came the acceptance of his life. He was a funeral director, mortician, undertaker. All titles meaning one and the same thing: he worked with dead people. That's what he did. It was who he was, but it was only one part of him. It was the rest of him that I wanted.

That said, I'd be lying if I didn't admit that the whole dead-people, mortician thing freaked me out. I mean, come on, who was I kidding? The gross factor was over the top. Something I'd never considered myself to ever be remotely close to other than going to a funeral.

He asked, "Can I call you when I get back home tonight?"

"Yes. No matter how late. Call me."

His call came three hours later. I was relieved because I hadn't been able to quit thinking about him. That he was dealing with a dead person made me ache for him. All the things he must be feeling and working through seemed unimaginable to me.

"Macie, I'm really sorry for leaving you like that. Please let me make it up to you."

"You don't need to make anything up. How are you doing? Are you OK?"

"What do you mean?"

"You know, the dead person and all."

"Oh, that. It went OK. No problems whatsoever."

I waited for him to say more but finally accepted he wasn't comfortable sharing something so private with me.

He said, "Are you busy tomorrow night?"

"Tomorrow's good."

The next day, I could hardly think; I was so distracted with the thought of seeing him but was able to accomplish my normal Monday routine at the salon. Back at the house, I dressed for our date. I have an eccentric way of dressing, so I tried to tone down my wild side. Most hairdressers tend to be somewhat unconventional dressers—at least, most of the ones in my salon were. When I opened the door to him, his eyes roamed over me. I couldn't tell if I was still too much or if I'd hit a home run. But man, he sure hit a homer. He looked as if he'd just walked off the cover of *GQ* magazine.

Once in his Ferrari, I couldn't help asking about it. His explanation: he felt he owed it to himself...deserved it. That wasn't the kind of answer I'd been expecting, but I guess if I worked with death every day, I might want to drive something remarkable when I was out in the living world. He took me to a restaurant that I'd never been to. The prices weren't even on the menu. We ordered and sipped wine, which made us both loosen up a little.

He said, "I know absolutely nothing about you, so can we start with you? Then I'll fill you in on myself."

I laughed. "Sure. What do you want to know?"

"Just start talking."

"OK. Let's see. I'm an only child. I went to cosmetology school and then got a BA in business. I bought my grandmother's salon. You've met her twice now."

He nodded.

"After I bought her place, the city came in and widened the road. All the businesses on the north side were bought out. I received one hell of a settlement, which made it easy for me to get a business loan and relocate to Wood Borough Plaza. I purchased the land and built a building. I own Wood Borough Salon and have my own makeup line."

I could tell he was impressed as he touched his glass to mine.

"Macie, you're really quite something. I thought I had you pegged the first day I met you. You seemed to be a girly girl with your short skirt, high heels, and jewelry. At the movies, you were dressed in that see-through getup and had a bow in your hair."

"It wasn't see through."

He raised his eyebrows and said, "You bat your beautiful sapphire eyes at me and then invite me to Rollerblade. I thought you were quite the tomboy. Now, I find out you're this successful businesswoman. I'll admit, when I saw your house, I thought you were probably a spoiled trust-fund kid. Never worked for a thing in your life."

I truly was at a loss for words and slightly pissed, but I finally said, "I told you I had to work Saturday."

"I know, but I thought you were going out with Pretty Boy again and just didn't want to admit it."

"I don't lie," I said rather rudely. "I would've told you if I was seeing him again."

"How old are you?"

"I just turned twenty-eight. How old are you, John?"

"Twenty-nine."

"And you already *own* a funeral home?"

"I took it over when my father died a couple of years after I was out of college."

I waited for him to continue. It was his turn; I wasn't going to pull the info from him.

"I don't know if you remember, but our funeral home burned down several years ago. Dad rebuilt it with the insurance money."

I actually did remember the incident now that he had brought it up. There were so many uncouth jokes about the free cremations and about whether the firemen should have rescued the bodies inside.

"Anyway, I took over after his death. It was already running smoothly, so I really didn't do much but move to the head of the class. Mom helps, as you know." He grinned at me. "I was able to find another makeup person. I can do it myself, but I hate it. I have one brother, Charlie. You might've seen him at the funeral. He works there too. He isn't right. He's extremely good help, but he's..."

I could tell he was searching for the right words. I took his hand, squeezing it with encouragement. The waitress arrived with our salads, so the moment was paused.

He peppered his salad vigorously and said, "Charlie's slow. Looking at him, you can't tell anything's wrong, which is a blessing and a curse.

Women think he's hot but then realize that he isn't normal. He's the most caring and gentle person I know."

"I hope I can meet him and your mother."

He sighed with relief and smiled beautifully at me. After eating a bite of salad, he asked, "What do your parents do? Are they still together?"

"My parents have been together forever. Dad's a chemist. That's how I was able to get my own makeup line; he developed the formula. Mom's a dental hygienist."

"God. I couldn't do that all day. Stick my hands in other people's mouths."

I choked on my salad and put my napkin to my mouth. I took several sips of water. "I can't believe that came out of your mouth."

"What?" he asked. He actually looked puzzled, as if he couldn't make the connection.

"You...of all people. I mean, you work with dead people, for goodness' sake."

"I know. That's just it. They're dead. She's working with stinky, gross mouths." He shuddered. "I could never do that or be a podiatrist, proctologist, or nasal surgeon."

I laughed. Mom would love this. "I'd let you tell her that, but they're busy moving Dad's father back from Wisconsin."

Our meal was so good that I was in a state of bliss. My fish was possibly the best I'd ever had, and the risotto was divine. Afterward, we strolled around the shops for a few minutes to enjoy the cool evening and then drove back to my house. I offered him several different beverage choices. He selected a beer, so I had the same. We sat on the couch facing each other. He said, "So tell me about this Chance guy."

"There's nothing to tell. We aren't together anymore."

"How long did you date?"

"About six months or so. He's a cheater. I won't allow that."

"So why did it take you so long to break up?"

I shrugged. Enough about Chance. "Tell me about your last girlfriend."

"Robin liked my money but didn't like what I did for a living. She was always ashamed to admit she dated a mortician. She could've handled me being a drug lord easier. And then there was Charlie. She never wanted to be around him."

"How long were you together?"

"A little over a year."

"Did you love her?"

"It's pretty hard to love someone who's embarrassed of you and your family."

"Now I'm asking you the same thing you asked me. Why did it take you so long to break up?"

He thought for a moment. "I wanted to change her mind about Charlie."

I nodded. "Who else?"

"No one really that I was ever serious about. Well, there was someone in high school, but she died."

"Oh gosh. I'm sorry."

"She ran track. At first they thought she'd died of heat exhaustion, but they discovered she had some underlying heart condition, which triggered a lethal arrhythmia."

"God, that's awful."

He nodded and said, "How many other ex-boyfriends do you have out there?"

I laughed. "Too many to count. They leave because I'm not available a lot during the wedding season. Men aren't very understanding creatures."

"Well, I am."

We smiled at each other. The rest of the evening, we talked about our childhoods; he shared more about Charlie. One thing was perfectly clear: Charlie was a high priority in his life. He felt responsible for him and his mother. I didn't want to ask too many personal questions, but I got the distinct impression that either he wasn't close to his dad or something had happened in the end to sever their goodwill toward each other.

At midnight, he stood to leave. I walked him to the door. He pulled me into his arms, and my hands immediately went into his hair. Honestly, I'd been waiting for that moment ever since I saw him at the movies. When his lips touched mine, I knew that I'd do anything to make it work with him. If I didn't care so much about what he thought of me, I would've taken him to my bed, but I wanted to prolong the sexual tension for a little while longer.

When he pulled away, he said, "I've wanted to do that since the first time we met at the funeral. I really haven't been able to get you out of my head. Your pretty face. Your gorgeous eyes, which made me so sad when they were full of tears. Your lovely hair. Your sexy body."

He took a breath and asked, "When can I see you again?"

I was so flush from his little speech that my voice seemed nothing more than a whisper. "I'm free tomorrow night and Thursday night."

"OK then, tomorrow night." He kissed me again. I believe he was waiting for me to make the next move, make the offer, but I held strong. I didn't want to be a second-date whore.

CHAPTER 3

The next morning, I woke to find a text on my phone.

"I enjoyed last night. Can't wait to see you tonight."

How sweet. I liked this guy.

That evening he took me to a sushi bar. I didn't love sushi but didn't hate it either. He quite adored it, though. Afterward, we drove around for a while and then went back to my place. He again wanted to talk about my previous boyfriends—almost as if he thought I was still pining for someone. Also, he seemed concerned that I'd date someone else while I was dating him.

"I want you to know that I'm an exclusive dater. I only date one woman at a time."

"OK. That's nice to know."

He stared at me as if waiting for me to continue. Finally, he said, "I'd like to know that you're the same way. When you tell me that you have something else to do, like tomorrow night, I want to know that it's not another man."

"I wouldn't do that. I already told you how I felt about cheaters. I have a huge shipment coming in tomorrow afternoon. I simply want to get it inventoried and put away."

He sighed with relief. "I just don't want to play games. I knew the first time I saw you that I wanted to be with you. I simply don't want any bullshit."

"OK. No bullshit." I slid over beside him, and we spent the rest of the evening kissing, talking, and laughing.

The next morning his text read, "You're an amazing kisser. Can't wait until my lips are on yours again."

Thursday night was a repeat. We went out to eat and came back to my place. Toward the end of the evening, I could tell that he was antsy, wanting to crawl into bed. He had his hands inside my top, rubbing my back, and he kept running his fingers under my bra strap. I had the worst case of PMS and certainly didn't want our first time to be less than perfect. I finally decided that honesty would probably help defuse the situation.

"John, I know you think I'm putting you off, and I guess in a way I am. The thing is, I'm not one hundred percent this week, and next week I really won't be in the mood either, so if you could just wait until next Saturday, I'll be good to go."

He smiled. "Got it. Thanks for letting me know."

All the tension between us eased once a date had been set.

His text the next morning: "You're worth the wait."

That weekend was crazy busy with weddings. Saturday morning, I arrived early to set up the food and drinks. I purchased bagels and different spreads and provided mimosas, coffee, and tea for the morning group. For the afternoon group, I provided bite-size sandwiches and two different wines. For some reason these two groups didn't eat much of the food. Instead of going out like we usually did, Valley, Lucy, and I ate the leftovers.

By Sunday afternoon, I was totally worn out. Not only was I sick of brides, but I had horrible cramps. As I soaked my tired body in the bathtub, I couldn't help thinking about how well I'd done that weekend. I'd made a killing on the bride packages, and I'd sold several makeup kits. Once women had seen how great this makeup was and how wonderful they looked, they wanted some of the miraculous stuff for themselves.

John came over that evening with pizza. I was so grateful to him and so glad to see him that I really could've cried. He was so supportive of my business and didn't give me any shit for not being with him.

The rest of the week, we spent evenings together, learning more about each other. Every morning I'd find the sweetest text on my phone. One that made me smile read, "Mom & Charlie are anxious to meet you but I'm keeping you to myself for a while longer."

I really was anxious to meet his family, but he hadn't offered yet. My parents were still in Wisconsin, but the moment they returned, I was going to introduce them.

Friday night, John and I went to a movie, and I went to bed early. I had another big day Saturday, and then my wedding season would be over. Before he left, though, he wanted to make sure we were still on for the next day. I knew he was just as anxious for it as I was.

"I want to take you to a new restaurant that opened a couple of months ago. Then we can come back here."

I laughed. "Now, think about it. Once you step foot in this door, I'm not letting you leave until I've had my way with you. I should finish the last wedding party at four. I'll get home at around five, shower, and then wait for you. That's my plan."

He grinned. "That works for me."

His morning text: "I'm dying here. The hours are dragging."

My last group for the season was really a joy. She was a first-time bride and was so excited to get married. I loved her happiness and her hope for the future. By the time we finished, though, I only had one thing on my mind. I could hardly breathe; I was so ready.

In the shower I was giddy with excitement, and I wondered how John was feeling. I decided to dress as if I were going out on a date. When he rang the doorbell, I ran to the door and threw it open. He stood there, gorgeous and sexy, holding a bouquet of flowers. My knees felt weak as I pressed my nose into the blossoms. Dropping them on the table in the foyer, I pulled John inside and put my mouth on his.

He wanted to take things slow, which was new for me. I wasn't used to men taking the time for foreplay. He didn't even try to undress me at first; he simply kissed my neck and ran his tongue along my chin. He nibbled my earlobe and kissed the end of my nose. By the time he took me into the bedroom, I was so ready that I could hardly speak. I undressed him first; then he undressed me. We stared at each other, and he slowly lowered me onto the bed. He kissed me and teased me until I was almost out of my mind. When he entered me, I almost wept with joy. He made love to me in a way I'd never had before. He waited for me, and when I cried out, he didn't come in a heated rush but only satisfied me yet again. But when I came the second time, he did come quickly, as if he was barely hanging on.

The sex was intense, but it was more than that...more than anything I could define. We connected on some level that I'd never experienced before. I was totally drained yet totally alive.

He laid his head next to mine and said, "Macie, I love you. I'll wait until you're ready, but I'm going to marry you."

We raided my fridge and then made love again; he left around one. I told him he could spend the night, but he chose not to. He seemed to think that my neighbors would be bothered if he slept over. I didn't want to confess that Chance had stayed several times. I told him, "We can put your car in the garage."

He thought about it but then decided against it.

In the morning I found the flowers rather limp and unhappy in the foyer. I stuck them in a vase and dropped an aspirin in the water. Maybe they'd perk back up. I grabbed my phone, anxious to read his message, which I knew would be there. He didn't disappoint me.

"OMG Macie OMG."

Well, that said it all for me too.

From that night on, we were together. Thursday, he came to the shop so I could introduce him to Lucy, Valley, and the rest of the hairdressers. Also, I wanted to cut his hair. The women were quite impressed with my new guy. Most didn't blink an eye when I told them he was a funeral director. I chose my words carefully. "Funeral director" sounded like someone who directed funerals, whereas "mortician" and "undertaker" brought up images of cadavers (at least they did for me). I told them this tidbit after they met him. I knew once they laid eyes on him, he could've been anything (even a drug lord) and they wouldn't have cared.

Once I had him seated in my chair, I did what I always do with a first-time client. I combed through his hair to see how it fell naturally, and then I ran my hands through it. On him I did this longer than I normally would. I asked him if he wanted anything different. He didn't really know. I thought he should have a little more taken off the top and a little less off the bottom. I knew he wanted a neat collar line, but he didn't need to wear his hair that short.

I leaned him back and washed his hair while I stared at his wonderful face. I could have shampooed him the rest of the day, but even I knew this was getting ridiculous. His hair was fantastic, dark and thick, but he had a serious cowlick in the back. I finally sat him up and began cutting, taking extra care with his wayward tuft of hair. I gave him some new styling product and showed him how to use it. His hair had never looked better. Well, at least since I'd known him.

The next morning, he called instead of texting. "What did you do to my hair?"

I cleared my throat. "Didn't it lay down in the back like it should?"

"I didn't spend one second on it. It fell into place…like…all by itself."

I laughed.

"You're one hell of a hairdresser. Can you cut my hair from now on?"

"Of course."

"OK, but next time I want to pay you. I don't expect you to do it for free."

"I'm not charging you. You're my boyfriend. I don't want to argue about this. Let me do this one thing for you. Please."

"OK, but I usually get my hair cut every three weeks. You know, with my job and all, I need to look clean cut all the time."

"That won't be a problem. I'll always work you in. By the way, my parents are back. I want you to meet them, so could you plan on Sunday dinner at their house?"

"Sunday dinner it is."

That night he bombarded me with questions about my parents. I didn't want to spend the evening discussing them. There wasn't any doubt; I knew they'd like him and he'd like them. My parents were fun and open minded. They hadn't blinked an eye when I told them John owned a funeral home.

He picked me up Sunday. On the drive over to my parents', his hands were tense on the steering wheel. I wanted to ease his nerves but decided to let him stew in his own thoughts.

My dad immediately put him at ease, especially when John tried to be formal.

"Call us Marty and Deena."

Wine was poured, and my parents never stopped talking. John laid his hand on my knee as he sipped his wine. I watched him and saw my parents through his eyes. Here were two people who loved each other, enjoyed each other's jokes, and just wanted the best for each other. Both were attractive. Slender from working out every morning (together, of course). Mom had great arms, so she always wore tops that showed them off.

Obviously, I did their hair. Mom's was shoulder length and highlighted. Dad's was dyed, but that was a secret I did for him there in his bathroom.

Soon Mom was telling John how they met. "I was working part time at Macy's. Marty came in to buy his mom a Christmas gift. We saw each other, and that was it. He proposed on Valentine's Day; we married in June. A year and a half later, we had Macie."

John looked at me wide eyed. I leaned into him. "Yes, I was named after the department store where they met. Very original, don't you think? They spelled it differently to fool people."

He laughed hard. "I was totally fooled."

Dad said, "When you find the right person, you just know. The minute I saw Deena, I knew I'd marry her. She was eighteen; I was twenty. Both of us were in college, but our parents didn't object, and when little Macie was born, they loved babysitting. We've been very blessed."

I said, "OK, enough about all this."

John turned to me. "I like hearing all about your life. It's nice to see a couple who fell in love and stayed that way through all the ups and downs." He looked at my dad. "I know exactly what you mean about finding the right person."

Mom smiled sweetly at John. He'd obviously won her over. She said, "My mother was quite impressed with you and your mortuary. She's a funeral devotee."

Dad laughed. "That's an understatement if I ever heard one."

"Well, she is." Turning from my dad back to John, she said, "She thinks you're a great mortician. That's a career that people can be rather judgmental about. Not everyone could do that job. It takes a special person. You seem like a very caring and understanding man."

His morning text: "Loved your parents. Your mom's so young and beautiful."

Soon it would be my turn to win his mom's approval.

CHAPTER 4

Marabeth was well fed and wore an outdated hairstyle, but I liked her immediately. Charlie was drop-dead gorgeous, almost better looking than his brother. He took an instant liking to me, which I was grateful for. John had warned me that he would seem very normal and then something strange would fly from his mouth. He didn't know how to filter, so if he thought someone was pretty or fat or rude, he'd tell that person. John assured me this didn't happen with strangers, or else he wouldn't be working at the funeral home. It only happened when he felt comfortable with a person.

He became comfortable with me by the end of the meal. With his mouth full of chocolate cake, he said, "I think you're pretty, Macie. Much prettier than Robin and a lot nicer too."

"Well, thank you, Charlie. That's very kind of you."

"Do you know Robin?"

John spoke up. "Why would she know Robin?"

"Because she was your old girlfriend."

I said, "Nope, Charlie, I never met Robin."

"She was a bitch. She didn't like me. I saw her naked once. In the pool. She had big, big tits."

Marabeth looked at me and said, "Sorry," as John yelled, "Charlie."

There was a moment of uncomfortable silence. Then I couldn't help but laugh. I mean, really, who had this kind of dinner conversation? Charlie was so uninhibited, and in a way, it was refreshing. He just spoke his truth.

John looked relieved with my response. Charlie smiled at me, and really, from that moment he and I became friends. Maybe he sensed that I genuinely liked him and that I really loved his brother. Unlike Robin, I wasn't after John's money.

The rest of the afternoon, I played video games with Charlie. We were fairly well matched, although he didn't have to try as hard as I did to win. During the car ride home, John said, "I liked that you tried to beat Charlie. Most people always let him win. He's a nitwit when it comes to social skills, but he's very competent at other things."

Later in bed after he'd made me happy, John said, "I'm really sorry about the Robin comment. He hated her as much as she hated him."

"Well, at least I know why you were with her. I've always been pleased with my breasts, but now I feel inadequate."

"Macie." He leaned down and kissed both of my breasts. "I love you just the way you are. You've nothing to be jealous of or feel inadequate about. Trust me, if Charlie saw you naked, he'd say you had big tits too."

I swallowed. I wasn't a jealous person—at least, I'd never been in the past—but for some reason, this did bother me. "Why did Charlie see her naked?"

"We swam a lot in Mom's pool...in the buff. I didn't think he was home, but she shouldn't have exposed herself to him. I think she did it on purpose."

"She was beautiful, wasn't she?"

"Macie, let's not do this."

"Just tell me."

"Yes, she was, but I promise you, she and I never had what you and I have. We never made love like you and I do. Never."

I believed him.

His text the next morning: "You are perfect."

Since Halloween was just around the corner, I started planning our costumes. The other hairdressers and I always threw a huge party for our faithful clients. It had started out small, but over the years, it had become quite the party to crash. John was game for dressing up, so I threw out several suggestions. I wanted him to wear something that showed off his amazing physique. We decided on Tarzan and Jane.

The day of the party, he picked me up from the salon, and we went to his house to dress since our costumes were there. From the moment we put our costumes on, I never quit laughing. He did the best Tarzan yell, so, of course, we won the prize for the *best couple's costume*. I hadn't laughed that much at someone in a long time. In fact, I hadn't had that much fun with a man in I didn't know how long. By the time we got back to my place, we were so turned on after dancing and drinking together that we really sounded like Tarzan and Jane in the jungle.

That night he stayed.

When I woke, he was waiting for me. I'd always liked morning sex, but Chance was never a morning person. It only made things that much better to find out that John was. At breakfast he said, "I want us to move in together."

"OK."

He stopped, surprised by my quick response. Then a slow smile spread across his face. "My place or yours?"

"I don't care. You decide."

"My place is paid off. Is this place?"

"Yes. I paid it off with the money I got from the city, although I did use it as collateral for the business loan."

"I kind of like your place."

"Like I said, I don't care."

He kissed my nose. "I like how indifferent you are to material things. Doesn't this house mean anything to you?"

"Not really. I don't like new houses. The only reason I bought this was a client of Valley's was desperate to sell. I looked at the place and realized it would be perfect for me. I figured, when the time came, I wouldn't have any problems selling it."

"Do you mind if I move in here with you?"

I looked at him. He couldn't move fast enough for me.

He dressed to go back home. The only thing he had to wear was his Tarzan costume. The rest of the day, I laughed every time I thought about it.

A week later he was moved in, and his place was on the market. The only issue we had was with all our clothes. My closet was already full, so I had to move my seasonal things to the basement. He had two different wardrobes: his multitude of suits, shirts, and ties for the funeral home and all his nonfuneral clothes. I realized we were both clothes-horses; the man I'd fallen in love with almost had more clothes than I did.

The only downside to his moving in, other than the closet-space problem, was that he didn't text me in the morning anymore. I guess he thought it would be stupid since he saw me before we left for work. I'd always enjoyed that little love note every morning. I really missed them.

One thing became clear once John moved in: his hours were erratic. He received calls at any hour—day or night. Death, like birth, had no set hours. It could happen at any time. When he did receive a call, he'd leave promptly. He'd take the body to the mortuary and immediately do the embalming. I could count on him being gone for at least three hours. If cremation was requested, then he would come back home much sooner, as those had a state-mandated waiting period.

I realized that he had probably wanted to move in with me so I would truly understand his work schedule—the way our lives would be. It was different from anything I'd ever experienced, and I wished at times that he didn't have to leave, especially in the middle of the night. But it was his job, and he never complained. I just accepted that if it was his night to be on call, then he might need to leave at any time. Another thing I realized was how many people died. I'd never really thought about it.

But it happened every single day.

John's mom came to the salon for a hair appointment. I wasn't sure if she felt obligated or if John had bragged so much about me that she had decided to give me a try. (That cowlick must've really caused him problems in the past.) I gave her highlights, lowlights, and a new, perky style. I usually didn't overstep with first-time clients, but Marabeth needed some eyebrow work done. She had wonderful skin; she just needed some grooming. I politely made the suggestion, and she seemed relieved by the offer.

Honestly, when I was done, she looked ten years younger and, I thought, somewhat slimmer as well.

She hadn't been back to the funeral home five minutes when John texted me. "What did you do with my mother? This woman isn't her. She's a hottie! Thx baby." I giggled the rest of the day.

Something Marabeth had said, though, made me want to whack John on the head. She had given me the impression that Charlie wanted me to cut his hair but that John wouldn't let him ask me. I took matters into my own hands that afternoon and called Charlie myself.

"Hey, Charlie, do you want to stop in today or tomorrow and let me cut your hair?"

"Oh, Macie, would you?"

"Of course. Do you have a ride, or do I need to come get you?"

"I'll have Johnny bring me."

John texted me within what seemed like seconds. "Call me when you can."

I called immediately. "What's up, baby?"

"Macie, you don't need to cut Charlie's hair. He can continue going to his normal place."

"Why's that? Are you afraid I'll make him look better than you?"

He laughed. "It's just that he might embarrass you. I don't want that to happen."

"Listen, John, let's get something straight right now. I like Charlie. He won't embarrass me, and if he does, I'll survive. I'm not Robin, so quit treating me like her."

Absolute silence on his end. I'd hit my mark.

John and Charlie arrived during the busiest time. I'd just finished with my last client, so I was ready for him. He had lots of hair just like John, although his cowlick was minor compared to his brother's. I washed and cut his hair while he and I joked together about John. John relaxed after a bit and finally felt comfortable enough to leave us alone. He walked around and talked to Valley and then a couple of the other hairdressers. He wasn't really a flirt, but the girls sure flirted with him. Once I was done with Charlie, I took him by the hand and introduced him to Lucy and Valley. I'd already forewarned them about him. My main purpose was to show John I wasn't ashamed of his brother, and I wanted Charlie to meet my best friends.

Charlie was subdued toward them, but he did quite well. I kept his hand in mine the whole time. When we returned to my station, he sat back down while I cleaned up for the day. As I bent over to put supplies away, he leaned toward me and said, "I like you, Macie. I think your girlfriends are pretty."

"I like you too, Charlie, and my girlfriends are very pretty."

He reached for my hand and placed it against his cheek. John came up at that moment and looked at the scene before him. He started to say something but then closed his mouth. He leaned over and ruffled Charlie's hair. "She made you look better than me."

Charlie laughed. He stood up and waved bye to Valley. She blew him a kiss. Charlie pulled me close, his lips on my ear. "I'd like to fuck her someday."

The day before Thanksgiving, the temperature dropped. A freak Georgia cold snap. I was chilly all day. Just looking outside made me shiver. That night I took my shower and rinsed my hair with cold water like I always did. (Hairdresser's tip: Rinsing with cold water makes your hair shine.) Once out of the shower, I could not warm up. John was already in bed watching the news. I ran in the bedroom naked and shivering. I crawled under the covers and tried to warm up.

He shut off the TV and turned to me. Goose bumps covered my body. I was so cold I could hardly move. He instantly became aroused and climbed on top of me, ready for sex. I didn't really care, but I wasn't going to get into it like I normally did. He didn't ask, but I made no indication that he needed to stop. I lay motionless underneath him as he entered me. He was so horny that in a weird way I was touched that he wanted me so much. He was just crazy with desire. He lifted one of my legs so that he could push even harder. His breathing became erratic; then it was over. The whole episode shocked me but ended so quickly that I didn't know what to think. He collapsed on me and wrapped himself over me. I warmed into a nice, comfortable heat as John whispered in my ear, "You're everything I need. Everything."

I fell asleep to his warm voice in my ear.

The next morning, he acted bashful. Wouldn't look me in the eye. Finally, I went to him.

"What's with you?"

Sheepishly, he said, "I feel bad about last night. You had me so turned on that I lost myself with you."

"Bloody hell, it's OK. I liked that I made you happy. You seemed… well, I don't know…like I was the greatest thing you'd ever had. I didn't mind it at all."

He pulled me to him. "You *are* the greatest thing that's ever happened to me. You've no idea what this means to me. No idea whatsoever."

We ate a light breakfast and then went to my parents' for Thanksgiving. Marabeth and Charlie were also coming, as were Grande and my grandpa Fred, who Mom and Dad had moved back from Wisconsin. After Grandma Bea died three years ago, he'd been all alone without family—just his old friends. And, well, he wasn't getting any younger, and neither were his friends. He would need a helping hand someday. He seemed to be truly happy to be with us, although I knew he missed his friends. When the two of us had gone to lunch a couple of times, he had mentioned them with longing.

When Marabeth and Charlie arrived, I introduced them to Grande and Grandpa. I wasn't expecting Grandpa and Marabeth's reaction to each other. Sparks flew immediately. Grandpa bowed to her, and she batted her eyes at him. John cocked an eyebrow at me, and I shrugged, but I should've expected this. Even though they were getting up in age, they were both attractive people. Marabeth's haircut alone would turn any old gent's head.

Weirdly enough, Marabeth was closer to my grandparents' age than she was to my parents'. Of course, Grande had Mom when she was nineteen, and Mom had me when she was twenty, whereas Marabeth didn't have John until she was thirty-five.

Charlie sat between Grande and me. John sat directly across from him as if to watch his every move and guard each word from his mouth. But Charlie did very well as Grande joked with him. When he called her Mrs. Grande, I couldn't help but laugh. The more they chatted, the more John's shoulders relaxed and his tight mouth turned into a smile. He poured more wine into his glass and said, "Charlie's been bragging about his looks lately. How Macie has upped his game."

Charlie's smile was big. "She has. You're just jealous."

"I guess I am. You've always been the looker in the family."

"Macie's my favorite person. Your best girlfriend ever."

I leaned over and hugged him hard. "You, Charlie, are one of my favorite people."

Charlie looked at John, and John winked at him. I couldn't help but think that Robin had done a serious number on his family.

Lying in bed that night, John turned to me and said, "You're so good with Charlie. Your family likes him. They don't treat him like he's different."

"I don't see him as different, and I wish you'd quit saying that. He's a sweet man. Just childlike in a lot of ways. Why don't you simply let it go now? We like Charlie. He'll be fine with us. The one you need to watch is your mother. She's hot to trot for Grandpa."

Laughing, he leaned over and kissed me so tenderly that I was on top of him in an instant.

Our first Christmas was amazing. We opened our presents to each other first thing that morning. I loved everything he bought me. He was really a generous boyfriend, but I shouldn't compare him to Chance. Chance was generous; he just simply didn't have the money to buy the things that John bought. After opening presents, we went to his mom's for brunch. Later in the afternoon, we went to my parents' and had the evening meal.

Back home that evening, he wanted to light a fire and sip wine in front of the fireplace. While he lit the fire (which consisted of flipping a switch), I poured the wine. After we were nestled in and cozy, he pulled out a ring box. "Macie, I know you're going to say this is too soon, but I want to marry you. I know you're the woman for me, so I wanted you to know my intentions. I'll wait until you're ready. No pressure. When you want to tell people we're engaged, just let me know so I can tell my friends as well. I already asked your dad. He understands better than anyone how I feel. He's the one who said you'd probably want to wait. That I shouldn't be disappointed by your hesitation." He popped open the ring box.

Unable to speak, I gaped at the big, beautiful ring. But he was right; this was way too soon for me. He took the ring out of the box and slipped it on my finger. He said, "You don't even have to wear it until you're ready."

I nodded and then leaned over and kissed him. It wasn't that I had any doubts about him, but there were still so many things I didn't know. He'd never told me about his dad. I knew something had gone on there. I didn't need to know everything, but I guess I wanted to know the things in his life that had hurt him the most or that had set his future on the course it had taken. One time he'd started to tell me why he'd chosen the funeral business, but then he'd shut down...as if he didn't trust me to understand or trust himself to share the truth. Either way, he never told me.

"I love the ring, John. You're right, though. I'm not ready for this. Give me a little more time. I do want to marry you, though. I have no doubt about that."

He kissed me. "That's all I needed to hear."

I slipped the ring off and placed it back in the box.

CHAPTER 5

Lucy had a New Year's Eve party at her house. When I kissed John at midnight, my whole world was perfect. I had my family and my career, but most of all I had him—a man willing to wait for me.

A couple of weeks later, John came home in a weird mood. He seemed jumpy and out of sorts. I tried to pry his discontent from him, but he didn't want to talk. When it was time for bed, he watched TV while I showered. I rinsed my hair like I always did, but when I went to wrap myself up, I remembered the towels were still on the dryer. I dried off with a little hand towel and was totally frozen by the time I toweled the cold water out of my hair. Crawling into bed, I pressed my cold, shivering body up against him. "Please warm me up," I begged through chattering teeth.

He was on top of me in an instant—clearly wanting sex. It wasn't exactly what I'd had in mind, but I thought maybe if he satisfied himself, it would pull him out of his funk. Plus, I was too cold to care. He screwed with pleasure, and it was over quickly. I didn't understand this, but I did like how much he seemed to enjoy it. Afterward he whispered, "Macie, I needed that. You don't know how much I needed that." Then he fell asleep with his head on my chest. I stroked his hair as I lay awake and wondered. How strange his need was.

Two days later Grande called to say that her friend Cathy was in the hospital. They didn't expect her to go home. I stopped to buy a small bouquet of flowers and then realized they might not let her have them in her room.

Undecided what to do, I saw a necklace with a tiny cross. For some reason, it spoke to me. On impulse, I bought it.

When I entered her room, she did have several bouquets of flowers. My first thought: "Crap, I should've bought the flowers." My second thought: "She probably has enough blooms." Her face lit up when she saw me. I leaned down and kissed her cheek.

"How are you feeling?"

"You know, I've been better, but, Macie, as strange as this sounds, I'm at peace."

"I bought you a little something."

She opened the box, and her eyes misted over. "Why, it's beautiful. Absolutely beautiful. Put it on me."

I placed the necklace around her neck, hooked the clasp, and centered the cross. As she fingered the pendant, she said, "I wanted to ask you again to do my makeup. I know I'm asking a lot of you, but it's very important to me. I know I'll be dead, but right now, I'm still vain."

I laughed. She did too.

"So…you'll do it, right?"

"Yes, I'll do your makeup."

"I've already packed the makeup bag, so my husband won't have to worry with that. Your grandmother already has it."

I nodded because I couldn't speak.

"Macie, I've had a good life. A great husband. Wonderful kids. A granddaughter. Good friends. Your grandmother has been the best friend to me, and I've enjoyed your sweet friendship as well. You have a wonderful man in your life now. Just love him and enjoy your time together. Life is precious, and it goes by so very fast."

I wanted to say something—something meaningful, something profound—but my throat wouldn't work. She patted my hand in understanding. The doctor came in, and I was asked to leave. I looked at her one last time.

She grabbed my hand. "Thank you, Macie. Make me look pretty."

I stepped out into the hall and then ran. When I was outside, I burst into tears.

She died that night.

I knew nothing about applying makeup on a dead person. (A part of me thought, "How hard could it be?" The other part of me thought, "Very hard.") John assured me he'd be with me every step of the way. It wasn't that I was afraid to be alone with her body; I just didn't want to be. Every time I thought about actually applying the makeup, I'd get queasy. Surely John must've experienced this his first time out.

The thing was, I'd never actually asked John much about his job. I was curious, but then again, I didn't want the details. It felt almost like rubber-necking at a car accident and being horrified when you actually saw blood or a person on a stretcher.

I worked at the salon all day, but then it was time to face the dreaded job I'd agreed to. I'd tried to keep my mind occupied, but honestly, I hadn't thought about anything else all day, nor had I eaten anything. My stomach was a knotted mass of growling nerves.

I drove to the funeral home, where John was waiting for me. Shaking and almost ill, I entered his office, where he sat, nonchalant, reading his *Car and Driver* magazine. When he closed the door, I immediately burst into tears. He held my trembling body as I sobbed into his chest.

"Macie, calm down. I'll help you. You're making too big a deal out of this. Once you do the first one, then you won't have any qualms next time."

"There won't be a next time."

"You promised all those other women."

Why did he have to bring that up? I went into the ugly cry. He finally stepped back and blew in my face. I'd seen him do this with Charlie when he wanted him to settle down. For some reason, it did make me stop and catch my breath. He handed me a Kleenex and became firm with me.

"OK, now stop. Blow your nose; let's go do this. You tell me what to do, and I'll do the work. I've done it before, but like I already told you, I hate doing makeup."

He grabbed my sweater, holding it as I slipped my arms inside. He'd told me to dress warm because the embalming room was cold. I didn't need any explanation for why it was kept like a freezer.

I walked stiff legged to the embalming room. The moment I stepped inside, formaldehyde instantly hit my nostrils, almost knocking me to the floor. Repulsion shuddered through me. My neck stiffened, and my head wouldn't turn; I was so traumatized by the room itself. Petrified. And because it was so damn cold, I was frozen in place.

He took my hand and said, "Just stand here for a minute and familiarize yourself with the room. Nothing in here is scary."

The hell it wasn't.

"It's just a room where I prepare the body for the families. I make their loved ones look as good as I can, so they can have peace of mind about the end."

My knuckles turned white from gripping his hand. Working his hand free, he walked into the room as if to give me a tour. I didn't turn my head but let my eyes follow him as he roved around the large room. It had two porcelain embalming tables. He stepped up to one of the tables and grabbed hold of a handle.

"This raises the table up and down or from side to side. There's a plug here at the bottom. Everything that's drained from the body goes—"

"Stop."

He looked at me. I put my hands up. "Just stop. I don't want you to say anything else. I'll look around. If I have a question, I'll ask."

He nodded.

The whole process of preparing a body for a funeral was foreign to me, and I didn't want to know any of the details. I noticed that the plug he'd pointed out was positioned over the sink. The sink looked as if it could be flushed like a toilet. I wanted to walk over to it and puke but was afraid to stick my head into the bowl. There were four tables draped with sheets. I knew there were bodies underneath those sheets.

When I looked at John, he was staring at me. I must've looked like death myself, because he said, "How are you doing?"

I could barely nod, but I tried to. My eyes returned to the tables with the sheets, and then I looked back at him.

He must've seen the question in my eyes because he said, "I'm waiting for their families to bring their funeral clothes. Usually, it's the next day, unless it's an unexpected death. Then it can take a few days." He handed me some gloves. I stared at them until he said, "Put the gloves on. Let's get this done."

My hands were shaking so much that I didn't think I'd even be able to do this first step. After I managed to work my hands into the gloves, he grabbed my arm and pulled me over to Cathy. I'd seen the blue dress before and knew it was one of her favorites. She looked better than I'd imagined, but I couldn't get past the fact that she was dead.

He took thin plastic (like from a dry cleaner) and tucked it in around her neck. He pulled it across her to protect her dress. He laid out all the makeup, and then he brought out some makeup brushes. This was a surprise. I'd thought I'd be applying the makeup with my fingers. One knot of anxiety slipped away.

"I've already applied cream to her face. We may need to wipe some of it off. The more you do this, the more it will become second nature to you."

I wished he'd quit talking like that.

"After a person dies, their skin won't absorb like it did when they were living. I'm going to inject some tissue builder in a couple of areas that have sunken in. After that, we'll apply the makeup, and then we'll spray her face with hair spray."

He did the injections quickly and efficiently. First he inserted the needle under her eyes; then he did a couple in her laugh lines. He talked while he worked. "These grooves running downward from her nose to the corner of the lips are called the nasolabial. A little of this injected here and there makes all the difference." He looked at her hands and did a couple on those as well. Picking up the makeup brush, he opened the bottle of foundation. "This is your makeup, isn't it?"

I nodded. I'd lost my voice; I wasn't sure I'd ever get it back. He dipped the brush into the foundation and overloaded the bristles. When he daubed it on her chin, he left a huge glob. Instead of working with that, he dipped the brush again and plunked another huge glob on her left cheek. He dipped the brush again. Before he plopped it on her face, I grabbed his hand. I took the brush from him and removed one of the globs. Then with a clean brush and an experienced hand, I started applying the makeup. Working from the glob on her chin, I dabbed the foundation into a light, even layer. It went on beautifully. Once I had that done, I worked on her eyes. Using a couple of different smoky hues, I blended the shadow expertly. I was so intent on the job before me that my mind shut out the room, the other bodies, and that damn sink.

Cathy had short hair that she curled with hot rollers or straightened with a flat iron. I hadn't thought to ask John if all that equipment would be there; I'd just assumed it would be. As I put my hands in her hair, he retrieved a basket with everything I needed. I wished I had brought my own hairstyling spray, but the one he had, I'd used before. He took a pedestal-looking device and placed it under Cathy's neck. It raised her head, lifting it off the table, so I could easily work on her hair.

I misted her hair with styling spray and used the hot rollers. While I let them set, I checked her fingernails. She'd recently had them painted, but I decided to apply a fresh topcoat. After I finished her nails, I took the curlers out, styled her hair, and sprayed it with hair spray. The last thing I did was apply her lipstick. I then stepped back and observed my work. I smoothed a lock of hair and touched an area of blush. She was beautiful. Dead. But beautiful.

I looked at John for his approval. He raised his eyes from Cathy's face to mine. And I knew. His face said it all. From the warmth of his blue eyes to his huge smile, he was impressed, pleased, and, most of all, proud of me. All he said was, "Macie."

He grabbed a can of hair spray. "I just mist this over their face. It sets the makeup and keeps it looking fresh." He sprayed a light film over my makeup job. I packed up the makeup as he removed the plastic. He said, "Let's keep this makeup here. I liked how easy it was to use. Mom uses mortician makeup on everyone. I just realized that's one of her big mistakes. If she ever has to fill in for me again, I'll have her try using your makeup."

I sighed with relief when we left the room, but I was also filled with a sense of accomplishment and an unexpected peace that surprised me. I'd done Cathy a favor. I'd given her one last gift.

Back in John's office, he said, "Thank you. You did a remarkable job. Honestly, I can't tell you how impressed I am with your work. You're a natural. I wish you'd come to work for me. We'd make one hell of a team."

I smiled. He touched my chin and quietly said, "Are you ever going to speak again?"

I nodded but didn't say a word.

He laughed and kissed me lightly. "Let's go home."

The bunco women met at the funeral home for the visitation with the family. Grande and I went together. I knew Cathy looked good, but still, I was nervous about how the rest of the women would view her. It wasn't a pride thing on my part; I simply wanted Cathy to look nice for her friends.

When we entered the funeral home, Charlie was the first person I saw. He immediately came to us and squeezed me hard. He held out his hand to Grande as if to shake hers but then opened his arms to her. She walked into them, and he held her tight. As she stepped back and wiped her eyes, he leaned into her. "Mrs. Grande, I'm so very sorry this has happened to your friend. I'm your friend though, and you can talk to me anytime."

Tim, Cathy's husband, was the next to hug me tight. "She looks beautiful. Simply beautiful. The night she died, she hung on to the cross you bought her. She told me she wanted to be buried with it. I hope you don't mind. It meant so much to her."

I swallowed but couldn't speak. He spoke to the rest of the women, and then we all went to the casket. As we gathered around, Grande immediately said, "My God, she's lovely."

Birdie said, "She looks at peace. No more pain and suffering."

She began to cry, as did the rest of Cathy's friends. Their grief was too much for me. I left to let the women be alone. John was standing off to the side, and I went to him. He wrapped me in his arms.

"I'm proud of you, baby. I knew you could do it, and look how happy you've made so many people."

I looked back at the coffin. Cathy's little granddaughter was viewing her grandmother. She turned to her mother and said, "She just sleeping. She looks pretty like Snow White."

The funeral was the next day. I told Grande I'd drive her there. Cathy had been such a good friend of hers; I didn't want her driving home by herself afterward. She was ready and waiting—as immaculate as always—when I pulled into her drive. Her long legs were still quite shapely in her designer suit. Her beautiful gray hair was cut into a stylish bob, which, of course, I'd done. Grande was classy and knew how to dress even at seventy.

Grande's friends were already seated toward the front, so we slipped in beside them. Cathy's husband gave a lovely eulogy, as did Grande. Afterward, several of Cathy's family members personally thanked me for doing her makeup. I accepted their gratitude graciously, but I still wasn't certain I could ever do it again.

And yet I'd promised all those bunco women. Maybe they'd all outlive me.

CHAPTER 6

The more I thought about marrying John, the more I saw no reason to put it off. I loved him. He loved me. What, really, was I waiting for? I simply didn't want to rush into marriage. On some level, I'd always thought my parents had been somewhat reckless to marry so quickly. They bragged about it as if it was something to be proud of, but they couldn't possibly have known each other. Perhaps I'd watched too many shows about people not being who they said they were and then destroying the innocent person's life. I didn't think John was like that, though. I knew him. He was a good man with a kind and compassionate heart. There wasn't any reason to wait any longer.

He wanted to celebrate Valentine's Day at a swanky restaurant that had a small dance floor. We loved dancing together. He was light on his feet and could swing me around like a pro. I dressed in a smoking-hot red dress; he wore an outfit I'd bought him for Christmas. At the restaurant, we ordered and ate a lovely meal. After dancing for several minutes, we returned to our table to have our dessert. When the maître d' placed our crème brulée in front of us, I opened my purse and slipped the ring on my finger. We ate the dessert and were finishing our coffee when he noticed the ring. It took him a moment to fully understand the meaning, but once he did, I think he would have screwed me in the parking lot if his car hadn't been so close to the front door.

At home I wanted to call my family and friends, but he wanted to celebrate in a different way.

Decked out in green for Saint Patrick's Day, I was meeting John for lunch. I'd made sandwiches and sent them with him to put in his fridge. I would never eat with him at his work, but ever since I'd done Cathy's makeup, I'd somehow overcome my aversion to the funeral home.

I'd met some of John's twenty-three employees. Five were funeral directors. That seemed like a lot, but when I realized there were over five hundred services a year, the number seemed on the low side. John and the other morticians rotated being on call at night, although if one of them needed off for some reason, John would fill in.

He had three funeral assistants: Charlie; Anthony, a short, little man; and Roger, who I'd never met. I'd met his office manager, a gray, middle-aged woman. She'd been hired by his father, but John liked and respected her. All the rest of his employees did the numerous jobs required each day at the funeral home: cleaning, delivering flowers, retrieving the necessary paperwork, and so on.

Kelly, his makeup person, was the one I wanted to meet. She'd refused to use my makeup. They'd exchanged words. I wanted to try to smooth things over with her. She probably had makeup she was comfortable using. I didn't expect her to change just because John wanted her to, although he was paying for the makeup. I couldn't help but think this was some sort of power play on her part. There wasn't one thing she couldn't like about my product. (Well, there wasn't.)

As John and I were finishing lunch, a woman walked into the break room. I knew without being told who she was.

"Oh good. I wanted you two to meet. Macie, this is Kelly."

Without a bra, her nipples were obvious through her tight-knit T-shirt. Her cute, spiky hair suited her face. A mess of freckles sprinkled her nose. She was slender with small breasts. Probably a yogi. She wore flats, so I wasn't sure if she disliked her height or dressed for comfort. She wasn't beautiful, but I liked her looks.

I stuck out my hand. Hers was limp and unfriendly, but I took the high road and said, "I've always wanted to meet you. John speaks highly of you."

"Well, he must not trust me on every case, because he brought you in for Mrs. Carton."

"That was a unique situation. She'd asked me several months before to do her makeup. You weren't even working here when she asked, so it wasn't anything against you. I would've gladly let you have the job."

I thought my answer was nice and explained my position clearly, but she still seemed put out. I could tell she wanted to take me aside and set me straight. But she turned and walked away. I wanted to run after her, manhandle her to the ground, and tell her she would use my makeup without further complaint. Instead I kissed John good-bye and drove back to the salon.

Somehow, though, I'd break that bitch's attitude.

The next day, Grande called. "Do you remember my neighbors when I lived on Polar Street?"

"Barely. That was fifteen years ago."

"Paula, who lived across the street, her cousin died. I'm going to her funeral tomorrow."

"Did Paula call and tell you this?"

"No, I read it in the paper."

I rubbed my forehead. This notion Grande had about death in threes was weird. Until she'd gone to two more funerals, she wouldn't rest.

The following evening she stopped by to tell me about her day. John and I were eating our dessert. Cutting a big piece of brownie for herself, Grande said, "Paula didn't recognize me at first. But once she figured out who I was, we had the nicest chat."

John was always entertained by Grande, but that night he looked at me over her head and gave me bug eyes.

"Her cousin looked pretty good. I mean, I didn't know her, but I thought she looked nice. The funeral was poorly done. Just seemed like no one was in charge." She turned to John. "I'm so proud of you—the way you handle your business and how you treat and respect the families."

His face pinked up. That'd teach him to make fun of Grande.

About two weeks later, Sue Ann died. She and Grande had worked together for several years in Grande's salon. John was doing her funeral, which just happened to be on a Monday. I told Grande I'd go with her. For some strange reason, I was interested in seeing Kelly's makeup job.

When we viewed the body, I focused my attention on the makeup details. Kelly had done a nice job, but I wouldn't have used green eye shadow and would've definitely used a different shade of lipstick, and her hair needed a bit more work. Grande thought she looked good, but she, too, mentioned her hair.

I finally comprehended how important the makeup job was on a dead person. I'd been to funerals where the person had been sick for months and looked better dead than alive. (A horrible thing to think, but the truth.) This phenomenon made sense now that I knew a little bit about the funeral business. The tissue builder filled out the sunken areas, and wax could contour and hide a multitude of flaws and scars makeup wouldn't cover. How a person looked in the coffin depended on the expertise of whoever did the makeup job.

That night after eating, I was looking at different flower arrangements for our June wedding, and John was looking for a honeymoon package when he set his laptop aside. "I want to ask you something. Would you ever consider working for me?"

"Uh, I don't think I want to do that."

"Come on. You're a natural. After a few times, you'd get over the hump; it would become second nature."

"That's too big a hump to get over."

"You need to look at it as if you're doing a service for the family. They want to see their loved one just one last time. I keep thinking how nice Cathy looked. How grateful her family was to you. Would you just think about it?"

I said, "OK," but I was thinking, "Hell no!"

Over the next week, though, I really couldn't quit thinking about it. My mind kept coming back to Sue Ann. Kelly was the expert, yet I felt I could've done a better job than she had. Even if that lipstick had been given to her by the family, she didn't have to apply it so heavily. And bloody hell—go easy with the green eye shadow.

Two weeks later, Cathy's husband called to ask if I'd consider doing the makeup on his cousin's wife. "She died this morning. My cousin was at Cathy's funeral. He asked me to ask you."

Because I liked Tim so much and maybe, too, because I didn't know this woman at all, and after John's comments, well...I told Tim I would. The funeral wasn't at John's mortuary but in Macon, thirty miles away. I didn't have to worry about stepping on Kelly's toes. She was like a dog with a bone—protecting her turf. I called the funeral home and talked with the owner, Mr. Bower. I made arrangements to go out the following evening.

Tim drove me, which gave us the opportunity to talk about Cathy. He, of course, was having good days and bad. But again, he told me how relieved he was about the way she'd looked. "After Patsy Grover's funeral, she worried until she made herself sick. She was obsessed with how she'd look in that casket." He wiped at his eyes. "Honestly, Macie, you did her, me, my family a huge favor. You really did."

His cousin, Vance, met us at the funeral home with a bag of his wife's makeup and a picture, which I'd requested. I studied the picture and asked a few questions just to clarify a thing or two. Then I hugged him and said, "I'm sorry this has happened to you, but I'll do the very best that I can for you."

I'd taken a few things from my makeup line just in case her colors didn't quite work with her coloring. (Dead people didn't have the same glow as the living.) Also, I took my own hairstyling spray.

Mr. Bower took me to Betty. I went into the room, introduced myself to her, told her I'd be doing her hair and makeup, and let her know she could just relax. I laid out everything her husband had brought and a few of my things and then slipped on a pair of gloves. I rested my hands on hers, closed my eyes, said a prayer, and then focused on applying the makeup.

Mr. Bower had already done the tissue builder, but I thought I could've done it myself if he hadn't. Her hair was cut in a short bob, which was easy to style. When I was finished, I stood back and examined my work. Now was the true test. I wanted Vance to view Betty before we left. I could change things if something was off.

I walked out to the waiting room to tell him I was ready. To my surprise his two children were with him. My armpits immediately dampened. The daughter gave me a grateful smile. The son shook my hand.

Mr. Bower had moved the casket to the viewing room. I stood slightly to the head of the casket so that I could interact with them without intruding. Both children began to cry but were able to talk through their tears.

The son said, "She's peaceful."

The daughter said, "God, I'm going to miss her." She looked at me and said, "She looks beautiful. Thank you."

"Is there anything I can change or do different? Her hair? Her nail color? Lipstick?"

All three shook their heads.

On the ride home, Tim thanked me several times. And really…I felt I'd done something special. For her. For her family. And in a weird way, for myself.

When I arrived home late, John was waiting and in a rotten mood. Pissed that I would do a makeup job for another funeral home. I tried to explain myself without becoming too defensive.

"I just wanted to see if I could do it on someone I didn't know."

"You could've done that for me."

"I know, but I didn't want to get in a pissing war with Kelly."

"Kelly's irrelevant. She works for me. If I want you to do makeup on someone, then that's my prerogative."

"I don't want her to quit because I wanted to try this one more time. Don't be so sensitive."

He crossed his arms over his chest. "Well, so what's your conclusion?"

"I'm not sure yet. It gave me a sense of accomplishment that surprised me, and I did it all by myself without your being there." I tried to determine if he was still mad before I said any more. I couldn't tell, but I went ahead and said, "I wasn't totally pleased with Kelly's job on Grande's friend. Sue Ann's lipstick color wasn't the right shade, and her hair needed a little more work." (No need to mention the god-awful green eye shadow.)

His lips twitched as a slow smile spread across his face.

I looked at him, waiting, and finally said, "What?"

"Kelly's good. She was trained for this type of work, but there's a big difference between the two of you. She can do the work, but you're the one with the natural talent. An eye for detail. It's like my cowlick. I've had several hairdressers cut my hair. Only a couple of you knew how to work with it. It's like a special gift or something. A knack that can't be taught." He stepped toward me and put his hands on my face. "Would you consider doing makeup again and this time for me?"

"I haven't decided."

In April, a situation came up that I should've handled differently, but at the time I was at a loss as to what to do. I'd decided not to sell any more wedding packages. Since I was getting married, I wanted to spend my weekends with John. As much as I dreaded telling clients I was no longer offering the service, I found myself filled with relief. I no longer felt I needed to work my ass off for a bunch of brides. I offered Lucy and Valley the option to continue the business, but neither one wanted the job.

The sister of one of my previous brides was getting married in May. When I told her I wasn't selling packages anymore, she seemed to accept the fact, but later that day her mother called me, insisting I sell them a package. For some reason, she made me feel obligated. I decided one more wedding wouldn't kill me. Lucy and Valley said they'd help, but we agreed it would be the last one. I had a totally different perspective on working with brides now. Maybe since I'd done the makeup for two dead women, I had somehow changed.

When the Saturday arrived, I bought the wine and sandwiches. Everything went like clockwork until the bride's mother realized I was engaged to John Harnon. Robin's mother was her best friend. For the next hour, I listened as she told me how much John had loved Robin, all the things he'd bought for her, and the romantic places he'd taken her. It took everything in me not to take my shears and slice her fucking throat.

Back home, I was in a foul mood and pissed off at John. Finally, I told him, "You had nothing to do with this, and it isn't your fault, but I'm angry at you anyway."

"Will you at least tell me what happened?"

"You and Robin. I had to hear all about you and her today. All the shit you bought her. All the places you took her." I smacked my hands against his chest. He didn't know what to say, but he tried to calm me down, which only infuriated me all the more. I knew this whole thing was ridiculous, but I simply didn't want to be around him.

"I'm going over to Mom's. Don't come over there, or I'll leave."

"God, Macie. This is stupid."

"I know it is. But why didn't you tell me all the stuff you two did together?"

"Macie."

"Don't 'Macie' me." With that, I stormed out.

Mom listened as I bitched excessively. Finally, she said, "Did you tell him everything about you and Chance?"

"No."

"How about Shane Franklin?"

"Shit, no."

"You've never told him about Shane."

"No."

"Why not?"

"Because I loved Shane. It would be too hard to explain."

"Well, then." She crossed her arms and stared at me. What could I say? She said, "Let's do something fun and get your mind off all this. You remember my friend Tracy, the real-estate woman?"

"Yeah."

"She's showing that house you like so much. The one on River Rock Road."

"You mean that big-ass mansion?"

She laughed and nodded. "You want to see it? The owners are moving to Florida. Tracy's showing the house today to another couple. We could tag along."

I grabbed her hand and squeezed. I'd always wanted to go inside that house. It was huge and absolutely beautiful from the outside. I wasn't sure exactly when it had been built, but it looked old—as if it had been there for a century. It wasn't really a mansion, but I'd always called it that because it just seemed so large and majestic. Plus, it was fully bricked and had stone pillars on the front porch. I'd chew my right arm off to live there.

Twenty minutes later, we were standing in the front yard. The landscaping was immaculate, and the house was even better up close. The walkway leading to the front door wasn't poured cement but beautiful laid rock. Inside, the enormous foyer featured an amazing chandelier. A medium-size den was off to the right. A deer head with sad eyes hung from the wall. (Men always had to kill something and show off.) I pitied the poor thing.

As I moved on into the house, it was obvious the owner had totally remodeled. I couldn't tell if walls had been knocked down, but I was impressed nonetheless. The rooms were huge and painted in the warmest colors. Thick rugs covered the rich, wooden floors.

Mom waved to Tracy, who was with the other couple. Tracy said, "I'll be with you shortly."

Mom said, "We're just being nosy. Don't worry about us."

We entered the kitchen, where everything was upscale. The stove had six burners and almost looked daunting, as if it were saying, "Get your ass in here and cook." There was a stack of ovens—two regular and one microwave. The refrigerator was massive, and there was even one just for the wine. The eating bar was so large it looked like a gigantic island.

Leaving the kitchen, Mom motioned for me to go upstairs. She probably didn't want to disturb Tracy and her clients. The curved staircase ended in a loft. I wasn't sure what this space was for other than to spy on the people below. The owners obviously didn't know either because it had nothing in it. Not a chair or even a throw pillow. We entered a small library—mainly two walls of shelves and enough room for two comfortable chairs and a table. We found two more bedrooms and bathrooms.

Back downstairs, Tracy and the couple were on the right side of the house, so Mom and I went to the left, which was the master bedroom and bath. Although large and impressive, the walk-in closet was smaller than I would've expected. It was bigger than mine at home, but still, I was rather disappointed. There was another, smaller bedroom on this side of the house as well, and it also had a walk-in closet. The owner must have been a crafter, because the room had a large worktable, and in the closet we found stacked containers of what looked to me to be material, art supplies, and crafting paraphernalia.

When we heard the three of them leaving through the front door, we went to the other side of the house. I realized I'd been wrong about what I'd thought was the master bedroom and bath, because we were obviously in it. The oversized bedroom had a small sitting area; the bathroom had dual sinks, a tub big enough for two, a stool, and, believe it or not, a urinal. That'd certainly end all the arguments over the toilet seat.

The door to the walk-in closet was in the bathroom. I stepped inside, and my mouth watered. I turned to Mom; her eyes were huge. We couldn't even speak.

Tracy entered and said, "When the owners remodeled, this is where they knocked out walls. The other bedroom used to be the master suite, and this side of the house had two bedrooms and bathrooms. She wanted bigger everything—bedroom, bathroom, closet—so they tore out all the walls."

She must've hired a closet expert, because this one had everything.

Tracy said, "Have you been in the basement yet?"

We shook our heads. She said, "Let's go down there. It has a neat wine cellar, another kitchen, and a bar."

The basement didn't seem like a basement, with large windows on one side displaying the backyard. There was a game room with a beautiful billiard table. Tracy said it stayed with the house. I dragged my finger along the dark wood, imagining all the possibilities. John and I could play pool, and then we could lie on the table and do other things.

Outside, we toured the small pool house and the remodeled cottage. Tracy said it had originally been servants' quarters or something like that. (Holy hell.) The backyard was still torn up from the reconstructed pool, but she said it would be finished before the end of the month. She talked as if one of us was serious about buying the place. Realtors always looked at people as potential buyers, but this property was so far out of my price range. Even if I sold my house for the asking price, I still couldn't afford the place. Also, I had used my house as collateral for my business loan, so that was totally out of the question. And really, did I need a four-bedroom, six-bathroom house? Who'd clean the thing?

After the tour, I only wanted to go home and tell John about it. He was my best friend (male friend, anyway), and I didn't want to stay mad at him any longer. When I entered the house, he looked rather leery—trying to guess my mood. I circled his neck with my arms and kissed him. He relaxed and pulled me close. I didn't want to discuss our previous conversation or apologize either, so I told him about the mini-mansion. I blathered on like some sick lunatic, even telling him about the pool table. He laughed at my chatter and kissed me, and before I knew it, he had me naked and on my back.

We went to my parents' for dinner the next day. While I was listening to Dad talk about an idea he had for my makeup line, I overheard Mom tell John, "Don't let Macie give you crap about your old girlfriends. She wasn't an angel herself."

John laughed, which only encouraged Mom.

"She was just the sweetest baby and little girl, but my gosh, those teen-age years were something else."

"Was she ornery?"

"You've no idea. Marty had to pick her up early from cheerleading camp because of an improper incident. She and Valley almost got suspended from the squad for their behavior."

"She and Valley have been friends that long?"

"Yes, forever. And trust me, they weren't always nice girls."

I finally yelled, "Shit, Mom, don't tell all my secrets."

After lunch John went to play videos with Charlie while I met Lucy and Valley at the bridal shop to look for their dresses.

CHAPTER 7

I woke up at my parents' house. Excitement filled me; I was marrying John that day. The wedding had come together easier than I'd anticipated, but honestly, Mom had handled most of it. Lucy, Valley, and I had found dresses we loved, and tuxes for the guys were a breeze. Charlie and one of John's best friends were standing up with him.

Dealing with brides over the last several years had taught me not to sweat the small stuff because in the end it didn't really matter. I wanted our wedding to be fun.

And it was.

John was so darn handsome, especially in his tux. His eyes just seemed to sparkle, and his smile never left his face. Once we were pronounced husband and wife, we danced down the aisle, followed by our attendants, my parents, Marabeth, Grande, and Grandpa. It set the mood for the rest of the evening. We partied until we couldn't stand up any longer and left the next day for two weeks in Hawaii.

The day before our return home, John handed me a small wrapped box. Tearing off the wrapping, I uncovered my ring box. When I opened the lid, a key was stuck inside. At first, I thought he'd bought me a car, but it didn't look like a car key. I looked at him quizzically.

He said, "It's a house key."

"A house key?"

"To the mini-mansion."

I snorted. "Right."

He didn't say anything but simply looked at me.

"John, are you serious? You bought that mansion?"

"I did."

"No."

"Yes, I did."

My mouth popped open. I couldn't utter a word. He kissed my cheek, bit my earlobe, and whispered in my ear, "I never bought Robin anything like this. You know why? Because I didn't love her. I love you, Macie. You and only you."

"John." I wanted to say more, but where did I start? He didn't need to buy this for me to prove something to me.

"What, baby?"

"When did you do all this?"

"That next day. When I told you I was going over to play videos with Charlie, I actually went with your mom and met Tracy at the house. I made them promise not to tell you. I waited until now because I didn't want to ruin our honeymoon."

"How would it have ruined our honeymoon?"

"That's all you would've thought about."

I laughed because he was probably right.

"I've wanted to say this ever since that day you threw a hissy about Robin and me. The reason I never took you anywhere is because you worked. She didn't work, and she planned all the trips. I would've taken you if you could've left the salon for a week or two."

"You bought the mansion for me because you feel guilty?"

"No. I liked the closet." He kissed my nose. "When we get home, we're moving. Mom wants to buy your house. She likes the size, and I think she'd like a new start."

Something dawned on me then. The last time Marabeth was at my house, she'd explored a little too much for my comfort. Seemed rather snoopy and meddling. When I caught her in my pantry, I'd thought she was checking out my food—as if I wasn't feeding her son properly. Now her nosiness made sense.

"How much are the payments? Can we even afford this?"

Confusion knotted his brow. That's when it hit me. He'd written a check.

Bloody hell, he really was rich.

The moment we arrived home, we headed over to the mansion. He'd arranged to have the entire place cleaned. Over the next two weeks, we moved things that we wanted from my house and the things from his house that he'd put in storage. We shopped for new sofas and a new bed. My full-size bed would look like a Tinkertoy in that big room.

On Saturday, we worked in the closet arranging our clothes. It was embarrassing how much we both loved clothes and how much we loved this fabulous closet. It had an island of dressers in the middle. There was even a special place for John's ties and my purses. The ceiling was high enough for another row of rods to hang the things we hardly ever wore (perfect for our Tarzan and Jane costumes). After we had everything arranged and all our stuff put in the dressers, we still had room to spare.

John turned to me. "God, Macie, we need to buy more clothes."

We were officially moved in. Even though we had a new bed, I wanted our first lovemaking to be on the pool table. He thought we should at least play a game of pool—just to keep things interesting. I didn't see the point since it didn't matter who won or lost; the end result would still be the same. I tried to win, though—I really did—but he was a much better player than me. Every time I missed a shot, he'd say, "Macie, Macie." When he won, he threw his arms in the air as if it were some great big competition. I tried to look unhappy, but all I wanted was him naked on that table. He said, "I won, so I get to decide how we're going to do it."

"Fair enough." I stood before him waiting further instruction, but then his mouth was on mine, and there wasn't much talking from that point on. Afterward, as we lay on our backs exhausted and looking at the basement ceiling, I asked him, "Do you think this felt will hold up?"

"I'm not sure, but if it doesn't, I'll have it re-covered."

"Have them put on the thickest felt they can find." I rolled over to face him. "What sold you on the house?"

"You. How excited you were about it."

"No, I mean, what was it about the house? The four-car garage? The wine cellar?"

"Honestly, I'd already decided to buy it before I even saw it. You loved it so much, and that's all that mattered. But when I saw the huge closet with my own eyes…well, I would've paid the asking price for that alone. I was so tired of trying to find my stuff in your little closet. Plus, this damn pool table. I never could get the thought out of my head once you mentioned it."

Over the next several weeks, I had to pinch myself every time I pulled in the drive. That this place was really mine and that John was really my husband were sometimes more than I could take. We had our first party the Fourth of July. John and I gave tours of our house all day.

The next day was Saturday, and since I'd quit working Saturdays altogether, I was home when Grandpa showed up. I offered him his usual, which he accepted. As I fixed his bourbon and Coke, he acted nervous; his eyes darted around, not making eye contact with mine. Bloody hell. Was he going to tell me he had cancer or liver disease or—? I couldn't think of anything else at the moment.

He asked, "Is John home?"

"He's in the back picking up trash."

"I'd like to speak with you both at the same time."

"OK."

John was lugging a trash bag when I yelled for him to come inside. As he grabbed a beer from the fridge, I whispered that Grandpa wanted to talk to us. He raised his brows at me, but I only shrugged and chewed my lip. His fingers closed over mine, and we returned to the living room.

Grandpa cleared his throat and said, "John, I'm in love with your mother. I want to marry Marabeth. I wanted your approval for some reason; I'm not really sure why. Perhaps it has something to do with Charlie.

I know he needs to stay with her; I won't force him out or make him uncomfortable in any way. I have my own money, and she has hers, so there won't be any funny business you'd need to worry about. Charlie can—"

John reached over and laid his hand on Grandpa's arm. "Fred, you can quit talking. I'd be happy for you to take Mom off my hands."

Grandpa laughed with relief. I was so touched by John's actions and quick humor.

"Macie and I have been talking about letting Charlie live in the cottage. Macie's convinced me that Charlie needs his own life. His own place. That we've babied him too much. He can't drive, but other than that, Charlie's very self-sufficient. Mom needs her own life; I know you'll make her happy. The money isn't an issue. We'll have a sit-down and write something up, so Charlie will always be taken care of. It's time to get that done anyway."

I asked, "When are you getting married?"

"I haven't asked her yet. I wanted to talk to John first."

"Well, when she says yes, you can get married in our backyard. I'd love to plan your wedding for you, Grandpa."

"I just hope she says yes."

John laughed. "There's no question on that one."

"Oh, bloody hell."

They both looked at me. I turned to John and said, "Your mother will be my mother-in-law as well as my grandmother."

John doubled over in laughter.

Marabeth, of course, said yes. She and Grandpa didn't want to wait around, so the wedding was planned for the first of August. Charlie was eager to finally have a place of his own. When I took him out to the cottage to tour the place, he said, "I'm going to ask Valley over for drinks after I get settled in."

"OK. But, Charlie, you do understand she only wants to be your friend and not your girlfriend. She has a boyfriend. They've been together for a while now."

"Sure. I know that."

The next week Charlie moved into the cottage. He didn't want to wait for his mom to get married. Plus, she was packing everything up anyway. He might as well move out; at least I thought so.

Between John's stuff, my stuff, his mother's stuff, and my grandpa's stuff, Charlie had an assortment of furniture and accessories to pick from, but I wanted him to decorate the cottage to his liking. Why should he settle for everyone else's discards? I told him I'd go with him to buy new things if he wanted to. He was so happy just to have his own place, though, that he had the cottage furnished in no time. I worked with him hanging pictures and making the place look homey.

When we were done, he said, "The only thing I need is some lamps for my bedroom."

"OK. Let's go in the house and see if there's something that'd work for you."

I wanted some new lamps for our bedroom, so I showed him my bedroom lamps first. I could tell he liked them but didn't want to admit it to me.

"You can have them."

"What will Johnny say?"

"He won't care. These really are too small for this room anyway."

Before he could say anything else, I reached down and unplugged the cord. When he saw I was serious, he walked to the other nightstand and did the same. Back in his cottage, we plugged the lamps in. He smiled with approval. "Now I don't have to worry about someone stubbing their toe in the middle of the night."

I wondered who that someone was.

Monday, after restocking my makeup at the salon and doing my normal clerical work, I went shopping for bedroom lamps. A client had recommended a store that carried unusual things but had warned me it was somewhat pricy. Almost immediately, I found two lamps I absolutely loved. They were rather expensive but were so unique. I debated back and forth and finally called John for his approval since in actuality he'd be paying for them.

"Macie, if you like them, buy them. You don't need my permission."

"I know, but they're overpriced. They're a thousand for each one."

"I hope they come with light bulbs."

I laughed. I really loved this guy.

"Are they really that much?" he asked.

"Hell no. They're only twelve hundred for the pair."

"Was that some kind of reverse psychology?"

I laughed again. "I'll see you tonight. When you get home, come in the bedroom naked. I want to see you in the glow of our new lamps."

When I got home, Marabeth had just dropped Charlie off at the cottage. I hated how dependent he was on her and John. I knew he wasn't as helpless as John and Marabeth thought. He depended on them because they'd taught him to. Working with him on the cottage, I saw him as the man he could be. He had his own ideas, his own interests. He did speak out of turn at times, but shit, who didn't? I truly believed that, with a little work, even that could be curtailed to some degree. I'd taken Charlie with me several times to the grocery store and once to an estate sale. When he'd say something inappropriate, I'd just tell him, "Filter, Charlie. Filter what you're saying." He'd blink at me and usually change the subject.

I walked to the cottage and invited him to the house for a beer. He trotted over and helped carry the lamps inside. We set them up in the bedroom. Even though they were overpriced, I had to admit they were perfect.

Grabbing two beers, we plopped down on the sofa and immediately started talking. That's the thing I loved the most about him: his openness when talking with me.

"I love my place, Macie. Thank you for talking Johnny into letting me live here."

"I didn't have to talk him into it."

He shrugged as if he didn't believe me. He said, "I can have a date over now. Before, I felt like a teenager bringing someone home to my mother's house."

"I want you to have your own life, Charlie."

"Well, I sure can now." He took a swallow of beer. "My sperm doesn't have any swimmers."

At first I thought I'd misunderstood him, but he continued, "My nuts swelled up and hurt for two days."

"You had a vasectomy? Did you have this done recently?"

"Nope. I was sixteen. Johnny said I got that instead of my driver's license."

OK. That seemed kind of a cruel thing to say. "How did you feel about it?"

"I had a cute girlfriend at the time. I was very happy with it." He poked me. "You know what I mean."

"I sure do. What happened to your girlfriend?"

"She found someone else."

I glanced at him, but he didn't seem upset. I really didn't know what to do with this information.

He must've thought he needed to explain more, so he said, "My parents didn't trust me, you know, with girls. They were afraid some female would trap me with pregnancy." Then he said as if in confidence, "My family has money."

I wanted to say, "No shit. Look at this mansion." Instead, I put the beer to my lips and drank down a big gulp.

He changed the subject. "I like your grandpa."

"Yeah, he's nice. I think your mom and him will be happy. You're OK with them getting married, aren't you?"

"Hell yes. Because of that and because of you, I got my own place."

Our backyard was perfect for a wedding. John and Charlie stood with their mother; Dad and I stood with Grandpa. The whole day was fun. Lucy couldn't come, but Valley did. She and Charlie were together the entire day. She seemed to truly enjoy him. My only hope was that Charlie didn't read too much into the friendship. I trusted Valley; she wouldn't hurt him on purpose, but Charlie was overly infatuated with her. He'd even switched to her for his haircuts. She was very sweet with him, and he loved flirting with her.

That night John climbed on me for the quick sex he liked so much. He did this on a fairly regular basis. We'd never discussed this peculiar preference of his, which I'd come to think of as "cold sex." It usually happened when I was freezing and not really in the mood, but I never told him no. Honestly, I liked how much he seemed to enjoy himself. I would never say this to him, but he had a Jekyll-and-Hyde personality in the bedroom. Sometimes he was the best lover I'd ever had. Very giving and patient. Then at other times, he liked this emotionless sex...almost as if he was merely masturbating on me.

Usually, I lay still and waited for him to finish, but that night, I wanted in on some of the action. After he'd entered me and was working himself into a frenzy, I raised my legs and wrapped my arms around his back. He instantly stopped, lost his erection, and slipped out of me. Shocked, I didn't know what to say or do. He was embarrassed, as men always were when they had a failure-to-finish episode. He rolled off me, so I turned to him and laid my head on his chest. We went to sleep without saying anything.

The next morning, he left the house early. I wasn't sure if he'd gotten a corpse call or if he was avoiding me. At some point, though, we'd need to talk about this. First and foremost, there wasn't anything to be upset or ashamed about. Second, I thought maybe my actions had somehow ruined his quickie. If they had, he could tell me. I was open minded enough to hear that from him. I certainly told him what I liked and didn't like in bed. He could do the same with me.

He arrived home a couple of hours later, acting as if nothing was amiss, so I did the same. All day I thought of ways to start the conversation, but it never felt quite right. That night in bed, he pulled me on top of him; we completed the act just fine. Maybe some things in a marriage didn't need to be discussed.

CHAPTER 8

It was the anniversary of our first meeting, August 16. That we were already married amazed me. John wanted to celebrate, and I didn't have a problem with it, although I didn't think our first meeting had been me at my best. Also, the fact wasn't lost on me that Mrs. Grover had been dead a year.

Personally, I'd rather celebrate our second meeting at the movies or our third date Rollerblading. But John told me he was so moved, so affected by our first encounter. My honesty about Mrs. Grover's eyebrows. My laughing hysterically. My crying uncontrollably.

He said, "After the funeral, I couldn't quit thinking about you in your short black skirt and your long legs. I liked the way you treated your grandmother. You had this charisma about yourself that I was drawn to. I just thought, 'If I ever get a chance with this woman, I'll do anything to make her happy.'"

Who was I to argue with all that? So celebrate we did.

After he was asleep, I lay awake and thought about how much my life had changed because of that one day. I suppose everyone could say the same thing about meeting the person he or she would eventually be with. Finally, I understood my parents' crazy love story.

One thing was different in my marriage compared to my parents': John and I never discussed money. From the moment we returned from our honeymoon and moved into the house, I hadn't paid another personal bill. All the household expenses—gas for my car, even my personal charge card—were paid by him. That he paid my credit-card bill made me uncomfortable. Other than clothes, I wasn't a spendthrift. I watched my money very closely, but now I felt uneasy buying things I normally wouldn't have given a second thought to. Nowadays, the only thing I paid for was anything to do with my salon and my makeup line.

I wished it didn't bother me, but it did. I felt like a kept woman instead of a partner. I knew he had money, but I wanted to discuss things. Even his buying this house, without discussing it with me, bothered me. But I understood his reasoning. I'd made it so blatantly obvious that I loved the place; he knew he couldn't go wrong buying it for me.

Also, he'd hired a weekly cleaning crew, which I liked and loathed all at the same time. Most women would love to be in my shoes, and really I shouldn't have cared, but in a way, I felt out of control or maybe just the opposite—I felt controlled.

Labor Day weekend was exceptionally warm. Since I was off, I spent most of my time in the pool. John, of course, was busy all weekend with holiday accidents. As I dove off the board, I noticed something on the bottom of the pool, wedged in the corner. I swam down and retrieved a bikini top. It certainly wasn't mine, so I knew Charlie had a girlfriend, or at least someone he was intimate with.

When he returned home, I walked back to his cottage. Once inside, I held up the top. His face broke into a huge grin.

"I had a little party the other evening when you and Johnny were gone."

"Obviously."

"She was fun, but we aren't seeing each other again."

"Why's that?"

He looked at me as if trying to decide whether he should tell me or not. "I found out she's married."

Well, that explained a lot. Charlie wouldn't knowingly mess around with a married woman. We chatted for a few more minutes; then I broached a subject I'd been thinking about for some time. "Charlie, have you ever tried to drive?"

"No."

"Did you ever want to?"

"Yes, but I knew I'd never be allowed to."

"Do you still want to?"

He grinned. "I'd like to try it one time."

"I think we should go out next weekend. John's going with Grandpa and your mom to some old-car show. If you don't go with them, we could go practice."

He hugged me so hard my breath stopped and a vertebra in my back popped into place, but I understood how exciting this was for him. He was twenty-six and had never driven a vehicle.

Neither of us said anything to anyone…totally our secret. The moment the threesome left, Charlie was at my back door. He was a pile of emotions: excitement and nervousness all rolled into one. I'd racked my brain for places where we could drive that'd be safe for us and the innocent public. The only place I came up with was the huge parking lot at the high school. No one would be there since school was out.

In my car I began with the first lessons. The seat belts, the pedals, the rearview mirror, and safety, safety, safety. No phone usage of any kind. I made him repeat it—twice. "No-phone zone." Once at the school, I had a moment of wondering, "What the hell am I doing?" but it didn't last long.

Charlie was the driver I strived to be. Moved cautiously, listened intently, looked thoroughly, and let nothing distract him. We drove around the lot for at least two hours. When he was comfortable with my car, we drove out on the road around the school property. He was doing a magnificent job when I yelled, "Stop! There's a kid."

He slammed on the brakes. The seat belts locked as we were thrown forward. He turned to me wide eyed. "Did I hit him?"

"No, there wasn't a kid. I was just checking your reflexes. You did perfect."

He patted his heart. "Fuck, Macie. That scared the shit out of me."

"Well, you did great. Quick reactions, and you hit the correct pedal."

He slowly grinned at me. I said, "Here's what we're going to do. We're going to practice every chance we get. Then I'll enroll you in driver's ed. If you can pass that, then we'll buy you a car."

He nodded. I thought I saw tears in his eyes.

For the next month, it was as if we were having an affair. We'd sneak around and drive Sunny (my car) all over the place. If John got a call in the evening, then I'd call Charlie.

"Bloody hell, someone died."

"Whoopee," he'd yell.

He needed to drive at dusk and at night, so I thought it was good experience. If John needed to work on a Saturday, then Charlie and I'd drive around for hours. He was the best driver. It infuriated me that he'd never been allowed to get his driver's license when he was sixteen. That they'd never even let him try. There was no good reason. No good reason whatsoever.

I knew it was probably illegal for him to be driving without a learner's permit, but I was afraid if he went to driver's ed. without having a tad bit of confidence, he'd be easily intimidated by the instructor. I didn't want him cowed or made to feel stupid.

Sunday afternoon John was called to pick up a body. I immediately called Charlie. "Let's pretend you're taking me on a date. I want you to come to the front door and walk me to the car. We'll drive around. Then you can take me to Sonic and buy me a drink."

Within ten minutes my doorbell rang. I opened the door, and his grin was so big that my heart melted. I handed him the keys. He took me by the arm, walked me to the car, opened the door for me, and helped me inside. We drove around for about an hour; then he took me to Sonic. I told him what I wanted. He placed the order and paid the carhop.

As we were sipping our drinks, he turned to me. "I like that woman with the black hair. She has nice boobs."

"OK, Charlie, you know that isn't the thing to say when you're on a date."

Shocked, he said, "I forgot we were on a date. I was just talking to you as my sister-in-law."

I laughed. "OK. That's fine. See that guy over there, the one in the red shirt? I think he has a really nice ass. And the one standing by the black truck is hot too."

Charlie looked at both of them, then turned to me, and said, "I was with this woman, you know, having sex with her, and she didn't move."

"Some women, believe it or not, don't like sex. I wouldn't take it personally. Are you seeing her again?"

"Nope, she's gone."

"What do you mean 'gone'?"

"Gone. Gone. Gone." Then after a beat, he added, "Married."

"Oh." I nodded. "You've had a lot of girlfriends, haven't you?"

He smiled. "A lot more than Johnny, that's for sure. But he went to college and then went to work, so he didn't have as much free time as I did."

Since he'd brought it up, I decided to pursue this. "Was John ever with anyone else like he was with Robin?"

"No, not really. Robin chased him until he finally dated her. She had big plans for them."

"What about the girl in high school that he was crazy about?"

He jerked his head around. "What did Johnny tell you about Fiona?"

"Nothing. Just that she'd died during a track meet or something."

"Oh. Well, she was three years younger than him. They dated, but she was too young to...you know. I'm sure he wanted to, but she had, you know, that virgin thing going on."

I laughed. "Who did he date between her and Robin?"

"He didn't really. I mean, he had girlfriends in college but nothing serious that I ever knew about. Once he graduated and came back, he mainly spent time with the women at the funeral home."

"Oh. He dated his coworkers. I see. Well, that can sometimes get sticky. The whole working, dating, relationship thing. Once he took over for your father, then I'm sure that changed those relationships."

Charlie looked at me for a while and sucked on his strawberry chiller. Finally, he said, "If I get my driver's license, will you go with me to buy a car?"

"No. We'd better have John or my dad do that. I'm not good at negotiating. What kind of car do you want?"

"I wish I could have a Dodge Dart."

I doubled over with laughter.

He laughed too. "I saw one on a movie the other day. I liked the name. I'd like to say, 'I drive a Dodge Dart.'"

"Do you have a checking account?"

"No. Johnny puts my check in the savings for me every week. I have a lot of money."

"We're going to open you a checking account and apply for a credit card. You need to start making your own decisions. I'll be with you every step of the way, but you need to do this."

When we were ready to go, Charlie backed out skillfully. A few blocks from home, John called. "Where are you?"

"I'm with Charlie. We're almost back at the house."

There was total silence. I realized my mistake. I shouldn't have answered my phone.

"I'll see you when you get here."

I turned to Charlie. "We've been found out, so here's what we're going to do. You're going to pull into the drive like nothing's unusual. If John's angry, I'll handle it. None of this was your doing. I won't let you take the heat for any of it."

He nodded.

As we pulled into the drive, John was waiting in the yard. His arms were crossed, but other than that, he didn't look too upset. Charlie put Sunny in park and turned to me. A grin split his face from ear to ear. If this was all that became of his driving episodes—if he never got a driver's license—his happiness in that moment was worth every second.

We climbed out of Sunny; I walked to the front of the car. John looked at Charlie but never once looked at me. I never would've guessed in a hundred years what John did next. He walked up to Charlie and embraced him. It was one of the most moving things I'd ever seen.

He asked Charlie, "How long has this been going on?"

"Several weeks. Macie took me to a parking lot and taught me how to drive. Then she yelled at me when I almost hit a kid, but there wasn't a kid. She said I had perfect reflexes. From then on, we drove on streets and highways. Just all over the place, Johnny. We went to Sonic today. I pointed out the girl I liked, and she told me the two guys' asses she liked."

John's eyes left Charlie's and flicked over to me. I didn't know if I should smile or look contrite, so I put the straw in my mouth and took a big gulp of my cherry limeade. His eyes went back to Charlie's.

Charlie said, "She says I'm a better driver than she is."

"That's not saying much."

Charlie laughed hard. Then John said, "I'm mad about two things, Charlie." He looked at me again. I immediately began sucking on my limeade as if it were the best thing ever. "The first is that you both felt the need to hide this from me. The other is that you went to Sonic and didn't bring me back a root beer float. You know how much I like those."

A laugh escaped from me.

He said, "Tomorrow, you're driving me to Sonic and buying me one. Plus, I want to see these two guys Macie thinks are so fine."

Charlie was overjoyed at the prospect of driving John somewhere. I knew John couldn't believe that his brother could drive. Maybe, too, that he'd never thought of doing this himself. He told Charlie he wanted some alone time with me.

Charlie handed me my keys, and I thanked him for the cherry limeade. Inside, John kissed me and made love to me like I was some treasure. Afterward, he wouldn't stop talking about this miraculous thing I'd done for his brother.

"When Charlie turned sixteen, instead of getting a driver's license, my parents gave him a vasectomy. I've always felt horrible about it. I was away at college and found out after the fact, or I would've tried to intervene. I tried to make it sound like a good thing to him, but it only came across as an insult. I've always wished that I could take my words back, but I can't."

Rubbing his back, I was so relieved by his confession. Ever since Charlie had told me about that incident, I'd sort of been pissed at John for not standing up for him.

Later that night in bed, he started in again. "You see Charlie different than the rest of us. You've made me see him in a whole new light. I've always tried to protect him. I still do. I still think he needs my protection, but I guess I carry it too far."

He swallowed hard. "That's the real reason Robin and I broke up. I knew she didn't like him, was ashamed of him, but I thought after she got to know him, she'd see what a great guy he was. Then I overheard her refer to him as retarded. I hated that bitch. I hated her. I broke up with her right then.

"When you and I first started dating, I didn't want you to meet him because it would've broken my heart if you would've felt the same way. But, Macie, you love him as much as I do. You love him and treat him so sweet that it almost breaks my heart."

"Oh, John, I want him to have his own life. Let's help him do that."

The following month, John and I attended the National Funeral Directors Convention. Even though we would be gone less than a week, I asked Dad and Grandpa if they'd ride with Charlie. He was taking driver's ed. and needed to log driving hours. They both agreed, which was a huge relief for me. I was concerned Charlie would try to drive by himself.

At the convention I'd made arrangements to have a booth in the exhibit hall for my makeup line. Honestly, I wouldn't have thought of this myself, but once John suggested it, I knew it was a good idea.

My booth was a hot spot. John knew a lot of people and gave my makeup a high recommendation. I gave away numerous sample kits and sold several orders. I knew if I could get this makeup in the hands of the right people, they'd want to use it on a regular basis.

During our short time away, Charlie had formed a special friendship with my dad and Grandpa. Probably all the time spent driving together. Our families blended so well, which brought me a special kind of joy. Over the holidays—with Grandpa and Marabeth now married—it had just seemed as if we were one big happy family.

And Charlie—he was the best brother-in-law, the best friend to me. He'd matured. I couldn't say exactly how, but he just seemed different.

His friendship meant everything to me.

CHAPTER 9

The day Charlie was issued his driver's license, he and John went car shopping. I wanted to tell John to let Charlie pick out the car he wanted, but before I even opened my mouth, John said, "I can't wait to see what kind of car Charlie wants. I don't care if it takes us a whole month of looking at every new-car lot in town; I want him to buy his heart's desire."

It didn't take that long, though. Charlie had been researching cars, and like anyone in the market for a new vehicle, he looked at anything and everything that was on the road. Suddenly, a Dodge Dart was beneath him; he chose a new Audi sports car.

The weekend they went to pick up his car, I threw a big party for him. As he celebrated his success, I couldn't help but notice his transformation. He was a different person. He walked different, talked different, and had a new attitude. He was, truly, his own man. He said, "Macie, I'm whole now."

I laughed. "You've always been whole."

"No, not really."

Marabeth, overhearing our conversation, wiped her eyes. "He's right. You've given him everything his father and I wanted to."

She pulled me into a hard hug and sobbed on my shoulder. I patted her back until she regained control.

For Valentine's Day, John had asked me to plan my schedule so I could take off early. Everyone in the salon was leaving at four, so I didn't have to change anything. When I arrived home, I immediately took a shower to remove all the hair stuck to me. After I was dressed and ready to go, he blindfolded me and led me out to the garage. Once the blindfold was removed, I was staring, totally speechless, at a new yellow Audi sports car.

"This is from Charlie and me. We wanted to thank you for all you did for him. He wanted you to have the same kind of car as him. I honestly would've picked something else, but when Charlie saw this one on the showroom floor in your favorite color, he pointed and said, 'That's it.' I couldn't tell him no."

"My gosh, you didn't need to do this." But as the words were coming out of my mouth, I was climbing into the car. He laughed and walked around to the passenger's side. I drove us to the restaurant but could hardly read the menu as I was so excited about the car. I thought the gift was magnificent, but I was more touched by the fact that Charlie wanted us to have the same type of car. His heart was so kind. It did bother me, though, that John had let Charlie pay for half of the car. I finally said, "I really don't like Charlie spending his money on me."

"He insisted. I couldn't talk him down. He wanted to pay for the whole thing. The only way I convinced him to let me pay for half was by telling him that it would make me look bad since his gift would be better than mine."

I laughed.

"I'm not joking. It really did bother me. Him buying you the car and that he'd found a yellow one."

"I still don't like him spending his money that way."

"Charlie's rich. Don't worry about him."

Once we'd finished eating, John asked if I'd like to do anything special.

"Yeah, let's drive around."

He grinned. "OK, but then maybe we can go home and play some pool."

We drove around for about an hour. I loved the car. I'd already called Charlie and left a voice mail thanking him for such a sweet gift. I knew he was probably out driving around himself.

Back at the house, we went to the basement to play pool. Our games had become very competitive. John had always won, but I'd come awful close a few times. That night, though, I played well and won, although I wasn't totally convinced that he hadn't let me. But since I had, I took full advantage of the privilege. I knew exactly what we'd do. As the winner, it was my prerogative to decide how the rest of the night went. (John always had me do a striptease or give him a lap dance. Men were such simple, simple creatures.)

I took full control. "You're doing exactly what I say, John."

He grinned. "OK."

"You're going to keep your hands to yourself. Don't touch me unless I tell you to."

I unbuttoned his shirt and slowly removed it. I began kissing him—his mouth, his neck, his nipples, his stomach, working my way down to his belt. God, he had the best body. I undid the belt slowly and removed his jeans. I liked seeing him in his briefs, but I removed those as well. I said, "Wow, you could play pool with that hard thing."

He tried to push against me, but I held him back. Once I had him naked, I just kissed him, licked him, and nipped at him until he was a begging mess. Then I stood in front of him and took off my dress but kept my bra and panties on. This was one thing that turned John on, the anticipation of removing those two small garments. I kissed him again and started stroking him.

Finally, he said, "Macie, I'm getting blue balls here. I really am."

I giggled. "Oh, John, you are not."

"I am. I really can't take any more of this. They're actually beginning to hurt."

I cupped them in my hands. "Did I really win this game, or did you let me?"

"You did."

"Tell me the truth, or I won't stop with the torture."

"You really won. I promise. But I will tell you this: I'll never let it happen again."

"You can lift me up onto the table."

This was one thing I loved—the way he could lift me up. He had powerful upper-body strength from all the dead weight he lifted at work. Once up on the table and on my knees, I crawled around in front of him. He watched my every move. I turned so that I was facing him. "OK, you can kiss between my breasts."

He buried his face in them and then kissed up to my ear. "I'm begging you. Please let me come up there and finish this off."

"OK, you can come up here."

He swung up onto the table in one quick second. Before I even said he could, he had my bra unhooked and thrown on the floor.

"Now, John, I'm still in control here."

But really I wasn't because his hands were in my panties pulling them off. Then his finger was inside me. I tried to sound firm, but my voice came out more like a whimper as I said, "I told you not to touch me until I said you could."

He put his mouth on mine to shut me up. Then he was on top of me and inside me. From that point on, I couldn't even think clearly except to know he'd never let me win at pool again.

In June, we celebrated our first anniversary on a little secluded island that John had discovered online. He was the most romantic guy, but I kept reminding myself that money could buy a lot of romantic things in life.

Back home the following week, one of Lucy's aunts died. They weren't close, but Lucy planned on attending the funeral. The day of the viewing, I stopped by the funeral home to have lunch with John. He asked if I wanted to look at the body before Lucy did. I didn't think Lucy would care one way or the other what her aunt looked like, but I thought, "What the heck."

The woman was in her midforties. Kelly had done a fine job on her makeup, but I thought she could use a little more color on her cheeks, and her eyebrows needed a little more work. Asian women had the most beautiful skin and always kept their eyebrows plucked and sculpted in a perfect arch. I probably noticed her eyebrows because I did so many wax jobs at work. Kelly's failure to take the time to pluck a few strays seemed lazy to me. She probably thought, "What difference does it make?" Well, it did. It made a difference.

I asked John to bring me some tweezers and the makeup bag I'd previously left there from Cathy. He returned shortly and stood by my side as I applied a little more blush and dabbed off some of her lipstick. (Kelly was heavy handed with lipstick for some reason.) I was plucking the last of three stray hairs near her eyebrows when Kelly stepped into the room. I immediately smiled and said, "She looks perfect. You did an amazing job."

She looked at the tissue with the lipstick and said, "Obviously, you didn't think so." She turned and stomped off.

John didn't seem upset, but I knew Kelly needed to be reassured her work was OK. I told him he needed to talk to her. I would've myself, but I needed to return to the salon. I had a full afternoon scheduled.

When John arrived home, he was in one foul mood. "Kelly quit. She doesn't want you checking her work or doing any touch-ups. I told her it was my business; I could run it the way I saw fit. I also said that starting today she was using your makeup. She told me to go to hell and walked out."

He was pissed, but honestly, I couldn't blame her. She was threatened by me, and if the tables were turned, I would've felt the same way. But I knew John wanted to use my makeup at the funeral home. When we returned from the convention, he'd told me he didn't feel right that I was selling it to other funeral homes and he wasn't even using it in his own.

I felt responsible for Kelly quitting. If I'd just left those three eyebrow hairs alone, this would've never happened. I asked, "So, what now?"

He looked at me. Oh, bloody hell, I knew what he was thinking.

I rubbed my forehead. I'd been back and forth with this—a private struggle in my own mind. I'd fought the idea but had come to realize there wasn't any difference putting makeup on a live woman or a dead one. Well, clearly, there was. Of course, there was. A live one talked. A live one could make me mad. Could make me want to pull my hair out. A dead one couldn't.

If I was honest with myself, I'd admit I missed applying makeup but didn't want to do the bride packages anymore (couldn't handle any more bridezillas). I knew John wanted us to work together. Even though I'd only done one makeup job that he'd seen, he'd liked how it had turned out.

I said, "I don't want to give up my salon. Could I do this in the evening or first thing in the morning?"

"You could do it whenever you want to. Men take a lot less time than women. I don't want you working too much, though, Macie. I don't want you working day and night."

"Let me just try it. But I want you to promise me, if I don't like it or can't handle it, you'll let me walk away without giving me any grief."

"OK."

Thus began my moonlighting job in the funeral business. I'd never imagined this for myself, but I quite liked it. Dead people were at peace, and it seemed, especially with the women, I was doing them a favor. After a while, I just felt honored to do this last thing for them. And also, I loved how much John respected me and bragged about me at the funeral home. I had become his makeup person, and I must say, I was quite good.

The only problem: I had no free time. I became a working machine. I still used Mondays to stock the salon and take care of the clerical duties. Tuesday through Friday, I cut and colored hair. I tried to cut back on my hours, but I had my regular client base and didn't want to lose them. I referred any new client to one of the other hairdressers.

Every morning before going to the salon, I'd go to the funeral home and work until I needed to leave. Once I left the salon, I'd eat a quick supper and return to the funeral home. Some evenings I wasn't there very long. Other times I returned home after eleven, which made for a long, tiring day. Weekends were hit or miss.

The bodies were always dressed and ready. I never had to deal with that part of the process. John seemed to comprehend I wasn't ready for anything more than a very small part of the business. When I arrived, the corpse would be in a small room just outside the embalming room. Normally, this room was only used when another hairdresser was brought in. (Some family members wanted the woman's regular hairdresser. Lord, I certainly understood that.) John knew my uneasiness with the embalming room—the sheet-covered bodies and that awful sink were more than I could take—so he simply moved my work into a more comfortable area for me.

Since John and I never discussed money, we never even brought up the idea of a salary. I honestly hadn't thought about it until a salon client offhandedly remarked on my second job. At first, I thought she was referring to my makeup, until I realized that she was taking about the funeral home. I wasn't sure how she knew about it because I certainly didn't broadcast those details.

All day I thought about the fact that I was basically working for free. But I would feel weird telling John to pay me a wage when he paid for every single thing in my life.

In October, we attended the national convention again. I set up a makeup booth in the exhibit hall, and for the second time, I did quite well. Now that I'd done several makeup jobs on cadavers, I truly knew the process and understood what my makeup could do. Because of the convention, my sales jumped to a whole new level, making me a nice profit. John saw the potential of my makeup line and wanted to advertise in one of the magazines for funeral directors. I'd never thought to promote it that way, but I agreed—it was an excellent idea.

CHAPTER 10

By our second wedding anniversary, I realized I couldn't handle all the jobs. I felt as if I had two careers (my salon and my makeup line) and one job (the funeral duties). I was considering selling my salon to Lucy. I struggled with the decision because the salon was my baby. I'd built it on my own, and as prideful as this might sound, I was pleased I'd accomplished so much at such a young age. Also, I still wanted my own identity apart from John. I'd never changed my name, mainly because of my makeup line. He'd never said one word about it, and I really believed it was a nonissue for him.

Lucy assured me I could still sell my makeup at the salon even though I'd no longer own it. I could still cut hair if I wanted to, which I thought I would. I knew if I asked John, he'd tell me that he really wanted me totally out of the salon business. He thought I worked too much as it was, and of course, he wanted me working with him.

Also, I wanted to start our family. There wasn't any way I could keep my schedule and have a baby. Something had to give. If I sold my salon, I wouldn't be tied to a schedule. I could make my own hours at the funeral home and work on my makeup line whenever it was convenient for me. I saw the benefits of the change.

With a heavy heart and a knot in my stomach, I agreed to sell my business to Lucy. The night before I signed the papers, I had a major breakdown. I didn't have the guts to back out and didn't want to renege on Lucy. If she'd been someone else, I would've called the whole thing off in a heartbeat, but I just couldn't do that to her. For the first time, I think

John realized how much the salon meant to me and how little I wanted to do this.

In the morning, I woke with dread, knowing I was making a huge mistake. But I went through with the deal.

For the next two weeks, I was literally sick, as if I had an ulcer eating away at my insides. When I thought about what I'd done, I knew I'd made the wrong decision. Every time I told a client I couldn't reschedule them, I almost bawled. John tried to pull me out of my funk, but I needed time to adjust. He found out real quick what not to say to me. One night—probably tired of my less than stellar attitude—he made a comment about how much money I'd made from the sale. That we were a team now...partners at the funeral home.

I shouted at him, which I'd never done before. "Money isn't everything. And we're not a team. The funeral home is yours. Your family's. The salon was me. My life. My dream."

I left the house in a huff and drove over to Grande's. She seemed better able to cope with my moods. She understood how I felt about the salon, whereas my mom had never owned a business. Mom had always seemed to take John's side. When I told her I was selling the salon so that I could work with John, she'd said, "That's wonderful. He needs your help. Supporting his business is the right thing to do."

Like always, Grande was supportive but realistic. "Macie, I don't know if it was the right decision or not, but you've made it, so you need to move on. You're a wonderful makeup person and can still use your talent but just in a different way. This is still an amazing career."

I agreed with her that it was a good career, but the fact was that no one would see my work other than the people attending the funerals. My handiwork would be closed in a casket and buried. It wasn't as if I'd be getting referrals from the deceased on their stylish hairdos.

I returned home late that evening. Well, actually, early in the morning. I drank until I was three sheets to the wind and collapsed on the sofa. When I woke the next morning, John poured me a cup of coffee.

He didn't know what to say, so he merely sat staring at me as if I were a wild beast that couldn't be trusted. I knew how his mind worked and swore if he said he'd buy me another salon, I'd hit him over the head with my coffee cup.

We stared at each other, neither one of us saying a word. When his phone went off, I was grateful for that dead person's perfect timing. Once John left, I crawled into bed. After waking hours later, I showered and then had a long talk with myself. I decided to accept my decision. I'd made it. I'd done it. Now I needed to get over it.

When John returned home, he entered the kitchen, carrying a bag of takeout. I was starving, and somehow, I'd shed my unhappiness. I walked to him and pulled him to me. He sighed with relief that my ugliness was gone.

After selling my salon, I had lots of free time. Well, maybe not free time, but I wasn't on a tight schedule anymore. I shared booth rent with another hairdresser, working Tuesdays and Thursdays. I missed the hubbub of the salon, but I'd reconciled with my choices. John wouldn't admit it, but he was thrilled with my work schedule. He'd cut back himself by turning more of the actual funeral services over to Charlie, who was great with his new responsibilities.

Although the funeral job was fulfilling, it was just that—a job. Not a career. John wanted me to love it the way he did. Maybe not love the business, but love working with him. He considered us partners and tried to convince me that we were, but I never felt that way. More like I was working *for* him instead of *with* him. There was a big difference between the two.

Another hard thing was telling people what I did for a living. I used to love saying that I owned Wood Borough Salon. Now, I hated admitting I worked on dead people. One day at the grocery store, the checkout lady offhandedly asked where I worked.

"A funeral home."

Her face turned sour. "What do you do there?"

"Makeup on the deceased."

Horrified, she acted as if I were the grim reaper. She hurriedly sacked my groceries, never looking me in the eye again.

Also, and this one, admittedly, was petty, I couldn't wear the clothes I liked and used to wear at the salon. John had never said I had to dress differently, but he'd once told me that he never let Kelly talk to the families because she didn't dress appropriately. He obviously thought her nipple exposure wasn't the best thing for a bereaved family to witness.

I'd bought some new clothes—business attire. Now I had my own funeral-clothes section in our closet, the same as John. I liked the suits; I just didn't think they represented the true me. When I met with the families, though, they saw a professional instead of some floozy without undergarments.

Now that the funeral job was my main job, I spent more time there than at the salon and did more than just hair and makeup. John and I had never talked about my responsibilities, but he had just assumed, and I had just accepted that I'd do more. Working with grieving families was one of my new duties, and it was more rewarding than I would've believed. When they had questions about what clothing to bury their loved ones in, I tried to help with their decision. I was good at smoothing over any fighting among the family members. Some wanted to bury their loved ones in some favorite old outfit, while others wanted them buried in new clothing—they just didn't want to actually go buy the new clothing.

I didn't mind doing this at all. In fact, I enjoyed it. I'd find out the deceased's favorite color. Especially with women, I asked their clothing style. Did they like dresses, suits, bows at the neck, and so on? Also, a picture was worth a thousand words, although I couldn't believe how many times people brought in their parents' wedding picture. Bloody hell. What was I supposed to do with that?

Several times a month, I'd find myself in Dillard's or Macy's (of course, I had to support that store). Shopping for a man's suit took very little time. From one glance at a picture, I could tell the man's style. What he liked in a tie—plain or stylish. Women, on the other hand, could take me a while. But I always seemed to find the right outfit, and the families were always pleased with my decision. The only thing that made me uneasy about the new clothes was the fact that we actually split them up the back to get them on the body. As I sliced my way through the cloth, I always wondered, if the family knew this, would they still want to spend the money for new clothing? But really, what difference did it make? Either way, no one was ever going to wear the clothes again.

In a short period of time, I learned a lot about the funeral business. Well, at least one small part of the business: making death presentable by preparing a body for viewing. Some of it I would've rather not known, but I'd admit that certain aspects of it fascinated me. John taught me so much about the human body's facial structure.

With expertise and patience, he trained me to use wax like a pro. After I got the hang of it, I used it on almost every older person I did. Some younger bodies needed it too, but not always. My first makeup job on an accident victim, though, was one of the hardest for me. She was an older woman (fell off a ladder—broke her neck), and her chin was sort of gone. John showed me how to use wax to rebuild and contour her face. He was so patient with me, especially when I'd get squeamish. He'd say, "Now, Macie, you can do this."

Once we were finished with her makeup, I was impressed with the end result. John said, "You're absolutely the best makeup person I've ever had."

He made me so proud of myself. After that experience, I thought I was up for anything.

One Friday afternoon, a motorcycle-accident victim was brought in; John would be working on him in the morning. That evening he said, "The whole left side of his face is missing. The family wants an open casket if at all possible."

"That's crazy. They should have him cremated."

He looked at me and said, "I told his brother I'd rebuild his face."

Not only was the family crazy, but John was insane. But then I realized, even though I was more than a little freaked out, I wanted to observe his reconstruction process.

"Can I watch you do this?"

He grinned and pinched my butt. "Macie, Macie. You never cease to amaze me."

Driving to the funeral home the next morning, John patted my leg. I knew he was pleased I was going with him. Delighted that I was interested in his work. But I was having second thoughts. My only hope was that I could stay in the room during the whole process and keep myself from upchucking into that dreadful sink. My uneasiness must've filled the car, because he said, "I'm so happy you came with me this morning. You'll be great help."

I swallowed and didn't say one word. I doubted I'd be much assistance.

In the room, we dressed in disposable gowns, gloves, and eyewear. This act alone made me so apprehensive that I wanted to tell John I'd come back and pick him up when he was done. He knew me well enough by then to know I was waning and immediately began his soothing chatter as he laid out the equipment he'd need.

I willed myself to stay. Willed myself to be a team player. John pulled the table forward so he could start the work. I braced myself for the first sight of the man's face. John warned me again by saying, "His face is partially gone."

He pulled the sheet back, and holy shit, he hadn't lied. Well, in a way he had. It wasn't just his face that was missing but the whole left side of his head. My first thought was, "This is nothing but raw meat."

John watched me—would I faint or hold strong? Horrified, I backed away, hitting my bottom on the cabinet as I took several deep breaths. Then I raised my eyes to John. He stood, waiting for me to make my decision of whether to stay or go. I knew he wanted me to stay, so I stepped forward and nodded.

"That's my Macie."

And the work began.

With plaster of paris, wax, glue, and a lot of patience, he literally re-made the left side of the man's face. Six hours later I started applying the makeup. That time I did use mortician's makeup, which helped to camou-flage severe flaws. When we were done, I had a whole new respect for my husband. And he had a whole new respect for me.

The next day John called the parents to view the body. He wanted to make sure they were pleased with everything before the public viewing. I normally wouldn't have gone with him, but he wanted me there. I wasn't sure why, but I didn't argue.

The young man's parents and his brother arrived a few minutes after John and I had moved the casket into the viewing area. Grabbing each other's hands, they walked to the coffin. When the mother saw her son, she immediately broke down into these awful wailing sounds. The dad and brother quietly wept. I hated witnessing it and didn't understand why John wanted me to. I had to wipe my own eyes. I didn't think it was proper for me to cry in front of the family, but I simply couldn't help myself. I glanced at John because I knew he'd be disappointed in my lack of control, but I saw tears in his eyes as well.

Then a miraculous thing happened. The mother looked at John and me and said, "Thank you for this. Thank you for giving me this last look at him."

The three of them stayed for about twenty minutes; then they left. Before walking out, the brother came to John. "Thank you for all your work on my brother. I identified him at the morgue, so I know what all you did. Deep down my parents know he was severely banged up, but now they can release that image from their nightmares. You've no idea what it means to me, you doing this for them."

John simply squeezed the man's arm and said, "I was honored to do this for you and your family."

They left, and we were alone. The whole experience opened my eyes to something I couldn't even put into words. Maybe people needed to be at peace with the deaths of their loved ones. Also, I truly understood why John did what he did. If I hadn't understood it before, I definitely did now. I saw it through his eyes. Not everyone could do this, but he could. I was glad he'd insisted I come with him to witness this.

He said, "I wanted you to see for yourself how worthwhile all this is. That you give the families something they need."

All I could say was, "I love you, John. I really love you."

It wasn't until I started working at the funeral home on a regular basis that I realized Charlie was always the first to arrive. His early arrival had started several years ago because Marabeth went to an early morning exercise class. Since it was her responsibility to drive Charlie to work, she'd gotten in the habit of dropping him off before her class. Even though he now drove himself, he'd never changed his schedule—an embedded habit. He'd turn on the lights, make coffee, and then check the corpse being viewed that day. If he foresaw any problems, he'd either handle them himself or alert one of the funeral directors.

Sometimes I went in early on Tuesdays and Thursdays before going to the salon. On more than one occasion, he and I would be the only ones there for the first few hours. That was when I first learned about leakage, which absolutely gave me the fucking willies. I tried not to think too much about it, but it was an issue. Some of the bodies leaked once they were in the casket. For the most part, it only happened to the victims of an accident or to someone who'd been in the hospital on IV fluids. Thankfully, the majority of the bodies didn't have that issue. Fortunately for me, Charlie handled it before I arrived. He'd just say, "Leakage." I'd know then why the body wasn't ready for viewing.

Usually, though, I started my day helping John or one of the other morticians dress the corpses. I didn't hate the dressing part, but I certainly could've done without it. I'd liked it better when I was moonlighting and the bodies were ready for me when I arrived.

Several things shocked me about the process. For one, the bodies weren't stiff. I'd always thought once rigor mortis set in, it stayed. That wasn't the case at all. But still, it was hard dressing a dead person, who was of absolutely no help at all with the process.

The underclothes also surprised me. One: we always put them on the dead. Two: a lot of people purchased new ones or wanted me to. Why these facts shocked me, I wasn't sure. Upon further consideration, I realized I wouldn't want to go into eternity without any panties. And I wouldn't want my panties stained or worn out.

Something else I knew but hadn't put too much thought into was how many naked bodies John saw. They were dead, so it didn't really bother me, but still naked was naked.

If the deceased was a man, John would've already shaved him, but the women's hair removal he left to me. And believe me, I did my fair share of light shaving on the women.

Men, for the most part, went rather quickly. Sometimes I'd give them haircuts, and I'd definitely clip the hair out of their noses and ears. Some had quite a forest growing. I'd clean and clip their nails. Use wax (if necessary) and tissue builder, and then apply the makeup.

Women were a different story. I'd decide if I was using hot rollers. If so, I'd start with that; then I used the wax (again, if necessary) and the tissue builder. Sometimes, I wished these women could see how nice they looked after I used the tissue builder. It filled out their wrinkles, and they looked years younger. I'd then apply the makeup and style their hair.

Once I was done, Charlie and I would move the casket into the viewing room. We'd arrange the flowers and the visitation book. This was Charlie's part of the business—the actual preparation for the funeral. He was very meticulous about how he wanted things. I simply followed his lead, and over time, I became accustomed to his preferences.

If John or one of the other morticians brought in a corpse while I was still doing my makeup job, I'd move the body I was working on into another, smaller room. I'd never witnessed an embalming and never planned to. The embalming process was like a scary horror movie. I simply couldn't wrap my mind around that portion of John's job. He'd offered to let me watch, but when I became weak in the knees and damn near fainted, he got his answer and never asked me again. I did ask him questions, though, which probably drove him nuts, but he always answered, keeping the facts as gore-free as he could.

After dealing with dead bodies, I understood why there were showers in the bathrooms. Sometimes, a shower just seemed like the best thing. I'd yet to experience that, but I realized why the embalmers would want to clean themselves. Also, we disinfected everything. We used a ton of bleach in the embalming room. And, just as the tables and all the tools were sterilized, I cleaned my makeup brushes. It just was the thing to do.

I also blocked from my mind the cremations. Not all funeral homes had the equipment (crematoriums) for cremating bodies. I had just assumed they all did. Some of John's business was from that alone—cremating bodies for other funeral homes.

Lastly, the paperwork. Death required so much official procedure. When a corpse was initially brought in, we would log all jewelry and personal items. After the embalming, we had to fill out a death certificate, permits, affidavits, and authorizations. Also, John or his office manager wrote an obituary.

I came to the realization that death was a very busy and profitable business. And it was my new job.

CHAPTER 11

We celebrated our third anniversary with a trip to New York. I'd been there before with Valley, but John had never been. When we returned, I was sick with the flu. My stomach was unsettled, and the smell of the funeral home made me queasy. After a week of this, it finally dawned on me. I didn't have the flu—I was pregnant. On the way home, I stopped at the store to buy a pregnancy test. Once home, I waited for John. I wanted to share this with him even though I already knew the outcome.

We sat together watching the stick. When the answer was clear, John turned to me with such joy that everything seemed perfect in my life. We decided not to tell anyone until I'd been to the doctor. Our own special little thing.

Two nights later, we had cold sex. Afterward, he rolled off me and immediately went to sleep. Within an hour, I began to have cramps. When I rose from the bed, John woke up.

"I think I'm having a miscarriage."

He jumped up and rushed into the bathroom with me. It happened very fast, and I had no doubt whatsoever I'd lost the baby. John was instantly remorseful. Blamed himself for everything. Even though he'd gotten quite robust in his quickie, I didn't believe it was the cause of my miscarriage. I couldn't make him understand that his actions had nothing to do with my losing the pregnancy.

My doctor's appointment was the next day, so instead of finding out my due date, I was counseled on miscarriages. The doctor told me not to overthink this. It didn't mean anything was wrong with me; I should try again. That night as we lay in bed, John told me, "I won't do that again until after our family's complete."

"John, it had nothing to do with your screwing me. I wish you'd get that through your head."

"I won't do that to you again."

Hoping to change his mind and relieve his guilt, I said, "Let's compromise. When I get pregnant again, then you can stop. Until then, let's not change anything."

He was quiet for a moment. Then he pulled me into the crook of his arm. "OK."

I kept the miscarriage a secret. I didn't want that stigma on my shoulders for the next time I became pregnant. People would be holding their breath; I couldn't handle the pressure of their concern.

For the next several weeks, John was in a funk that concerned me. His guilt was ruining his sunny personality. I was upset about the miscarriage, but nothing like he was. Perhaps I hadn't really come to terms with being pregnant before it came to an end. I honestly wasn't concerned that I wouldn't be able to have a baby. Miscarriages were common. I chose not to fill myself with negative thinking. It wasn't anyone's fault. His or mine.

Just when I was about to suggest he talk to someone, John returned to his normal, upbeat self. I was relieved when he overcame his brooding. We took a short trip together, which rejuvenated us. After that we returned to our usual (or unusual) sex life. We played pool several times a month, and he resumed his quickies with zeal—seizing the opportunity while he could. He knew once I became pregnant, it would all come to an end.

Even though I'd only been pregnant for a moment, I'd already started thinking about the next time. I didn't want to find day care for a newborn for the two days I worked at the salon. I knew Marabeth and Grandpa would jump at the chance to watch the baby; I just didn't want to wear them out. They were kind of old.

Also, I'd come to realize an ugly truth: I missed working at the salon on a daily basis. It was becoming increasingly painful for me to simply rent a booth and not own the place. Every time I walked in the door, I was filled with regret. It would simply be better for me to not go in there at all.

My friendship with Lucy had changed as well. Even though I didn't blame her for buying the salon, it had changed our relationship. At times, I got the distinct impression she wished I'd simply disappear. I missed the way things used to be. I decided that when I had my first baby, I'd quit the salon for good.

Valley was stressed when I went in one morning; she asked if we could have lunch together, which was sometimes hard to do, but we made it work that day. We only had thirty minutes, but it certainly was an informative thirty minutes. She told me she'd broken up with Stuart, her boyfriend of two years.

"What exactly happened?"

She stared at her feet. "I've met someone else."

My eyebrows shot upward, but I managed to keep my mouth shut.

"Stuart wasn't the marrying kind. He was never going to propose. I finally accepted it and decided to move on."

"This other guy, is it serious?"

She nodded.

"I'd like to meet him."

She blushed, and with her ginger hair, she was aflame. "OK."

For some reason I knew it wouldn't happen in the near future. He was probably separated and waiting for his divorce to be final.

She changed the subject by saying, "I think Lucy's in over her head with this salon."

Valley had never said the actual words, but I knew she didn't like Lucy as the owner.

"Why do you say that?"

"She's raising everyone's booth rent, and she raised her prices. Some of her clients have already left. One of them asked if she could switch over to me. I can't do that to Lucy, so I told her no."

"Well, there's more to running a salon than people think. The utilities are high, and she has a much larger loan than I ever did. I had a lot of start-up money from the payout from the city. Also, I did those bride packages for five years. She hasn't said anything to me."

"Would you buy it back if the opportunity came up?"

"I don't know. I wish I hadn't sold it, but now that I have, I don't know what John would think if I went back to that workload."

I never gave the conversation any more thought after that, because the very next week, I learned I was pregnant again. John immediately changed into a worrywart. He insisted I wear a mask when I helped dress corpses in the embalming room, suddenly concerned about my breathing formaldehyde fumes. I didn't argue. Now that I was pregnant, all smells seemed more intense. My nose became overly sensitive, like a drug-sniffing dog.

Christmas Day, my parents had everyone over for dinner. We still hadn't told anyone about my pregnancy but had decided to share the news that day. I was four months along and starting to get a tummy. I'd found an ornament of a woman in a rocking chair with a baby in her arms. I bought three, and I wrote on the back of each one, "Grandma, let's plan on meeting around May 17."

I'd expected Mom, Marabeth, and Grande to be excited when they opened their packages, but my dad was the one who was probably the most thrilled.

Once our news was public, John and I started talking about names. We decided at the first doctor's appointment we didn't want to know the baby's sex, so we needed to come up with two names. I wanted the boy's name to start with a J. I was even open to naming the baby after him, his dad, or his grandfather. John was adamant the baby have his own name. I'd mentioned Jonathan, but John didn't want that either.

One morning he told me, "I like the name Jordan."

"That works for me. In fact, I like that for either a boy or a girl."

Placing his hand on my stomach, he said, "Then that's the baby's name."

From then on we always called the baby Jordan.

It seemed to take forever for me to show. I just had this little paunch, but then all at once I started growing. I loved everything about being pregnant. Loved looking at my stomach. Every evening I'd stand naked in front of the full-length mirror and admire myself. Some women didn't like the looks of their growing bodies, but I wasn't one of them. I relished my ballooning stomach.

I'd prance around in front of John. He'd put his hand on my stomach or lean forward and talk to Jordan. We'd become horny, but he wouldn't make love to me the way I wanted and needed him to. I'd lie underneath him squirming with desire. I'd try to pull him into me, but he'd hold himself back. It became torture for both of us, but I understood his reluctance. If I lost this baby, he wanted the assurance it was no fault of his.

One evening as I lay under him, he was so restrained that I gripped his butt and tried to pull him to me. I was almost in tears, and he was actually drenched in sweat as he held himself back. When I finally came, I was so irate with him, I wanted to kick him off the bed. Something was going to have to change, because I was getting irritable.

Afterward, I took a shower. He stepped in with me, and I unleashed my fury on him. He tried to calm me down, but nothing he said helped my bad attitude. He kept saying, "Now, Macie."

Finally, I smacked him on the chest. "Don't 'Macie' me." He stepped out of the shower and left me alone.

That Saturday afternoon, I returned home from buying maternity clothes. I wanted to try them on, and John wanted to watch. When I slipped on a nursing gown and showed him the opening, he was instantly turned on. We were on the bed in no time. As he started to roll me over, I knew I couldn't stand another one of his half-assed sex encounters. I crawled on top of him, and for the first time since I'd gotten pregnant, I thoroughly enjoyed myself. John held on to my hips and seemed almost relieved that I'd taken charge. He hardly moved underneath me, but he enjoyed himself just the same. After that, I always stayed topside.

A few weeks later, he was on call and came home late from the funeral home. I was in bed just the same as asleep. He crawled in beside me, laid his head on my chest, and began to cry. I held him as he begged me not to leave him. As I stroked his hair, I could tell he'd showered. He must've picked up a younger person who'd been in an accident. Even though dealing with death was his life, it was still hard for him to remove himself from its anguish.

"John, everyone dies. I won't leave you intentionally, but I can't stop the things that happen in life."

He kept repeating, "Don't leave me. Don't leave me."

I finally said, "I won't leave you. I won't."

The next morning I had to ask, "Who died last night?"

"She was twenty-eight. Just this beautiful young woman who had so much to live for."

I kissed his cheek. No wonder he'd been so upset. Though she was younger than me, we were close to the same age. Bloody hell, I hated this job sometimes.

I did her makeup that morning, which was easy since she was so young. Just like John had said, she was pretty. I felt for her family. I couldn't imagine the anguish they must have been going through.

The next day at the funeral home, I was helping Charlie move her casket. Once it was in place, I rechecked the body to make sure everything still looked good. As I scanned the young woman's dress, I noticed one of her buttons was undone. I buttoned her top and checked her makeup again.

The following week at the salon, I again had time to have lunch with Valley. I could tell she was in love. This was different from when she was with Stuart. With him, it had been as if she was settling...trying too hard to make it work. But this new guy made her glow. She blushed to her roots when I told her that he must be doing everything right. Her secrecy about him was the only thing that alarmed me. In the past we'd shared everything, and now she wouldn't tell me a single thing about him other than he was a few years younger than her.

"How much younger?"

"Three years."

I laughed. "Big deal, Valley. Does that bother you?"

"No. I thought it might, but it doesn't."

"Where does he work?"

"In his family's business. He has a really good job."

"Have you met his family?"

"Yes, they're very nice people. You'd like them."

Relief flooded me. If she'd met his family, then he couldn't be a serial killer or anything.

Almost a month later, as I was helping Charlie again, I noticed that another woman's clothing wasn't totally the way it should be. She was an older woman but very attractive for someone in her early sixties. I'd helped John dress her and even mentioned that I hoped my body was that amazing when I was her age. He'd laughed and said, "Look at your grandmother. I think you have a pretty good chance of that happening."

As I was making the adjustments to the woman's clothing, I glanced up at Charlie to comment on the strange occurrence (at least it seemed strange to me). The look on his face made me pause. A sick feeling came over me. I cleared my throat and said, "Charlie, this isn't right. I think I know what you're doing, and it isn't right."

He wouldn't look me in the eye, only stared down at his feet. I continued with my lecture. "You need to leave these women alone. You can't be messing with them after they're dead."

He kicked the carpet with the toe of his shoe. "I know it's wrong."

"Then I want you to stop."

He didn't say anything else, only continued to look ashamed.

That night I couldn't quit thinking about my discovery. Charlie had the perfect opportunity to carry out his deviant behavior. He was the first one there in the morning and had plenty of time to undress the women. Was he just looking at them, or was he doing even more? Was he removing women from their caskets and screwing them? He was strong like John, so the lifting of a body wouldn't be a problem for him. My stomach knotted with repulsion.

The conversation we'd had at Sonic came back to me. The one about the woman who hadn't moved. Then he said she was gone, gone, gone. But he'd covered by saying she'd gotten married. Had she? At the time, it hadn't sat well with me, but I couldn't really understand why. Now, I totally got the gist of the conversation.

For once, I understood why Marabeth and Jacob had taken such drastic measures with Charlie. Sexually, he was out of control. He had bigger issues than I'd fathomed. Now I comprehended John's need to protect Charlie. It was much more than I'd realized. Did John know? If he did, why hadn't he done something, such as remove him from the situation? But John couldn't know. He wouldn't have allowed Charlie to act that way.

Charlie needed to see someone—a therapist—to help him overcome his desire for these dead women. It was a sickness. Probably something that had started when they lived over the mortuary. He'd been able to sneak down at night and screw whoever was available. Maybe it had been the only way he could relieve his sexual needs as a teenager. Regardless of why he'd started, he needed to stop.

That Thursday at the salon, I arrived early to restock my makeup line. Lucy was already there. She sat down as she drank her coffee, watching me replenish my stock. An air of tension wafted between us, and I knew she was on the verge of confronting me with something. For the first time, I realized that maybe she didn't want me selling my makeup in the salon anymore. Even though I gave her a cut of my sales, perhaps she thought it wasn't enough since she had to deal with the customers when I wasn't there. If she wanted me to remove my product, all she had to do was say the word. Selling my makeup wasn't her responsibility.

She fidgeted for a moment. Then I knew: she wanted to ask me to buy the salon back. Her phone went off; she left to retrieve her appointment book. I sighed with relief. I hoped she would never put me in that position. I wanted it back but knew it'd force me to make tough decisions again. Decisions I didn't want to make at this time in my life.

In the afternoon, Charlie came in to have his hair cut by Valley. She was so nice and easy with him. I'd finished with my client and was returning to my station when I saw her lean down and whisper into his ear. He laughed, and they shared a look. She ran her hand along his neck, and by the way she held his ear between her thumb and finger, I instantly knew: he was her new love.

All the facts lined up. He was younger and worked in a family business. She'd met John and Marabeth. Suddenly I realized why she was so tight-lipped about her new relationship. She probably thought I'd be against them, which I absolutely was not. Maybe she thought John would be. On that account, she might be right.

Every emotion ran through me. First surprise, and then happiness. They'd be good together. She saw Charlie the way I saw him—the man he could be. The man he had become. The only thing that gave me heartburn was what I had discovered about him. How could I, with a good conscience, not tell her about his deviant attraction to dead women? It put me in an awkward position. The only thing I could do was make sure he had changed his ways. As long as he'd reformed, I'd keep his secret.

At the funeral home, I was extra observant of the women. When I was done with their hair and makeup, I checked their clothing to make sure everything was perfect. I rechecked them again the next day and the next—until their funerals. I'd become some weird chaperone, keeping the women safe from sexual assault. I never found anything that made me suspect him, although he could easily be messing with the ones in the embalming room who were waiting to be dressed. He had plenty of opportunity to fulfill his craving in the mornings before anyone else arrived. He could simply crawl underneath one of those sheets and have his way. My hope was, now that he was with Valley, she was satisfying his every fantasy.

I knew they were spending a lot of time together because I'd noticed that Charlie was gone a lot...sometimes not returning at night. At least I knew where he was and who he was with. I might've worried about him if I hadn't known. John mentioned his brother's absence a few times, but he didn't seem too concerned. I wanted to tell him but didn't want him to step in the middle of anything quite yet. I didn't really think he'd have a problem with Valley, but with regard to Charlie, John sometimes surprised me with his protectiveness. But then, I surprised myself with the way I was guarding his atypical sexual secret. Since I hadn't observed any more impropriety, I wanted to shout from the rooftop. I was so relieved Charlie had stopped his awful behavior. But some part of me still felt I was doing Valley a disservice by not telling her. If the roles were reversed, I'd want her to tell me immediately. I knew she would, so why couldn't I do the same for her? I guess a part of me was like John—I felt the need to protect Charlie.

CHAPTER 12

John and I decided on a room for the nursery. We talked about the former master suite but changed our minds to the smaller crafting room that we never used. He painted the walls a warm chocolate. We went several times to look at baby furniture before finally finding just what we wanted. After the furniture was delivered, my dad helped John assemble the crib and changing table. Mom, Grande, and Marabeth were already buying supplies...lots of yellow and green onesies. No one seemed upset by our decision to wait until the birth to find out the sex of the baby. In fact, I think my parents were excited about the suspense. Dad said, "It's one of the last great surprises a person can have in life."

John and I hadn't really discussed what my working hours would be after Jordan arrived, but he knew I was quitting the salon entirely. Even though this was the best decision for me, I was still sad about the choice I had to make. I'd miss the interaction with people. Also, I'd miss cutting and coloring hair. I still did hair at the funeral home, but obviously, it wasn't the same. And I hated to admit this, but the whole death thing was getting on my nerves. Well, maybe not death, but the grieving families. Dealing with loss and heartache every day was taking a toll. Perhaps it was because I was pregnant, but at times I was an emotional mess as I listened to people's sorrow. And then there was the messy stuff that came with death—the dreaded leakage.

One week, we had a body that would not quit leaking. It just seemed to ooze all the time as if still hooked to an IV. I went nuts when Charlie and I noticed it again. "Well shit, Charlie. Shit. Shit. Shit."

He sighed. We rolled the casket back into the embalming room, where John and Charlie cleaned and redressed the body. I tried to tap down my feelings, but that day I couldn't. I really hated this job. John and Charlie seemed to take it in stride, but for me, it touched a nerve. Made me uncomfortable. Actually, it made me sick. There were still parts of death that I didn't want to deal with or think about. Moments like that...I just wanted to return to the salon and never step foot in there again. John kept telling me that with time I'd get used to the messy and unpleasant parts of the business. That I'd overcome my aversion. Well, I had news for him. I'd never get used to it. Never.

Over the next several weeks, we had several cases like that. Charlie and I would check the body and see the leakage. Maybe it was my pregnancy, or maybe it was because there were so damn many, but I really couldn't take much more. I wanted out; I truly did. But John really wanted a partner. I was his first choice; Charlie, his second. He wanted Charlie to go to college, but Charlie wasn't interested in being a mortician, and there was no way in hell I'd even consider it. No doubt, John was disappointed in both of us.

On Thursday, Valley finished her morning early, so we walked over to the sandwich shop. Once we had our sandwiches, we sat outside to eat. As we were finishing, she took a deep breath and said, "I want to tell you something I'm not sure you'll be happy about."

I already had a fairly good idea what she was going to reveal, but I said, "OK."

She looked at me and in a shaky voice said, "The man I'm in love with is Charlie. We want to be together."

I squeezed her arm. "I already knew, Valley."

"Did he tell you?"

"No. I figured it out when he came in to get his haircut. Neither of you could hide your feelings for each other. I'm totally OK with it. You'll be great together."

"How do you think John will feel?"

"I'm not sure, Valley, but it doesn't matter. Charlie's an adult. He can make his own decisions. He doesn't need John's approval or his mother's as far as that goes. You guys decide what's best for you."

"He's the sweetest man I've ever known. And my God, he's gorgeous. Sometimes when I look at him, I can't believe he wants to be with me. That he loves me. When you taught him how to drive, he changed. I liked him before, but he just flirted. I tried to ignore my feelings for him, but there were times when I was making love with Stuart that Charlie was all I could think about. When Charlie asked me how serious I was with my boyfriend, I knew that I wasn't. If Stuart had finally asked me to marry him, my answer would've been no. Once I broke up with Stuart, Charlie drove to my house and took me on a real date. Everything changed from that night on."

Listening to her, I wondered how John would feel about it. I couldn't see any reason he'd oppose their happiness. We both knew Valley. She wasn't a gold digger. I could tell she was seriously head over heels in love. A little voice told me that it would be a good time to disclose Charlie's little secret, his little weakness. I could save my friend a future heartbreak. If she were to discover his penchant for kinkiness, how much would she hate me when she found out that I knew all along?

But I simply couldn't burst my friend's bubble. I just couldn't do it.

The next day as Charlie and I were working together, I told him I knew about him and Valley. "I'll keep your secret until you two want to tell everyone."

"You won't even tell Johnny?"

I shook my head. "It's not my place to tell your brother about your love life."

He grinned. "This is just like when we used to go driving around together."

I'd reached my sixth month of pregnancy. At my doctor's appointment, everything was right on schedule. I was at a healthy pregnancy weight. Jordan was the perfect size. My morning sickness was long gone, and I felt wonderful. John always tried to attend my appointments with me, and that day, he just beamed with pride. His fear of my losing the baby had faded to nonexistence. After I'd passed the first trimester, I think he believed we were totally in the clear. Then when I began to show, he accepted that it would really happen for us.

After my appointment, we drove to the funeral home. He went to his office, and I went to find Charlie. He and I were setting up for an afternoon funeral. The casket was already in place, but we needed to rearrange the flowers. Several more sprays and wreaths had arrived. We both liked the flowers arranged in a certain way and hated an off-balance room. Charlie knew how it drove me crazy, so he was already moving some of the pedestals around. When he saw me, his face broke into a big grin.

"How did your appointment go?"

"I'm getting fat, Charlie. Jordan's growing like a weed."

I looked at the arrangements that had arrived and the way Charlie had positioned the pedestals. He said, "I thought we'd put this big spray beside these two plants and put those wreaths over there." He pointed to the other side of the room.

I grinned at him. He was quite good at this, but of course, he'd been doing it for years. I nodded my approval. Then I walked to the casket to check the body. The woman was in her midforties. Not overly attractive, but I'd done a good job making her look her very best. I checked the details of her makeup and hair. Everything passed my inspection. My eyes moved down to her clothing. I noticed her dress had been rearranged...the belt was off-center. As I stood with Charlie, I tried to control my anger. He looked off to the side as I chewed him out.

"This shit has to stop. If you don't, I'll be forced to tell Valley. She has a right to know. In fact, you need to tell her that you have this problem. At least she'll be forewarned."

His lips trembled as he glared at me. "You better not tell Valley. I mean it, Macie. If you do, you'll regret it."

"Are you threatening me?"

"You're threatening me."

"OK. Yes, I am. This is the last time, Charlie. If I see another woman like this, if I even suspect that you're still doing this, then I'll tell Valley. I will."

He grabbed my arm. "You better not. You better not. I thought you were my friend. I thought you cared about me."

"I do, Charlie. That's why I'm telling you to stop. So don't test me. This is your final warning. You could get John in a lot of trouble. This place could be shut down. If anyone found out, shit would hit the fan. Do you understand what I'm saying?"

"Don't talk down to me!"

"I'm not talking down to you. I just want you to understand that what you're doing isn't right."

One of the funeral directors entered the room, so we quit arguing. My hands were shaking so much that I could barely straighten the woman's dress. I was mad, and Charlie was furious, so we left without saying any more to each other.

I planned to tell John about our argument that evening, but he was in such a good mood, and really, how could I tell him something like that? I simply didn't want to deal with it and wanted to think about something else—anything else—to rid my mind of those sickening thoughts.

John was talking about taking time off after Jordan arrived. I listened to him yak. He was going to be the best father. Very hands on.

I asked, "Did your dad spend a lot of time with you and Charlie?"

He became quiet and then said, "Yeah, he did. He took us fishing all the time. He was very patient, especially with Charlie. Dad liked to ride go-karts, so we did that a lot."

"You hardly ever talk about him. I've always wondered if you were close."

"We were when I was young. When I...things just went south."

"What about after you graduated? You worked together for a few years before he died."

"That was a good and bad time." He rubbed my stomach and changed the subject. "Can I get you some ice cream or maybe those frozen bananas that you like so much?"

I giggled. "Sure." I knew the father/son discussion was officially over, but I'd learned more than I knew before.

CHAPTER 13

I loved how big I was getting. Jordan moved all the time, and I enjoyed feeling all the action inside me. Sometimes at night, I'd wake to find John's hand on my belly. He'd whisper to me, "God, I'm happy, Macie. You've made me so happy."

He'd rub my back and feet after a long day, or even a short one. He'd get up at midnight if I had a craving for french fries. He just pampered me. Even our sex life was OK. Once I'd taken control of the situation, I'd never given up my position. At times, I knew I made John nervous, but I'd asked my doctor, and she'd assured me that having sex while pregnant was OK. John was just apprehensive about everything, so I really couldn't be mad at him for that.

As I straddled him one night, my belly rested on him like a swollen watermelon. He held my hips, keeping me from moving too vigorously on him. It really amazed me how much control he had. That he didn't push inside me like he used to. I knew he wanted to, but he just restrained himself. Afterward, as I lay beside him, I asked, "Are you anxious for our sex life to return to the way it used to be?"

"I can deal with this. Don't worry about me. I just try to keep you happy. You scare me with your excitement."

I laughed.

Lucy and Valley gave me a baby shower. I received a lot of nongender baby clothes since I didn't know Jordan's sex. My guests asked me what I thought I was having. I said that I didn't have a clue, but judging by the Harnon track record, boys seemed to be the only sperm seeds they had.

Thursday at the salon, one of my clients brought me a gift for Jordan. She was moving back to England, so it would be her last appointment. I pulled the tissue paper out to find the sweetest little yellow booties along with several pairs of socks and a receiving blanket. I picked up the booties and stuck my finger into one. I could just see a little foot snuggled inside. She said, "There's one more thing in there."

I dug to the bottom of the gift bag. There was something wrapped in tissue paper. I pulled the paper away to find a lead crystal shot glass with a beautiful gold rim. I looked at her quizzically.

She smiled and said, "There will be days when you just wonder why the bloody hell you wanted a baby. A little sip will take the edge off."

I laughed so hard. A mom—speaking from experience.

I said, "I'll miss you. You know that I blame you for my cursing—using bloody hell."

She nodded while laughing.

At home I showed John the gift. As I dangled the booties in one hand and held the shot glass in the other, he said, "I can't wait until Jordan is here with us." He leaned over, pressed his cheek against my stomach, and said to Jordan, "If I ever come home and you're tipsy from your mom's breast milk, I'll take her little shot glass away."

My belly shook with laugher.

Charlie invited his mother, Grandpa, John, and me over for Sunday dinner. I knew what it was about, but I didn't tell John anything. I didn't want him to have time to overthink things. When we entered the cottage, Valley was in the kitchen. John raised an eyebrow at me but didn't seem upset. I went into the kitchen and helped her with the last-minute details.

After Grandpa and Marabeth arrived, Charlie poured everyone wine except me and Grandpa, who wanted his usual bourbon and Coke. Charlie took Valley's hand and calmly said, "Valley and I are together. We love each other, and that's it. We are together."

Marabeth seemed genuinely happy for them as she squealed and hugged them both. John slapped Charlie on the back and said, "When you find a woman who knows how to cut your hair so your cowlick won't stand up, then that's the woman you should marry."

Valley's face showed relief and then glowed with happiness, whereas Charlie's showed only his determination. No matter what anyone thought, he was going to be with her. I respected him so much for that.

We'd lost our close relationship. He was still friendly in public, but deep down, the undercurrent of his resentment was strong. I knew he'd do anything to protect his relationship with Valley, just as I'd do anything to protect John's business and good name. I was still pissed at him for his disgusting compulsion and had tried to talk with him about it again, but he'd rebuffed me. I knew he hadn't told Valley that anything had happened between us, because she would've told me if he had. She loved how he and I were with each other and would've been heartbroken if she'd thought that we were on the outs.

Charlie had taken ten days off to vacation with Valley. A little celebration of their coming out, so to speak. Since he was gone, I worked longer hours to assist in his place. One day while helping Anthony move the casket, I noticed the woman's blouse was slightly rumpled. I looked closer at the woman. She was in her late fifties and had died of a heart attack. She was attractive—looked younger than her age for sure. As I stood rooted in place, Anthony asked, "Is anything wrong?"

I cleared my throat. "No." I straightened her blouse and smoothed an area of her hair.

The following Monday, March 17, two things happened. I reached my seventh month, and one of the local morning news anchors died of an aneurism. She was a beautiful, healthy young woman. Her death shocked everyone. Because she was such a public figure, the media made a production of it. The nightly news, of course, ran a story about her life, her career, her husband, and her two children. I placed my hands on Jordan. I hoped I never died before I saw my baby grow to adulthood.

Tuesday at the salon, everyone wanted to talk about Avery Power. When I did her makeup later that evening, I was almost sick with grief. She had beautiful skin. (Botox had been her friend.) I didn't need to do much at all to make her look pretty. And, of course, her regular hairdresser was coming in to style her hair. After I was done with her makeup, I went home and cried. Even though I hadn't personally known her, I felt a connection with her because she'd been in my home every day through the TV. John tried to comfort me, but I was inconsolable.

"She had two little kids, John. Now they're motherless. She was so healthy, so beautiful. Even in the casket, she's simply beautiful."

He wiped my face. "I think you're beautiful."

Later that night, I was tired, truly exhausted, so I went to bed early. John came in just as I was on the verge of sleep.

"I need to head out. I just got a call." He leaned over and kissed my head. I heard him leave, but after that, I fell asleep.

When I arrived at the funeral home in the morning, the first thing I did was check Avery. Her funeral wasn't until Saturday. The family was waiting for her brother to return from Africa and wanted her in the viewing room until then—letting people pay their respects. I thought it was overkill and wondered what Avery would've wanted, but it was their request. Since I knew there'd be spectators in and out all day, I wanted to make sure that everything was in order.

I instantly noticed that the pearl button wasn't pushed through the buttonhole completely. It was a minor thing, something I could've easily missed, but I didn't think I had. The only reason I doubted myself was that Charlie was still on vacation. He wouldn't return until late Thursday or early Friday. I straightened her top, fixed the button, and scrutinized her makeup. Everything was as it should be.

That night I, again, went to bed early. I knew I needed to cut back on my work hours, as I was exhausted every evening. I was asleep almost the instant my head hit the pillow. I never knew when John came to bed, as I was dead to the world.

Thursday, after finishing at the salon, I stopped at the funeral home to apply makeup on an elderly gentleman. John had already called saying that he'd be at home with supper waiting as soon as I finished. Before leaving, I stopped to check on Avery. As I looked at her, I could tell she'd been taken out of the casket. Her hair was different, and her hands weren't positioned exactly the same.

Once I made it home, John and I ate supper. My mind was whirling with all the possibilities of why she'd need to be removed from the casket. Finally, I asked, "Did something happen with Avery?"

"What do you mean?"

"She's been moved for some reason. Like...someone took her out of the casket."

"Oh, that was me. Last night, when I went back to do an embalming, I noticed she was leaking."

My mouth dropped open. "Why would she be leaking?"

"Who knows? Sometimes it just happens. No rhyme or reason."

My stomach turned over. I wasn't an expert on dead bodies by any means, but from what I did know, this didn't make sense. Avery had died of an aneurism. She shouldn't be leaking. She just shouldn't. I pushed my plate away, as I was no longer hungry, nor could I have swallowed if I was. John glanced at me, then rose, and began clearing off the table.

That night, I couldn't sleep. I tossed and turned. My mind worked its way through a hundred ugly thoughts. In the morning, I had a major headache and was physically exhausted. John talked nonstop about the new pool cover he'd decided to buy. I didn't even pretend to listen.

I worked at the funeral home until one and then went home to lie down. My headache wasn't as bad but was still there. As I pulled into the drive, I noticed Charlie's Audi. I walked over to chat with him. He was tanned, relaxed, and thankfully quite talkative. I couldn't believe how glad I was to see him. As he yammered on and on about their vacation, I wanted to ask him about all the times I'd accused him. I wanted him to tell me the truth...just tell me. But I simply couldn't ask the question—because a part of me just couldn't bear to hear the answer.

John came home around five to eat. By that time I was feeling somewhat better. Charlie had made me laugh; I'd taken a short nap; and my headache had disappeared. After eating, John walked out to talk to Charlie. Then he left to return to the funeral home. It was "friends and family night" for Avery. Before leaving he said, "I'll be back around ten."

I cleaned off the table and went through the mail. An uneasiness filled me. I called Mom, but she never answered. I thought about calling Grande but remembered she was playing bridge that night. I decided to drive to my parents' house anyway, but they weren't home. As I was pulling out of their drive, Mom called. "Hon, we're at the Browns', playing cards. Did you need something?"

"No, I'm just bored. I'll go home and watch a movie or something."

I drove back home. The thing eating at me—gnawing on my brain— was the simple fact that John should have been home at eight thirty or nine. "Friends and family" always ended at eight. There'd be stragglers, but they wouldn't last until ten o'clock. And after everyone left, what was there to do but turn out the lights?

Ten was too damn late.

At nine sharp, I arrived at the funeral home. John's Ferrari was the only car in the lot. I went to the back door. My trembling hand inserted the key. As I opened the door, the chime sounded throughout the building. Dread engulfed me. Everything hardened in my body, as if rigor mortis had set in even though I was still alive and breathing. I walked stiffly toward the viewing room...but stopped halfway there. I couldn't bear to see if the casket was there or not.

I placed my hands on Jordan. Somehow it calmed me enough to keep walking. I entered the viewing room, my hand on the light switch. Filling my lungs with air, I flipped the switch, flooding the room with light.

The viewing area was empty.

All the air left my body. I didn't need to look further. Didn't need to find John with Avery. I wasn't one of those women who needed to see pictures or to actually catch my husband in the act. In fact, I'd rather not see the proof. The knowledge was enough for me.

I turned and wobbled out of the building. Once outside, I gulped in the night air. As I stumbled toward my car, John came out the back door. I wanted to shout at him but couldn't speak. Distress filled my every pore.

When he came to me, his shirt was untucked, and I could smell it on him. The smell of death. He'd fucked death. He'd fucked Avery. Had been fucking her ever since she'd arrived. Been fucking her for days.

I stumbled away from him. At the curb, I fell on my knees like a panting, rabid dog vomiting into the dead grass. Hurled until there was nothing left. John didn't even come to me but stayed, planted in place. I finally stood, wiping my mouth on my sleeve. Walking to my car, I held up my hand to stop him from talking or coming to help me.

I could barely drive home. My whole body was quaking. I thought I was losing my mind…felt as if I'd stumbled into someone else's nightmare. Arriving home, I stripped off my clothes. In the shower, I cried so hard I could hardly stand up. Finally, I shut off the water, dried my hair, and dressed. What was I going to do? How was I going to handle this?

I thought about leaving. Staying at my parents' house or Grande's. But what would I tell them? What reason could I give? My stomach was churning—filled with acid. I rubbed Jordan. At least I still had Jordan. But my mind was totally crazy. I knew what insanity felt like. I was there.

Totally sick again, I went to the bathroom to puke. After a few dry heaves, I tried to drink some water. A heaviness encased me, as if everything in me weighed a ton. I rubbed my back. I rubbed my neck. My whole body was uncomfortable. I decided to call my dad. I needed help. Something was wrong with me. I was having a psychotic episode—losing myself. The wetness between my legs was warm, familiar, unwelcome. Back in the bathroom, I yanked down my pants. I was spotting heavily. Grabbing a towel, I considered my options.

John wasn't one of them.

I walked over to Charlie's. Flickers of light came from his window; he was watching late-night TV. When he came to the door, he stopped short, his eyes focused on the towel I held between my legs.

"Could you take me to the hospital? I'm spotting. Charlie, I…"

He immediately went into action by grabbing his keys and steering me toward his car. As he drove, I talked to Jordan. "Please stay with me. I'll get us out of this. We'll leave. I'll hide us. No one will find us." Then I chanted to him until we reached the hospital. "I can't lose you, Jordan. Please stay with me. I can't lose you, Jordan. Please stay with me."

Charlie drove above the speed limit, but we arrived safely. I was taken swiftly into a room, and my doctor was called. My parents were the first to arrive and then Valley. Obviously, Charlie was calling everyone.

John entered a few minutes after Valley. I was too stressed and worried to tell him to leave. He looked like death himself. For a fleeting moment, I wondered if Avery was finally back in her coffin.

I relaxed with Mom by my side. She was so encouraging as she held my hand. On my other side, John never touched me. I wanted him there, but I couldn't stand the sight of him.

At first, everything the doctor and nurses did worked. Then everything quit working. Everything they tried failed. And then, it didn't matter anyway because Jordan died inside me. Some would call it a miscarriage. Others a stillbirth. All I knew was I'd lost Jordan. My son. I went to a place I'd never been. A place I'd never wanted to go. A place I was afraid I'd never return from. A part of hell only some women would understand.

They cleaned Jordan up and placed him in my hands. He was light as a feather. Perfect in every way. His little head was so sweet. Perfect little ears and nose. His eyelids were like tissue. I looked at his little hands and feet, his tiny fingers and toes, his button of a penis. My little Jordan. My little boy. My little baby. I'd killed him. The horror and revulsion churning inside me had killed him.

When they took him from my hands, I wailed. I'd heard mothers wail on TV and at the funeral home. I'd always thought how pitiful it sounded. But now, experiencing it myself, I knew wailing simply wasn't enough. I wanted to beat my chest, pull my hair out. My pain was so intense that I really thought I'd die from it. At the moment, death would've been a blessing.

John's grief was soundless compared to mine as he cried by my side. This wasn't how it was supposed to be. Finally, I was given something to knock me out. I hoped I wouldn't ever wake up.

At noon the next day, as I was preparing to leave the hospital, John came in the room. I knew he was coming because he'd called my mom and asked her if he could stop by. Her look was quizzical when she asked me. But since I'd already made arrangements to stay at their house, she knew something drastic had happened between us other than losing Jordan.

When he stepped into my room, he looked as if he hadn't slept in a week. Honestly, I had no feelings for him. Well, in truth, I did. I detested him. I never wanted to see him again.

Slumped down in a chair next to my bed, he sat for a moment without speaking. Then he looked at me with bloodshot eyes and said, "I can take you home. I don't need to be at the funeral home this afternoon for Avery's services. Both Peter and Doug said they'd fill in for me. In fact, Peter insisted."

"Tell Peter I don't want you taking me home. And anyway, I'm sure you want one last look at Avery." Before he could say anything—apologize, grovel, or do whatever men do when caught with their pants around their ankles—I asked, "Who's living at the mansion? You or me?"

He swallowed, ran his hands over his face, and said, "You can have the house. I'll take Charlie with me."

"OK, fine. You can leave now."

That was it. We didn't speak again for months.

Mom took me to her house. I returned to my old bedroom. They'd changed things—paint, curtains, and the rug—but it was still mine in every way. Same furniture. Same bathroom. Mom left me to nap, which was impossible. My mind simply wouldn't shut off.

The following afternoon, I did something strange, but it gave me great satisfaction at the time. I called Kelly, John's former makeup person. I really expected her to hang up on me, but I think her curiosity got the best of her. I told her I'd quit Harnon Funeral Home. She might like to reapply.

I wouldn't be an issue for her anymore, and she wouldn't even have to use my makeup. She said she'd think about it. I knew, without a doubt, her butt would be in John's office the next day.

I wasn't going back there. If Kelly didn't take the job or if John decided not to rehire her, then I didn't care what kind of bind I left him in. For all I cared, he could have his mother go back. She could draw her sorry-ass eyebrows on whomever she wanted to. Why I even cared that he was without a makeup person was beyond me. But really, I wanted him to know, with certainty, I was severing all ties with him…personal and business.

Neither Mom nor Dad asked any questions. They knew I was in shock—a state of grief only time would heal. Probably believing, though erroneously on their part, that I'd recover. That John and I'd reconcile and life would go back to normal. I knew he had called every night I was there. I overheard Mom tell him, "Just give her some time, John. She'll be OK. She'll return to her old self."

I stayed with my parents for four days, giving John time to move his stuff from the mansion. I didn't want to take a chance on seeing him. Returning to the mansion on Wednesday, the first thing I did was check the closet. All of John's clothes were gone. I walked out to the cottage, and it was bare as a bone of Charlie's things. After that, I don't even know what I did. It was as if I wasn't even alive; I couldn't function.

Three cleaning women showed up the next day. They'd been cleaning the mansion ever since we'd moved in, but I'd never met them. I couldn't say that I met them that day either since we never spoke. They didn't seem shocked I was there as they worked around me. Using a feather duster here and there, they simply ignored me as if I were a statue. John must've told them not to approach me because I might attack.

I stayed in the same clothes for days on end. Wouldn't shower, and half the time, I ate like a dog. If there was a three-day-old piece of toast, I ate it without a thought. Either Valley or Lucy stopped by every evening. Concern showed in their eyes, but honestly, I didn't really care. Grande came over every morning. Probably wanted to make sure I hadn't done myself in overnight. I wasn't suicidal, or at least I didn't think I was. I certainly welcomed death, but I wouldn't have inflicted it on myself.

When Marabeth appeared at my door by herself Sunday evening, I didn't even want to let her in. With wet eyes, she sat nervously on the couch, wringing her hands, barely able to speak. As I watched her, it dawned on me that she'd known about this all along. She'd worked at the funeral home with John, so she would've seen things…known he had a problem.

I wanted to smack her. In fact, I wanted to put my hands around her throat and strangle her. I watched her lips move but didn't listen to her. Didn't give a shit about her psychoanalysis or whatever it was she was spewing. What kind of damn mother was she?

The moment she left, I had a nervous breakdown.

The following Thursday, the cleaning women arrived again with their dusters and their happy chatter. That time I left the mansion and went to the cottage. I sat in a heap until they moved on with their jovial selves. When I went inside, the first thing I noticed was the missing pizza box. I was so pissed at those bitches that I could've screamed. I called Mom. She too was shocked. "They opened your fridge and threw it away?"

"No. It was on the counter."

"For God's sake, Macie, I brought that over three days ago. You'll get food poisoning."

"Who cares?"

"I do. Have you even showered or brushed your teeth today?"

When I didn't answer, she used her mom voice on me. "Macie, you need to stop this crap, and I mean now. Gingivitis is an early stage of gum disease."

As she lectured me, my tongue ran across my teeth. They were rather furry. Before she could go into a full hygienist's rampage about interproximal decay, bleeding gums, and abscessed teeth, I stopped her. "Mom, I know all about this. You've preached to me since I was six years old."

"Well, obviously, you didn't listen."

As she went on and on, I wanted to chew my arm off. I knew then, after almost two weeks of acting like a zombie and eating like an animal, I had to change. Even though the mansion was huge, the walls were closing in on me. I needed air. I needed out.

The next night, Lucy and Valley arrived together. I thought it might be some sort of intervention, and in a way, it was. Valley said, "Are you ever going to shower again?"

That seemed rather harsh, but maybe I stank. I said, "I will Monday because I've decided to return to the salon on Tuesday."

Shocked, Lucy asked, "Are you sure you should? I mean, did your doctor say it was OK? It's only been two weeks today since…"

They both looked abashed that she'd almost said the words…*lost the baby…went nuts…turned into a weirdo.* I wasn't about to admit I wasn't going back to the doctor.

"It's OK. I need to get out of this mansion. You can't keep rescheduling all my appointments. Surely I can find it within me to work two days a week."

Monday evening, I took a shower, shaved my legs and armpits. (Wow… that hair had really grown.) I proceeded to brush my teeth for three minutes. Since neither John nor I used mouthwash, I grabbed the peroxide and took a mouth full. I swished until the foam became so great I couldn't hold it in my mouth any longer. Maybe that'd help kill all the bacteria and get me back in my mother's good grace, although I wouldn't tell her about the peroxide.

CHAPTER 14

My first day back at the salon was uneventful because I was in a state of oblivion. I heard my clients' words of sympathy, but I tuned them out. Nothing they could say would help me or heal my hurt.

Over the following weeks, my clients became more verbal. They wanted to share stories of other women they knew. Women who'd had the same thing happen to them. Women who went on to have tons of children. Women who went on to have wonderful lives. I wanted to say, "Well, good for those women. Good for them. But were their husbands fucking cadavers?"

Now that I was back at the salon, I learned from Valley that Charlie had moved in with her. They'd been discussing it for a while, so when John told Charlie he had to move, Valley's door had swung wide open for him.

John called Mom or Grande daily to check on me. I probably should've been hurt that he didn't try to contact me, but actually, I only felt relief. He never came to the house, or if he did, I wasn't around. There wasn't any reason for him to anyway. It was still too early to mow. And I could call my dad if I needed a handyman for any kind of maintenance.

I learned from Mom, who'd heard it from Grandpa, that John was renting a hotel suite. (I bet his closet sucked.) He didn't want to move in with his mom or rent an apartment. Maybe he thought I'd give in, and he could move back home. I had news for him: that wasn't happening. My anger was so intense I couldn't even think straight. Several things were playing in my mind. Thoughts that I didn't want to have but that were wedged in like a tick in my hide. Things I didn't want to admit but finally had to.

First, my own stupidity. (Twenty-twenty hindsight was such a bitch.) Looking back, I saw some very red flags. That John was so easily turned on and liked sex so much when I was cold. I'd thought it was because I was so damn irresistible. How dumb could I have been? All the little inklings. All the little signs. Bloody hell—my intuition. My gut instinct. I'd wanted to believe it was Charlie. Wanted to believe everything John told me. I'd just wanted to believe.

Charlie stopped by one evening to check on me. I didn't think John had sent him but wasn't sure. We talked about him and Valley for a few minutes, and then I asked, "Did Kelly get her job back?"

"She did. Johnny didn't want to do the makeup. I didn't want to either. He doesn't like her, but she…" He shifted uncomfortably in his chair.

I knew what he'd started to say. I already knew that Kelly had a thing for John. Goodness, what woman wouldn't! He was gorgeous. I knew she didn't like me, but I always knew it was more than that. She wanted John for herself. Well, she could have him.

Finally, I couldn't ignore the elephant in the room any longer, so I said, "I'm sorry I always thought it was you, Charlie. I wish you would've just told me. I know you knew."

"I told you, but you didn't want to listen."

"When did you tell me?"

"At the Sonic. You asked about his dating history. I told you he mainly spent time with the women at the funeral home."

My mouth fell open. In Charlie's eyes, he had told me, but how was I supposed to figure out John's fetish from that? Bloody hell, my mind didn't work that way. Whose did?

"How long has this been going on?"

"You need to ask Johnny all these questions."

"Just tell me, Charlie. Just tell me what you know."

"The only thing I know is that when he met you, he quit. Then you got pregnant, and he started again. That's all I want to say."

Tears rolled down my face. I didn't even bother wiping them away. I was so used to crying at any given moment that I didn't care anymore who saw me or what they thought.

"He loves you so much, Macie. I'm worried about him."

I didn't say one word. He talked a bit more but finally got up to leave. I had to ask. "Did you tell Valley?"

He looked shocked. "God no. This is a secret. A family secret."

I was relieved and, honestly, a little surprised he hadn't told Valley. That was one thing I didn't think Charlie would do—keep secrets from her. I realized that he protected John just as much as John protected him.

I was trying to decide what to do with my life. I couldn't live in the mansion. Every time I walked by Jordan's room, it crushed the very life from me. One day I decided to just go in and sit. Maybe if I dealt with the room, dealt with never bringing my baby home, I'd be able to adjust. But as I looked at the things Mom and Grande had bought—all the shower gifts, washed and ready; the baby mobile above the crib—it only made it worse. Then I saw the little yellow booties. That was the exact moment I decided to leave.

I started making plans. I needed a new job, a new life where no one would know my history. I wanted new clients, new neighbors. I didn't want new friends, but those too would probably be better for me. The only downside of moving (honestly, there were several) was trying to start over in the hair business. It took time, sometimes years, to build a clientele. I'd have to start at the bottom. If I rented a booth, I wasn't even sure I could make a profit because I wouldn't know anyone. If I did commission instead of booth rent, then I'd make a lot less money since I'd only receive a percentage from my work. Either way, I'd be forced to do walk-ins, which I didn't mind, but I couldn't count on them for a living.

Money wasn't a huge issue. I had the money from the sale of the salon. Also, John had paid for everything once we were married. And all the money I'd made on my makeup since that time I'd stuck in the savings.

Then there was this: if I divorced him, I could demand a huge settlement. We'd signed prenuptial agreements since we both owned our own businesses. But I knew he'd pay anything to keep me from talking...to keep my mouth shut. Bloody hell, I could write a book. A tell-all. I'd never thought of myself as a vindictive person, especially toward John, but I realized that I very well could be. But even though I had all these evil feelings, all these emotions of hurt and betrayal, I had this dot, this tiny spot I couldn't overlook: I still loved John and wanted to protect him.

As my due date drew closer, the hardness in my heart grew into a tight mound of animosity. That John had treated me this way, had ruined my life...well, I couldn't reconcile myself with that.

Deciding I couldn't—or, maybe, just didn't want to—listen to my clients' words of encouragement, I contacted all of them and canceled their appointments. I looked online for an opening anywhere in the United States.

Then a fluke happened. A sign that I was doing the right thing. Tim Carton called. He told me he'd just heard I'd lost my baby. "I know losing a spouse is different than losing a baby, but you will recover. You will, Macie." He told me he was dating again. He missed Cathy but was lonely. He then said the weirdest thing—the thing that made my ears perk up.

"You remember the mortician, Mr. Bower?"

"Yes, I did a makeup job for him."

"He called me the other day. Asked if I'd contact you to see if you knew anyone who was looking for makeup work. That's how I learned about your baby. I called your grandmother."

"Is he hiring?"

"No. Ron, his brother-in-law, is. He has a large funeral home in Atlanta."

"I'd like to talk with him."

Tim gave me all the information he had. The minute I was off the phone, I called the number. After talking for several minutes, I agreed to go in for an interview, although he acted as if that wasn't necessary. He'd hire me over the phone.

The next day, I left early and drove into the city—into the hub of Atlanta. I could become lost there. No one would find me, and no one would know anything about me.

Ron wore his money: expensive suit, Rolex watch, diamond ring, excellent haircut. As he gave me a tour of the funeral home, it was easy to see where the profit came from. The place was huge. Before I could ask, he said they held over two thousand funerals a year. (Whoa, that's a lot.) I could almost smell the money mixed in with the formaldehyde.

Back in his office, we talked hours, wages, benefits, and my job duties, which would consist of hair and makeup, and helping dress the bodies. That was it. No flower arranging. No moving of the caskets. I'd never talk to or help the families with clothes. In fact, I'd never meet the families at all. No outside hairdressers were allowed in. The families had to accept the in-house hairdresser and makeup person. In my opinion, which I kept to myself, this funeral home lacked compassion. They told the family how things were done instead of listening to what the family wanted.

Each morning there'd be at least one body dressed and ready for me. For the next six to eight hours, I'd do nothing but dress bodies, style hair, and apply makeup. It sounded like nothing but a conveyor belt of cadavers. Should I need a day off, they also had a part-time person as well, but Ron made it clear they'd rather not use him unless totally necessary.

"Some Mondays will be a long day. We use Ricky on weekends if the family wants the funeral on Monday and absolutely can't wait; otherwise we'll have you do their makeup. I'm not happy with the way Ricky does the makeup on women, and he can't get the hairstyling right either. Even if he looks at a picture, he does his own thing. Punks them out. Makes them look as if they're going to a party. Plus, I don't like him. Every time

I've brought him in here to talk the matter over, he giggles." Ron raised his eyebrows at me. (I detected a homophobe.)

Really, I knew I probably shouldn't take the job, but in a way, it seemed like a perfect fit. Even though I was sick of the funeral business, it came with excellent pay and wonderful benefits. I wouldn't have to deal with the families, see their grief. And it would move me out of the mansion into a new life.

I wasn't sure how other mortuaries worked. To avoid any misunderstanding or surprises later on, I requested that he supply the makeup, but I wanted to use M. E. Cosmetics. Also, I wanted him to purchase new brushes (the ones he'd shown me were shit). He didn't bat an eye, and I signed an agreement form. I gave him as little personal information as I could. Just enough to satisfy him. I told him my husband and I were separated. I'd been working for him, and I needed to find another job. I asked him if he knew of any available apartments close to the funeral home.

He said, "Let's go to lunch. On our way I'll show you a new place that's just been completed. I think it'd work for you."

The apartments were about a fifteen-minute drive from the funeral home. I liked the area, and the fact that I could move in immediately was a strong selling point. Upon returning to the funeral home, we shook hands. Then I drove back to the apartment complex. I rented a three-bedroom apartment. One of the bedrooms would house my makeup business, which would strictly be from online sales. I didn't expect Lucy to handle my line anymore since I wouldn't be there to restock my product.

Back home, I called my parents and asked if they'd be home. Driving to their house, I prepared myself for what I envisioned would happen. Before I could even tell them that I was moving, Mom said, "Have you gone to the doctor for a checkup?"

"No. There isn't any need."

"Of course, there is, Macie."

"No, Mom, there really isn't. I don't want to hear them say this was a fluke or something." I wasn't sure what other reason they could give me.

"I still think you need to have a checkup."

She wouldn't give it up, so I changed the subject by breaking the news that I was moving. Mom became so upset that I wished I'd told them over the phone.

Dad knew better than to try to change my mind, but he said, "I'll worry about you. That's a big change. A long way away."

"Oh, Dad, it is not. You can drive it in no time at all, and you know it. An hour and a half."

"You know what I mean."

Well, I did know what he meant, but I had to do it. I had to.

The next day was Jordan's due date. I woke in a funk because I should've awakened either with a baby in the crib down the hall or with a belly so big that I could hardly move. Instead, I woke with nothing. The weird thing was how much I wanted to call John. My need for his comfort, my ache to be with him, surprised me. I couldn't even keep up with my back-and-forth feelings for him.

I didn't expect anything from him that day, but I was certain that he knew what day it was. At ten, my doorbell rang. An older woman stood with a bouquet of flowers. I thanked her and took the flowers inside. There wasn't a card, but I knew who they were from.

Four days later, Mom and Dad helped me move, which wasn't a huge deal because I wasn't taking any furniture. When I rented the apartment, I'd had the option of having it furnished. Even though I wasn't crazy about the kitchen table and chairs, I still chose that route. I didn't have time to shop for furniture and didn't want to take any from the house. I wanted a clean, fresh start. I did take dishes and cookware. We'd received multiples of so many things when we'd gotten married. I had a box of dishes that I'd never even opened. I packed those and my favorite glasses. I took everything of mine from the closet except for my Jane costume.

Before leaving, I walked into Jordan's room, picked up the yellow booties, and pressed them against my face. How I wished I was slipping them on his little feet. I put them back with the rest of his clothes. I grabbed the crystal shot glass and left the room.

I laid the mansion key, the yellow Audi key, and my wedding ring on the counter, propped against the flowers he'd sent. I thought it gave the whole crappy thing a personal touch.

I walked out.

When Mom and Dad saw my apartment, I think they were disappointed. It wasn't that I'd be living there instead of the mini-mansion but that my life had come to this. I was moving away from them, I'd be alone, and my marriage had failed. They couldn't be any more disappointed than I was.

As they were saying their good-byes, I said, "I don't want John to know where I'm living. I don't want him coming here. I trust you, but if he shows up here, I'll move again, and I won't tell you where I'm going."

The only thing Dad said was, "You're burning bridges you won't be able to rebuild."

"He started the fire, Dad. I'm just trying to save myself from the scorching flames."

John called two days later. I was sitting on one of the ugly kitchen chairs, eating an overripe banana. I thought about not answering. We'd never talked since the day in the hospital, but he couldn't hurt me here, and I could always hang up.

"John."

"You didn't need to go to such drastic measures. I would've stayed out of your life."

"Well, you definitely will now."

"You could've taken the Audi."

No need to comment on that. I could've taken a lot of things. I could've taken the very hide off his ass.

"I'd like to at least talk to you. We never talked. You never let me tell you one thing."

"We were married almost four years, John. You had plenty of opportunities to talk to me."

"I'd be willing to see someone...a therapist."

"Too little, too late. You should've done that a long time ago."

"Do you need money?"

"No, and I certainly don't want yours."

"I just want you to know that if you want a divorce, I won't fight you on it, but I'll never file for it. I still have hope that we can work this out. I love you, Macie. It never had anything to do with you."

I snorted. "That's the problem, John. It had everything to do with me. I need to go." After ending the call, I grabbed my bottle of bourbon and my little crystal shot glass. Bourbon and banana weren't the best combination, but after a couple of sips, the banana taste was all but cleaned out of my system.

Since John had brought up money, I wondered how much he would've given me. I wasn't worried, but still, I knew I needed to be very frugal if I ever wanted to buy another salon. I wasn't sure what my future endeavors would be, but I knew I wouldn't stay in that apartment forever and work for someone else. I needed my own business—my own livelihood. I'd sold my business, and what had it gained me? Of course, I had the money from that, but I'd lost all the potential income I could've made. Also, it would be next to impossible to find a prime location like that again.

I'd learned the hard way to never allow a man to control my purse strings. When John had said he wanted to make me a partner, I should've done that and formally drawn up the paperwork. At least I would've had something concrete to show for my work.

Even though I had hard feelings toward John, I knew deep down that he'd never intended to screw me over financially, but I still blamed him for all of this anyway.

CHAPTER 15

The mortuary was called SafeHaven—a stupid name. As if they could send you to the next life safely and in heaven. I hated the job and realized what a good mortician and funeral home John had. He'd always had such respect for the dead. (Well, other than the sex part with the women.) He kept the bodies covered in the embalming room and never talked about them in a disrespectful way.

Now, every morning when I entered the embalming room, one of two things happened: either I'd find naked bodies in full display because Dylan had already arrived, or else he'd come in after I'd started work and remove all the sheets. Almost all were old people who no one even gave a thought to look at, but still, I didn't think it was right.

Dylan was so crude about the naked bodies, especially the women's breasts, that I wanted to shove my fist down his throat. I asked if I could have a different room or area to work by myself but was informed that this had never been a problem before and that it would be a pain. ("A pain in the ass" were his exact words.) I wasn't sure of the pecking order. Ron owned the place, but I wasn't certain what Dylan's title was. He acted as if he was in charge, but with his slick way of talking and his soft stomach, from too much fast food, he reminded me of a used-car salesman, so I knew not to trust his arrogance.

What I couldn't understand, though, was why Dylan was even in the embalming room to begin with. When we'd first been introduced by Paul, a mortician, I'd thought he was a mortician too. But he had nothing to do with preparing the bodies for burial. His duties were helping with the services by opening and closing the casket and driving the hearse to the cemetery. He shouldn't even be in there viewing the bodies to begin with. He was nothing more than a pervert.

I thought about discussing the situation with Ron, but since I was the only woman who ever went into the embalming room, he'd probably say I was overly sensitive. Also, when I took this job, Ron had told me that I would be in the embalming room. I couldn't really go back and say that it didn't work for me. At the time, I'd thought I could handle it. I'd assumed the only thing I'd be dealing with were all the bodies on the tables. I'd just never realized they'd actually be embalming during my shift. How dumbass stupid could I be?

I tried to block out everything that happened behind my back. The whole thing was so barbaric, such a brutal process, that I thought I'd scream. And it never stopped. It just never stopped. I really wanted to quit within the first two weeks, but I didn't want to admit defeat.

The other thing I'd never realized was how many funerals John did for free. For any child under two, the services were gratuitous. He only charged for the price of the casket. He never made this public knowledge, not because he didn't want to be inundated with baby funerals but because he didn't want it to seem as if he was doing it for recognition.

SafeHaven made a public display if they gave anything away for free. They made sure it was mentioned on the news. It was so blatantly obvious, at least to me, anyway, that they waited for big news events. One week, a home burned down. The grandmother was killed, and the family was really destitute. SafeHaven stepped in and made a big production of handling her funeral, but later in the same week, a couple lost their one-year-old baby in a choking accident. Both parents were without work, but the incident didn't make a big splash on the news. They had the little girl's funeral at SafeHaven and paid full price.

My first-month anniversary, ironically, was also my wedding anniversary. I drank two shots to lament both: the job I despised and the marriage I'd lost. My apartment lease would be up in five months, so

I made a pact with myself that I'd stay until then. Also, I pledged to begin searching for a building to open a hair salon. I'd done it once; I could do it again.

When I thought of all the things I'd lost, all my bad choices, I wanted to weep. My meeting John, I'd thought, had been the greatest thing that'd ever happened to me. Now I realized that, because of him, I'd lost my salon, my first house, my hairdressing career, my friends, and most of all Jordan. I was missing out on time with Grande and my grandpa.

One man had caused all this destruction. I blamed him for everything.

Every evening someone from home called. Either Mom, Dad, or Grande. Sometimes Grandpa would, but he wasn't a talker like the rest of them. Also, he knew that I was livid with Marabeth. I was certain she hadn't told him the real reason for my leaving, but he was smart enough to know it was something significant. I'm sure he, and probably everyone else, thought I'd left because I couldn't handle losing Jordan. If they really thought about it, though, they'd realize John was the one and only person who felt exactly as I did about our loss.

Then there were my girlfriends. Lucy and Valley kept me posted on the salon gossip. Lucy never once said a word about any financial problems, although Valley mentioned several things that made me think all wasn't well at the salon. When Lucy and I talked, she always tried to keep the conversation away from anything she thought might upset me. She never repeated any gossip she'd heard about John or me. All that information came from Valley. From her I learned that John had moved back into the mansion. In some ways this surprised me because I'd thought he'd probably want to sell it. But then again, the mansion suited him. If he could live there with all those memories, all those dreams shot to hell, then more power to him.

One night when Valley called, she was excited about the news that Charlie had proposed. I hated that I wasn't there to share it with her. We'd been through so much together, and the fact that I wasn't there for her happy times made me sad. She asked if she and Charlie could come visit me. I told her they could; I also told her the same thing I'd told my parents. If they breathed a word to John of my whereabouts, I'd move into the unknown.

She hesitated for a moment, undoubtedly trying to decide if she could trust Charlie to keep a secret from his brother. Finally, she said, "Let me check that out with Charlie. If I don't think he can keep from telling John, then we'll just have to wait until you decide to come here for a visit."

They arrived Saturday around lunchtime. I fixed sandwiches, and we sat on my small veranda. They both kept looking inside the apartment, which in all truthfulness was nice and big. But when compared to my previous abode, well, it was small, boring, and lifeless. And the ugly kitchen chairs probably were more than they could take. The conversation never lagged, but we avoided certain people and topics. Finally, I asked, "Charlie, how's the job going?"

"OK. Everyone misses you."

"That's nice of you to say."

Valley said, "By the way, do you remember Lucy's client Lisa Redder? She was in college and had that jet-black hair."

"Yeah, sort of."

"She was killed the other day. Some driver hit her as she was out jogging. Broke her neck. She died right there."

"Bloody hell, that's awful."

After we finished lunch, we carried our plates inside, and instead of returning to the veranda, we sat in my living room. As they sat across from me, they clasped hands. I knew they were about to tell me what they'd driven all this way to say.

Valley started. "We're getting married in two months."

This wasn't a surprise to me. I didn't think they'd have a long engagement.

"We want you to be a part of our wedding. I want you to be my matron of honor."

"Valley, you know I will." I reached over and squeezed her hand.

She became nervous. "John will be Charlie's best man."

"OK."

They both sighed and sank back into the couch. Charlie said, "We were afraid you wouldn't come."

"Now, Charlie, you know I wouldn't miss this for anything. Anyway, at some point in time, John and I will have to see each other. I mean, Grandpa is married to your mother."

Valley talked about the finer details. We set up a time in two weeks for dress shopping. I'd drive back and stay at my parents'. When they left two hours later, they were both happy and relieved with the outcome of their visit. I just felt alone once they'd gone.

That night, I couldn't sleep. I kept thinking about Lisa Redder. As sick as this was, it wasn't that she'd died but that she was probably in John's funeral home and he was on top of her right then. The more I thought about it, the more I had to know where her services were being held. I trudged into the kitchen and opened my laptop. At the bottom of her obituary, the funeral home was listed.

Harnon Funeral Home.

Damn it. I couldn't believe how jealous I was of her. She was dead, and I was jealous of her.

I went back to bed but never fell into a deep sleep. In the morning, I filled makeup orders and then had the whole day to do nothing. I hated Sundays. They depressed me something awful. Also, I had this nagging curiosity that I couldn't shake. I wanted to know who else might've died that John would've had a fetish for. I ate lunch, made myself a cup of tea, and spent the next few hours looking at the obituaries from the last few months. I'd heard of women checking their husband's wallets or computers for clues about other women, but I bet none of them had ever done this.

Midafternoon John called. "You can quit threatening people."

"What do you mean?"

"That you'll move away to the underground if they so much as mention to me where you live. You act as if I'm going to force you to return at gunpoint."

I didn't even comment.

"What are you doing this afternoon?"

"You don't even want to know."

"I do, or I wouldn't have asked."

"Well, I'm looking online at the obits to see who you've been fucking lately."

There was total silence on his end; then there was only dead air. I suppose that's one way to get rid of your estranged husband.

Two weeks later, I drove back home for the first time since I'd left. I desperately missed everyone, and I missed my old life. The one I'd thought was so perfect.

I met Valley and Lucy at the bridal shop. I was shocked when I saw Lucy. Her unwashed hair was stringy and hanging limp in her face. Her normally flawless eyebrows were unruly with unsightly stragglers, and she had an ugly cold sore on her upper lip. I opened my mouth to comment but then didn't know exactly what to say, so I simply followed them inside the store. We tried on dresses for most of the afternoon. There were several I loved, but I decided to let Lucy choose. She was shorter than me, and some of the dresses I liked didn't do her justice; but she only shrugged with a beaten-down attitude, so I picked the one I liked best.

Valley found her dress almost immediately. She was glowing with happiness, and I only wished that I was looking forward to her wedding day as much as she was. I dreaded seeing John. I dreaded having everyone stare at us, wondering what would happen, how we'd act toward each other. I dreaded the day so much that I tried not to even think about it.

Both asked about my job. Not wanting to lie but not wanting to admit how unhappy I was—that I was simply miserable there—I merely said, "It's a job."

Lucy and I talked about giving Valley a shower in three weeks. Lucy said she'd plan it all since I lived out of town. I told her I'd pay for everything because she was doing all the work. Her sigh of relief told me that she was truly struggling financially.

Back at my parents', Mom had invited Grande, Grandpa, and Marabeth for the evening meal. I knew she wanted to make it convenient for me to see Grandpa, and there wasn't any polite way to invite him without Marabeth.

The gathering turned out fine. I sat between Grande and Grandpa. Marabeth and I didn't ignore each other, but we definitely kept our distance. Every time she looked at me, though, I could've sworn I saw understanding in her eyes.

During dessert, Dad said, "I hope you're seeing someone for grief counseling."

"I'm not, but thank you for your concern."

Mom said, "I never told you this, but we lost our first baby. I miscarried in the first trimester. It broke our hearts, but then we had you."

"Mom, I had a miscarriage before Jordan."

There was an uncomfortable silence. Then she said, "The third time's the charm."

I said, "I don't believe that."

Grande grabbed my hand, her face stricken with sadness. She didn't believe in the "third time's the charm" thing either. No, she believed everything ran in threes. Funerals and lost babies.

On the drive back to my apartment, I thought about the whole weekend. How hurt Mom had been after learning about my miscarriage. When I was able to get her alone, I tried to explain why I hadn't shared the information with her. "You would've just worried, Mom."

She said she understood, but I didn't think she really did. She wanted so desperately to help me. For me to talk to her and tell her my problems, my heartache. We'd always been so close, but how could I tell her all that'd happened to me? How could I tell her the very things that burdened my soul? I couldn't share that awfulness with her. And also, on some level, I felt the need, the duty as a wife, to keep this awful thing a secret. Somehow, I'd been sucked into this nightmare of secrecy that I didn't know how to handle. I wanted to and knew I needed to talk with someone about all these emotions eating at me. In a way, I actually understood why John had never sought help. It would be hard for anyone to admit something like this…even to a therapist.

Back at my apartment, I wasn't glad to be home, but I was glad to drop the upbeat, normal act I'd faked all weekend. I could be myself. My screwed-up, unhappy self.

CHAPTER 16

Entering the embalming room Monday morning, I was affronted by a display of naked bodies. Again, disgust filled my soul. I dreaded going in there every day, but that morning was possibly the worst I'd had so far. Dylan was standing over a young woman who'd obviously been strangled. Her exposed body was beautiful, and I couldn't help looking at her.

When Dylan saw me, he said, "Boy, we have a beauty here today. Come look at her, Macie. She has a rack any woman would be proud of."

I came totally unglued. "Dylan, shut your fucking mouth. You should be fired. God, I hate working with you."

Turning on my heel, I stormed out and went straight to Ron's office. He hadn't come in yet, so I sat down in front of his desk. Maybe I could get a grip on my emotions as I waited for him. Hearing someone behind me, I turned to see Dylan's panicked face. He asked if he could talk with me. I should've said no, but seeing his desperation, I followed him into a small conference room.

"I'm sorry if I offended you. I need this job."

My hands were shaking, and I wanted to spit on him. When I didn't say anything, he ran his hands through his hair. "I have kids, a mortgage, two car payments."

"Then shut your filthy mouth around me."

"OK. I won't talk...at least when you're in the room."

My heart pounded as I returned to the embalming room. I needed to calm myself and get to work since there were so many bodies from the weekend. Two bodies were already dressed and waiting for me. When Paul, the funeral director, was ready to dress two more gentlemen, I stopped to help him. Paul was a quiet man. I wasn't sure if it was his normal personality or if he acted that way because of Dylan.

He said, "You doing OK?"

"Yeah. Thanks."

After lunch I started on the men. I clipped and filed their nails and cut the hair protruding from their ears. One had exceedingly long nose hair, which I trimmed into a better look. One gentleman reminded me so much of Grandpa that I ached to see him again. That I'd moved away from both of my grandparents still broke my heart.

Arriving back at my apartment ten hours later, I knew I had to come up with a plan B—and soon. I grabbed my bottle of bourbon and my little crystal shot glass and poured myself a stiff drink. A bad habit was forming, as I was starting to do this a lot. I swallowed the shot and looked at the bottle. What the hell. I poured another and gulped it down.

If I was honest, Dylan wasn't the only reason I was upset. Seeing that beautiful woman had taken me to a place I didn't want to go. If she had been in John's embalming room, he would've screwed her. Even though Dylan was vulgar, he wouldn't have had sex with her—I was certain of that. I was so sick of all of this. Sick of thinking about it. Sick of John's sickness. I poured myself another drink.

For the next three weeks, my work went smoothly, probably because Dylan avoided me. There still were uncovered bodies in the embalming room, but at least I didn't have to hear his critique every morning. I spent my evenings looking on the Internet for a salon location and job openings for hairdressers. Nothing really seemed quite right.

I left Saturday morning for Valley's shower that afternoon. Mom and Grande both attended the shower with me. Marabeth was there too, but she kept a respectful distance from me. I had a great time seeing all the hairdressers I used to work with. I knew some of Valley's family, so I chatted with them for a while too. Several times I was asked when I was moving back, and others acted as if they didn't know that I wasn't with John, which was ridiculous because everyone knew. Mom avoided any probing questions, but Grande simply put people in their place if she felt they were out of line. God, I loved that woman.

I spent the evening at my parents'. They missed me and made no secret of their hopes that I'd move back. I tried to soothe them by saying that I'd be back in no time for Valley's wedding. "August is just around the corner. I'll come as early as I can and stay as late as possible."

Since Valley's rehearsal dinner was on a Friday night, I asked Ron if I could leave by noon. "I'll come in early, do all the women; the part-time guy can do the men."

He relaxed immediately and approved my afternoon off.

Luckily, Friday morning I didn't have very many women to work on. By eleven, I was working on the last one. The part-timer arrived at eleven thirty. I knew who he was the moment he walked in...mainly because of his pink shoes. I introduced myself, and he said, "I'm Ricky."

"I can't thank you enough for helping me out today. I finished the women, but there are two men who need to be done."

He nodded and said, "I like your outfit." He giggled and touched my leather belt. I couldn't help but laugh. We talked for a few more minutes; then I was in my car, heading home. I planned to arrive at the salon early so Lucy could do my hair.

Entering the salon, I was shocked by the condition of the place. I'd always kept it maintained in a classy, upscale way. Several lights were burned out. Shelves weren't stocked with product. (I'd taken my makeup out of her store, but she still should've been selling hair supplies.)

Three of the ten booths were unattended. The place was falling into disrepair. A shabbiness had settled over everything. Disappointment filled me. This salon had been my dream, and now it had fallen apart as well. Since I'd arrived earlier than I'd hoped, I had time to chat with the other hairdressers. Nobody said anything about the place, but an undercurrent of discord was apparent.

When Lucy was finished with her client, she and I hugged. She cut and colored my hair, but neither one of us said anything about the salon. I didn't want to embarrass her, and maybe she was ashamed that she'd let it become so neglected.

Back at my parents', I dressed in a short, dressy dress. I knew I'd see John, and as crazy as it was, I wanted to look good for him. Wanted him to still want me—to still desire me. A part of me was dreading seeing him again, and yet I couldn't wait, all at the same time.

At the church, the first person I saw was Valley's brother, Skylar, whom I'd always liked. He bragged about his dual wedding duties: walking Valley down the aisle and serving as Charlie's groomsman. Then he expressed his sympathy about Jordan.

I'd come to realize that people were in a no-win situation with me on this. If they did mention Jordan, I was pissed. If they didn't mention Jordan, I was pissed. I was pissed no matter what. That night, though, Skylar's words touched me. Maybe because he was so sincere, or maybe because I simply wanted to hear Jordan's name mentioned.

John waited until the last minute to arrive. When I finally saw him, his back was toward me—his unruly cowlick sticking up like a corkscrew. I bet he was irritated with his new hairdresser, who evidently wasn't Valley. The way my stomach flipped over just from seeing his back, I knew that I still loved him. When he finally turned and saw me, he nodded. I was relieved that he didn't try to talk to me. I just wanted to get through this first meeting without any drama.

Lucy, Valley, and I practiced walking down the aisle. Then we listened to the minister explain the order of the wedding. When it came time for John and me to walk out after the bride and groom, he held his arm out to me. I took it, and we walked down the aisle without saying a word.

Next, the wedding party met for the meal. Grandpa asked me to sit with him. I wasn't sure if he was doing it to help me out of an uncomfortable situation or if he really wanted to sit by me. Either way, I was so grateful to him I could've cried. After the meal, I didn't linger. I said my good-byes and returned to my parents'.

The minute I walked in the door, Mom asked, "How did it go?"

"Perfect. We never said a single word to each other."

She stared at me for a long moment and said nothing else.

Lucy and I dressed for the wedding and then helped Valley with her dress. She was beautiful, and Lucy and I looked pretty good ourselves. I couldn't believe how calm I was. I'd been dreading that day—seeing John and knowing that everyone would be watching us. I knew now that John and I could be civil in public and not cause a scene.

As I walked down the aisle, I was struck with déjà vu upon seeing Charlie and John standing together—such handsome men. Memories of my own wedding flooded me. I couldn't look John in the eye. I simply couldn't, but I felt his eyes on me the whole time.

Thankfully, after they were pronounced husband and wife, Valley and Charlie chose not to dance down the aisle. I simply couldn't have danced with joy...especially with John. Linking arms was tough enough. As we followed the married couple, he finally spoke to me.

"God, you're beautiful, Macie. Simply beautiful."

My throat closed as my heart swelled.

At the reception, I danced with everyone but him. He didn't dance much, which was sad since he was such a great dancer. His mother, my mother, and Valley were his only partners. Skylar and I danced together several times. He asked me if John and I were divorcing.

"I don't know. We've never really talked. I left after I lost Jordan, so I've no idea what he wants to do."

"I'd like to come see you if you decide to divorce."

The thought of being with someone else was so foreign to me that I didn't even know how to respond. Plus, every time I'd looked at John, his eyes had been on me. It was as if he were drinking me in. Lapping me up. Another man would never look at me the way he did.

By midnight, I was ready to leave. My parents were saying their good-byes to Valley and Charlie. I didn't want to stay once they left. I made my way around the room, kissed Valley and Charlie, told Lucy I'd call her next time I was in town, and headed out to my car. As I was tucking my lengthy dress underneath my butt, John leaned down so that we were eye to eye.

"Can you stop by for fifteen minutes tomorrow? I'd like to talk with you before you leave."

There were a million things I could say, but even I knew that at some point the conversation needed to happen.

Sleep eluded me that night. I was so excited to see him, and yet I feared what he'd say. I was fairly confident he didn't want a divorce, but since he'd said he only needed fifteen minutes, that pretty much said it all. Perhaps Kelly had gotten her way with him, and he'd decided she wasn't so bad after all. If he did want a divorce, then I'd agree to it. If he was through, then I definitely was too.

But I was hoping for answers. I wanted to know why.

In the morning when I told Mom and Dad that I was leaving early because I was stopping at John's before driving back into Atlanta, they couldn't hide their pleasure. I knew they wanted us to reconcile. They thought John was the greatest guy—the perfect son-in-law. And why wouldn't they? I'd given them no reason to think otherwise. I was the one acting crazy.

Driving through the old neighborhood, I longed to return to the past. To happier times. When I pulled into the drive and saw the mini-mansion, I could only stare at the beautiful house. I got out of my car and slowly walked up the sidewalk. The yard was maintained the way I liked. Flowers were in the large planters on the front porch, and he'd hung my summer wreath on the front door.

As I stood admiring the house, I realized how much I'd changed. The young woman I'd been before had had such a joy for life…she'd been such a happy-go-lucky girl. Now, I was totally removed from her. As if a veil (more like rose-colored glasses) had been lifted from my eyes and I could see the truth. I felt a hundred years older.

The front door opened; John stepped out on the porch. He didn't say anything, only stared at me. Then finally he said, "Macie."

I walked up the steps to him. He didn't touch me or even kiss my cheek. I looked down at the flowers in the planters. Petunias were mixed in with calibrachoas. I raised my eyes to his, and he grinned sheepishly.

"I asked your mom to help me with these. She said she would as long as she could plant her favorites."

He motioned for me to enter the house. As I stepped into the foyer, a flood of emotions rushed through me. The one that shocked me the most was the feeling that I'd returned home. Inside, everything was still the same. Why I'd thought he'd change anything, I really couldn't say. I wondered if he was dating. If he'd brought his dates to the house. Did those women salivate at the thought of living there? Did he show them Jordan's room? Had Kelly been there?

He offered me something to drink. I declined. I would have welcomed a drink, but not the kind he was offering. He said, "Let's sit in the living room. I won't keep you. I know you want to head back home."

I nodded and put my hand on my throat, rubbing up and down to loosen my vocal cords. He watched me closely, perhaps trying to figure out my mood. I wasn't even sure what my mood was. This conversation could go in so many different directions. So many things could be said or left unsaid, and I wanted to know everything.

He started by saying, "I'm glad you came back for the wedding. It meant a lot to Charlie."

"Valley's my best friend, and Charlie...well, Charlie's special to me."

"I know he is. He misses you."

I didn't say anything to that. He cleared his throat. "I'd like to talk with you calmly without you hurling hurtful things at me. I know I've let you down, but I'd at least like the chance to talk this out."

My first thought was, "You can do that in fifteen minutes? Well, bring it on." Instead I said, "OK."

"I'd like to start by saying that there's a lot you don't understand, and there's a lot I wish I'd had the guts to tell you from the very beginning. So many times I wanted to tell you the truth—tell you about my past. The night I saw you at the movies—I never did it again until you were pregnant with Jordan. I didn't want you to miscarry again. I knew I needed to control myself with you. It was never more than a sexual release."

"I'm supposed to be OK with that?"

He cocked his head, as if puzzled by my lack of understanding. "It was like a crazy form of masturbation."

"Oh, John. You can't honestly believe that. Men imagine crazy things when they jerk off, but I don't think dead women are one of them."

"I'll admit that it's not the norm."

"Not the norm! It's fucking deviant."

He held up his hands as if to block my words.

"What I want to know is how this got started. What made you do this? Who was your first victim?"

"Victim? They weren't victims. You act as if I raped them."

"John, they were victims. If you can't see that, then there's something fundamentally wrong with you...with your morals."

He ran his hands down his face. "I can see this conversation's going nowhere."

"You don't want to explain anything. You just want to blame me."

He looked shocked. "How am I blaming you?"

"By saying that my miscarriage made you go back to your perverted ways."

"I didn't mean it that way. I just meant that..."

I waited for him to continue. When he didn't, I said, "I want to know when this started and why you still need to do it."

He lowered his eyes. I had the distinct feeling that he was thinking of things to say to appease me. He wouldn't lie, but the truth wouldn't come out of his mouth either. He'd sit on the truth and pull out tiny tidbits—maybe embellish those truths to pacify my need to know.

Finally, tired of waiting for him to make something up, I stood. "When you decide that you're ready to talk to me, to tell me the truth, to tell me why I wasn't enough for you, then I'll come back. Until then, I have nothing to say to you."

I walked to the door. He followed, but before I opened the door, he said, "I'm going to get you back. You were and are everything to me. I lie awake at night and remember how we used to be. How much I loved kissing you. How much I loved making love to you. How we used to laugh together. All our times on the pool table. I can't even think half the time because you're always on my mind. I worry about you. I miss you so much, Macie."

He reached out to stroke my face, but I moved away. If I'd felt his touch on my skin just then, it would have been my undoing. He walked me to my car. As I opened the door, he said, "Wow, your car looks like it's had some rough treatment. Did you piss someone off?"

My car and several others at the apartment complex had been keyed the previous week. We'd called the cops, only to be informed that there'd been several reports of car vandalism. They suspected local teenagers. Also, shortly after I'd moved, a light hailstorm had left dimples that could be seen when the sun was just right.

"Sunny's parked outside all the time. I don't have a garage anymore. In fact, I lost a lot of stuff, John. My first home, my salon, my hairdressing career, my..." I stopped because I simply couldn't list all the things I'd lost. Filled with anger, I smacked my hands against his chest and then just summed it all up by saying, "I lost everything because of you."

I didn't give him an opportunity to respond. I climbed into Sunny and left.

CHAPTER 17

Over the next few weeks, I checked out a few buildings that I thought might be potential sites for a salon. One was promising, but I didn't quite have the funds for all it would entail. The lease alone was astronomical. I had a nice nest egg from the sale of my salon, but not enough to pull that off. Plus, last time I'd already established my client base, and I'd also had the majority of Grande's customers. In Atlanta, I had no one. I'd be begging people to come in.

My original plan had been to leave SafeHaven in two more months, but that wasn't going to happen. Unfortunately, my finances wouldn't allow me to buy and remodel a building without working at the funeral home. I was hoping I'd stumble across a salon for sale, but so far, no luck on that. I'd accepted that I would need another business loan. It was no wonder my stomach was in knots every day and sleep evaded me at night.

Some good things had happened at this job that I despised. Although I was the only woman who worked in the embalming room, I wasn't the only woman at the funeral home. Four worked in the office. One did the prearranged funerals; the other three did a multitude of clerical duties and met with the families. I was the only one who actually worked with the bodies. For some reason, this impressed them, and they thought I did the best makeup and hair they'd seen in a long time.

I'd formed somewhat of a friendship—some kind of a rapport—with two of them. Glenna and Elsa were both older than me by a few years. Glenna (married, no kids, seemed very happy) had shiny brown hair,

146

which, of course, I'd noticed. Elsa was living with her boyfriend, but her ring looked like an engagement ring to me. Her hair was short and black, her skin like porcelain. They knew very little about me because I didn't talk about myself at all. In fact, I was so unwilling to share anything about my life that I'm sure they thought I had some kind of secret criminal past. (Maybe I'd embezzled or was wanted for tax evasion.)

Glenna asked me to join them for lunch one day. I usually went home at noon, but that day I agreed—mainly because I was hungry and didn't relish going home to an empty apartment. We drove to a diner they both liked. After ordering, Elsa asked about my weekend. I didn't want to tell them I'd found a building Saturday that I was thinking about leasing or that I'd had several huge orders come in for my make-up. I didn't have anything to share about my social life because it was nonexistent. I wanted to give them something to satisfy their curiosity but had nothing to tell. Thankfully, our waitress brought our drinks, so the moment passed.

Elsa picked up her drink, took a sip, and finally said, "Macie, are you in the witness protection program, or are you hiding from an abusive husband?"

I wanted to laugh, but when I thought about it, the only thing I'd ever told them about myself was that I was an only child and was separated from my husband. I smiled. "I can understand why you'd think that, but I can assure you I'm not. I've just had an extremely bad year, and I'm trying to heal from a painful situation."

They seemed relieved and satisfied with my answer. I hoped that would quench their curiosity and they'd quit quizzing me.

That night as I was filling makeup orders, John called. I'd wondered when, or if, he'd ever talk to me again. He didn't ask what I was doing—probably afraid to after the last time—but did ask, "When are you coming back home to visit?"

"I'm not sure. I've no immediate plans right now."

"I'm ready to talk to you."

"About what?"

"Don't play games, Macie. I'm ready to tell you everything."

"OK. I'll come back, but let me be clear on something. I want to know everything, and if I think you're lying about anything, then that's it. I'll leave. You get one chance on this; that's it."

"OK. When can you come back?"

"I'll come back Saturday. I'll be there at one."

"Can I take you to lunch?"

"No."

"Can I—"

"No. I'll come to the mansion. You can tell me everything I want to know; then I'm coming back home."

"OK."

I went back to the bedroom and continued boxing up my orders.

All week I was on edge. I needed to know all of John's secrets to move on. Either we were going forward together, or I needed to move on toward a life without him. I wasn't ready to give up on us, but I wasn't ready to forgive and forget. I needed facts. I needed the truth. I needed a conclusion.

Saturday, I dressed in jeans. I'd originally planned on wearing a skirt that I knew he liked but had changed my mind. Neither of us needed any kind of distraction. When I pulled up in his drive, my palms were sweating. I had no idea what to expect. Would I stay married or file for divorce?

He must've been watching for me, because he opened the door before I was even out of Sunny. He stood on the porch and waited for me to go to him. That time he did take hold of my arm.

"How was your drive?"

"Uneventful."

Inside, he offered me a beer. I accepted and asked if I could use the bathroom. He raised his eyebrows. "You don't need to ask. This is your house too."

I didn't say anything, just turned, and walked toward the bathroom. I noticed that Jordan's door was shut. I wondered what he'd done with all the baby stuff. Was the crib still set up? Where were the yellow booties?

In the bathroom, I couldn't help but snoop. Everything was the same: the guest towels, the decorative soaps, the pictures on the wall. I looked for clues that some other woman had been there but found absolutely nothing. But if he'd had someone sleep over, she would've used the master bathroom, not the guest bath. As I walked back down the hall, I couldn't resist peeking into Jordan's room. I opened the door a crack—just enough to see that the crib was still there and so was the changing table.

Back in the living room, I sat across from him and swallowed several gulps of my beer. My plan was to let him talk, but he stared at me as if expecting me to ask questions. I decided right then to tell him exactly what I wanted and expected from him.

"John, I want you to talk nonstop for the next thirty minutes. I'm not going to pull the information from you. If I have a question, I'll ask. I want you to tell me everything, and if you don't, like I said, I'll leave, and we're done."

He swallowed a huge mouthful of beer and then started. "Our house, as you probably know, was at the mortuary. The whole backside and upper floor was where we lived. I know it sounds weird, but that's just how it used to be. I don't know if it bothered my mother, but honestly, I don't think Charlie and I thought too much about it. We were happy, and Dad spent so much time with us that our lives didn't seem strange to us at all.

"When I was a senior and Charlie was a freshman, he became friends with Fiona. She was a sophomore. I knew who she was, but she wasn't really in the group of friends that either of us ran with. She was quiet. Not really popular, but she wasn't unpopular. She just kind of was in the background, so to speak. She and Charlie had a class together and formed a friendship. Weirdly enough, he didn't like her as a girlfriend. He liked her as a friend.

"They had some school project they were working on together, and she came to the house. That's when I first really met her. I liked her. For some reason, she got under my skin. I mean, I couldn't quit thinking about her. I was dating someone else at the time, but I knew I wanted to be with Fiona. I asked her if she would be open to going out with me, and she said yes. I broke up with my girlfriend and started dating her. We had fun together. She was funny, and I really fell hard for her. She knew that I'd been with other girls, but she told me straight up that she was a virgin and wasn't ready to do anything yet. We messed around a lot, but I never tried to have sex with her or even talk her into it. When she was ready, I knew she'd let me know.

"She was excellent in track. An amazing sprinter and great at relays. I didn't go to the track meet that day. I really wanted to because I knew she'd win. When I got home that day, Charlie was crying. He said she'd died. I couldn't believe it. I just couldn't believe it. My father called her parents and said he'd do the funeral for free. He must've felt he should since she and I were dating. Who knows why he did, but that's what I've always thought. The night before the funeral, as I was lying in bed, I kept thinking about her—downstairs in her coffin."

He stopped and looked at me. "It was the most bizarre thing, Macie. The oddest feeling."

We both took a sip of our beers. My nerves were on edge. We were finally to the part that I needed to hear but wasn't exactly sure I wanted to hear.

He started again. "I finally couldn't take it anymore. I got up and went down to sit with her...be with her. I didn't want her to be alone. Mom always left a light on. Even though they were dead, she never left them in the dark. The light was on in the viewing room, but the casket was gone. I knew that sometimes things happened and Dad had to rework things. I walked toward the embalming room and saw that her casket had been rolled into the hall. I looked inside the casket, but she wasn't there. The door to the embalming room was open. She was naked on the table, and my dad was on top of her. His white ass moving up and down, pounding away on her.

"It was surreal, but I watched him until he was finished. When I turned to go, Charlie was standing behind me. I'll never forget the horror on his face. I was too upset to talk. As he and I were walking back to our rooms, Mom came down the hall. She looked at us, and I knew in that instant that he'd done this before with other women. All Mom said was, 'I'll see you boys in the morning.' It was as if nothing was wrong—nothing was abnormal. Charlie went to his bedroom. I could hear him crying."

He stopped talking. I didn't know what to say, but I couldn't help thinking, "If he was so horrified by this, then what had possessed him to do the same thing?" It was one screwed-up family.

He continued. "Nothing was ever said. The funeral was the next day. Mom had redressed Fiona, and she looked beautiful in the casket. I left for college that fall. The timing couldn't have been worse for Charlie. He became a mess. He'd always been different, but honestly, up until that time, it wasn't a big deal. He was smart in school. Had friends galore. But after that incident and me leaving for college, he went into an insane spiral. That's the best way I can describe it. He became sexually active. I mean, he screwed anything with a vagina, which was so bizarre, because I was just the opposite. I shut down sexually.

"Anyway, Charlie was damn good looking; he had no shortage of women. He became defiant with Mom and Dad. They didn't know what to do with him. They took him to see a therapist. Of course, Charlie wouldn't tell the therapist the truth about anything, so he was diagnosed as something he wasn't. The therapist encouraged my parents to take as many preventative measures as they could. My parents thought he'd outgrow it—you know, that it was puberty or just something wacky with his hormones. The therapist assured them that it wasn't. That Charlie was suffering from a mental disorder. That's why my parents chose the vasectomy and denied him a driver's license. The therapist convinced them Charlie was totally out of control. That he'd kill someone if allowed to drive. He made Charlie sound crazy, like an out-of-control maniac.

"Charlie just seemed to sink inside himself and become this different person. It was really sad to watch. It wasn't until you came along that he was pulled out of the mire. Then Valley did the rest when she fell in love with him. He's the man he was always meant to be. The man locked inside was finally able to break free."

He shook his head as if to get himself back on track and then took a couple of swallows of beer.

"I'd been going back and forth on whether or not I was going into the family business. After that episode, I decided to study and be the best mortician I could be. I'd put my father out of business. I'd expose him and ruin him. When I was away at college, the funeral home caught fire. It was determined to be faulty wiring, but the place was so damned old that I'm surprised it didn't happen earlier.

"Dad was wealthy to begin with, and now he had this huge insurance settlement. On weekends when I didn't have classes, he'd come and pick me up, and we'd tour other funeral homes. He said he was going to build a state-of-the-art funeral home so that I could take over. He'd work with me for a few years until I was comfortable. Then he wanted to retire with Mom.

"Once I was out of college, I came back to work for him. I'm still not sure why I did. Maybe I wanted answers from him or to understand him. Also, to be honest, I loved the funeral home he built. He'd done everything to make it the very best he could. It was the nicest one I'd ever seen, and he'd done it for me. I felt that he was trying to make up to me—a reconciliation. Ask my forgiveness. I wasn't sure how he knew that I knew. Had Mom told him, or had Charlie? I just knew that he knew about Fiona. Even though I hated him, Macie, I still loved him."

A tear slid from the corner of my eye. His pain was evident, and it hurt me to see.

"We worked side by side. I learned so much from him. How to work with the families. How to settle disputes. How to help people deal with their grief. He was an amazing funeral director. Really amazing. Now that he had this state-of-the-art funeral home, he hired more funeral directors and built the business into what it is now."

He swallowed and shifted in his seat. I pressed my knees together to control the shaking and prepare for what was coming.

"The first woman I had sex with was probably forty years old. She died from diving into a pool. I don't know why I did it, but as she lay on the table, I just had this overwhelming need. It was over quickly, and I didn't do it again for several months. But then I did it again, and I never stopped until I met you.

"At first, Dad didn't know. But then a situation came up that could've ruined us. I never used a condom. Never saw a need to. After I screwed this woman, the body was called back to the coroner. Her death had been determined a homicide; the police wanted more tests done. She'd already been swabbed for semen to determine if she'd been sexually assaulted. But if they'd chosen to redo that test, then my sperm would've been recovered. My face must've shown my fear...my guilt. Dad didn't say anything, but he comprehended, and he was scared. Nothing happened because they were testing for poison, not sperm. A few days after the body was buried, he came to me. Wanted to talk about 'my problem.' He acted as if this was something unheard of. Something unthinkable. I was shocked because I'd learned it from him."

He stopped and stared at his feet for so long that for a moment I thought he was done. That he wasn't going to tell me any more.

Finally, he looked up and said, "He told me he'd get me some help. They'd get me some therapy. That's when I told him I saw him with Fiona. He was so shocked that he fell back against the wall—literally collapsed with the knowledge that I knew about him. Two nights later, he took something. Anyway, in the morning he was dead. It was ruled a heart attack, but Mom and I knew that it wasn't...because he left us each a note. He didn't leave Charlie one—wanted Charlie to believe he'd died, not that he'd committed suicide.

"It took me a while to realize that he built this funeral home for me. He wasn't trying to buy my love back, win me over. He simply wanted us to work together. He wanted to give me a fantastic business. He knew I'd always take care of Charlie. That someday he'd be my responsibility, and he wanted to make me rich so that I'd have the finances to support us both. He really did have my best interest at heart. He really did love me."

I finally spoke. "John, of course, he loved you. From all the things you've ever told me about him, it was obvious to me that he loved you."

"If I'd just stayed in my room that night. If I'd never gone down to see Fiona, then none of this would've happened. Charlie wouldn't have lost himself. I wouldn't have this...this need that I have. My dad would still be alive. You would've never had a miscarriage. Jordan wouldn't have died, and I'd still be with you. I ruined so many things when I got up that night."

Now came the present. Where did this leave us? Now that I knew the history of his sickness, I wondered if I could move past it. I didn't think I could. I did have a few questions, though. "Didn't you ever feel bad for your behavior? Didn't you ever think it was wrong? I mean, you were so upset about Fiona, but then you did the same thing."

"I did feel bad when I screwed a nun. But she wasn't a virgin, which surprised me. We didn't do the funeral here, only the embalming. They had a Catholic funeral for her at the church. The only other one I felt some guilt over was a woman who was probably in her late thirties. She was a virgin...kept her maidenhead to her death, and then I took it from her. That kind of haunted me for a while."

I didn't even know what to say to either of those confessions. He said, "I can stop."

"Then why didn't you?"

"I didn't think it would upset you the way it did. As crazy as this sounds, I thought you might have figured it out."

"How would I have figured it out?"

"The quickies. The way I liked you cold and still." He stopped as a pained look crossed his face. "That night in the parking lot, your revulsion told me everything. You were absolutely repulsed by me."

He was right. That was a huge problem for me still. I couldn't erase the images from my mind.

"Mom had known about Dad for years and had accepted it. I just thought that you..."

"That I what?"

He shrugged.

"Well, I'm not your mother. I can't accept it. You cheated on me."

He looked totally surprised.

"Yes, John, you cheated on me. I told you from day one that I couldn't and wouldn't accept cheating. You agreed, yet you've screwed I don't know how many women."

"They weren't women. They were bodies. They were dead. It's totally different."

"It's not. Our vows said 'forsaking all others.' For me, that meant dead or alive."

"There was no connection between me and them. They were nothing. It meant nothing."

"It's not nothing, John. I'm not arguing with you on this."

"It is nothing. I haven't done it since that night. When I saw how much it upset you, I never did it again. You know, though, it isn't even illegal."

Bloody hell. What kind of comment was that? Just because it wasn't illegal, that didn't give him the right to do it. He was so screwed up that I came undone. I started crying because it was all so ugly. Finally, I said, "I need to leave. I need some space."

He stood when I did.

"Don't walk me to Sunny. Don't say anything else. Just let me leave."

He nodded. I managed to walk to my car. I'd originally planned on spending the night at my parents', but by that point, I only wanted to get the hell out of town. For the first thirty minutes, I drove in a daze. When I reached home, I immediately grabbed my crystal shot glass and downed two shots before I even set my purse down.

That night, I couldn't think about anything else but the conversation with John. It was almost information overload. I'd never heard of such a screwed-up, dysfunctional family. They were like some bad horror movie. The saying "Truth is stranger than fiction" was true in this case. I wasn't sure I even wanted to try to make things work with him. I really couldn't accept that he'd done this for several years or that he didn't seem to find anything wrong with it.

He'd said that he could change, that he had changed, that he'd stopped. I believed him when he said that he hadn't done it again. But I wasn't sure I believed that he would *never* do it again. That was the sticky part for me. I believed in forgiveness. I could forgive and forget. (Well, OK. I couldn't forget. Who could forget something like that?) If I did decide to stay with him, go back to him, one thing was for certain: I wouldn't have children with him. That was how I knew in my heart that I'd never totally trust him. I didn't want children with him because I had no faith in us.

CHAPTER 18

My foul mood was still with me when I went to work Monday morning. I hated my job, hated my life, and hated the decisions I was being forced to make. When I entered the embalming room, the first thing I noticed was a sheet over one of the bodies. Dylan, dressed in cutoffs and a ratty T-shirt, was talking with Paul. I looked at him curiously. He came and stood in front of me. "My grandmother died yesterday." His eyes rested on the sheet-covered body.

I knew I should say something like "I'm sorry" or "That sucks" or even "I'll do my best job on her," but I said none of those things. I'm not exactly sure what came over me—what possessed me to behave the way I did—but I walked over to the table and yanked the sheet off the body. The old woman was naked and as thin as a stick.

I said, "This is an equal-opportunity embalming room. We don't show favoritism to anyone." I wanted to make a rude comment about her flat chest ("pancake tits" or "flat as a flitter"), but I did have some couth about myself.

Red with fury, Dylan pushed me up against the wall. I thought he was going to slap the shit out of me, but instead he said, "That's my grandmother."

"Dylan, every single corpse in here is special to someone. The day that you understand that fact, the day that you get that through your thick skull, will be the day that you become a human being. You should treat every single corpse in here as if it were your grandmother."

"I don't need a lecture from you on how to do my job."

"I think you do. I think you should go work in a strip joint. At least, those women want to be looked at. They want you to admire their rack."

He leaned in, his face only inches from mine. "You're a spiteful bitch. No wonder you're separated from your husband. You're impossible to get along with."

He turned and stomped out. Well, he was right about one thing. I was a bitch. I didn't know when it had happened, but it had, and I did the name justice. I pressed my eyelids shut as I fought back tears and tried to control my emotions. When I finally opened my eyes, I saw Paul quietly staring at me. All I saw was respect.

I worked on the body that was awaiting me. After that, I helped dress three corpses and did my usual job on them. As I was walking down the hall to leave at the end of the day, Ron saw me and motioned me into his office. My first thought was I was going to be fired. As relief washed through me, my second thought was I wouldn't ever have to come back here again.

In his office, I sat down and crossed my legs. He said, "We're having an office luncheon Friday. I'd like you to plan on being there."

"Is this like a staff meeting?"

"No, no. Just a friendly get-together. I just like all the employees to know each other. Some haven't met you."

I wanted to say something, but nothing was forthcoming. I nodded, which he took as my agreement to attend.

The next day when I entered the embalming room, Dylan's grandmother was covered with a sheet once more. Well, I did it again, and I'm not ashamed to admit it. I yanked that sheet off and hid it in another room. Until there were sheets on every single corpse, there'd be sheets on no one. Paul had a smirk on his face but didn't say a word. The other mortician kept his head turned, so I couldn't see his face. The only downside was that Dylan wasn't there to see my wayward behavior.

The following day, I helped Paul dress Dylan's grandmother. I wanted to say something to him but wasn't sure what I could impart that'd make my actions seem acceptable. I decided the best thing to do was not to bring it up.

When I was alone with the body, I did apologize for my bad behavior. As I plucked two dark hairs from her chin, I told her, "Your grandson's an asshole, and I'm a bitch. I really am. But the asshole in him brings out the bitch in me."

I guess that really wasn't an apology, but at least it eased my conscience.

Friday at the luncheon, I was introduced to numerous people. Afterward, I could only remember a few names, but everyone knew me and was overly friendly. Of course, that was because I was the new girl. Dylan totally ignored me, which was exactly what I'd expected. Ron gave a little pep talk at the end—more for the office than for my department. It wasn't as if we could bring in more business.

That evening I watched sitcom reruns—thought maybe some humor would help me. At eight, Grande called to talk. I knew she wanted me to move back when my apartment lease was up. I decided it was as good a time as any to tell her of my plans to open a salon there in Atlanta.

"Macie, please don't do that. You'll never be able to come back if you get embedded that deep."

"I need to return to my first love: hair. I hate this job. I hate the people I work with. Well, one of them, but he's making me sour on everyone else. I hate my life, Grande."

She started crying, which broke my heart. I shouldn't have been so honest with her. She only wanted to see me happy and well adjusted. I was neither. Finally, she said, "Have you signed any papers on a lease?"

"Not yet, but I've talked to the bank and given them a business plan. They were impressed with the money that I can put down, so I'm fairly confident I can get the loan."

"At least let your dad and me check out the property before you do anything."

"Grande, I don't think that either of you could look at it with an open mind. It'd be a waste of your time, and you'd hurt my feelings with your disapproval."

"I just don't want you to make a bad decision and lose all your money."

"I've lost everything else; I might as well lose my money too."

"What happened, Macie? What happened to you and John?"

"Lots of shit. A lot of shit happened."

Entering the embalming room Monday morning, I stopped short. Sheets draped all the bodies. I knew better than to make any kind of comment. Dylan was back, and he eyed me with pure hatred. I couldn't blame him. I hated myself for my crude and thoughtless actions. The right thing to do would have been to try to smooth things over with him, but my pride wouldn't let me. Also, I thought my actions were justified. Looking at the covered bodies, I felt some good had come from it.

After finishing my morning, I walked by Elsa's office to say hi. I wanted to make more of an effort to be friendly to her and Glenna. She wanted me to have lunch with her. I hadn't been to the grocery store yet, so my cupboards were bare. Lunch sounded good.

Sitting in the sandwich shop, I asked, "Where's Glenna today?"

"She took today and tomorrow off. Went with her husband on a business trip."

"She seems happy. He sounds like a nice guy."

"He is." She leaned forward on her elbows. "This is a cruel thing to say, but he isn't much to look at. He's short and bald, but she's crazy about him. They don't really go together. I was so shocked the first time I met him. I guess that's why I'm telling you this—to save you from the shock."

For some reason, this struck my funny bone. I laughed hard. She settled back, grinning, and said, "I've heard some rumblings about you and Dylan."

I'd wanted to ask her or Glenna if any rumors had been floating around but didn't want to be the first to give a hint that there was trouble if nothing had been said yet.

"What did you hear?"

"That you told him off. The other men don't like how callous he is with the dead, but none of them wanted to stand up to him."

"Why not?"

She looked surprised. "You don't know who he is, do you?"

"No, I guess not."

"He's Ron's brother-in-law. He's married to Ron's sister. She's the baby of the family. Ron's something like seventeen years older than her. He isn't crazy about Dylan, but because of his little sister, he gave him a job."

"You sure know a lot about this."

"My cousin is best friends with Ron's wife."

"Oh, so you get the scoop from your cousin."

"Lord no. She and I don't get along. She tells her mom, who tells my mom, who tells me. So it's anyone's guess how accurate the information is by the time it comes to me."

I laughed. "Well, you can tell your mom to tell your aunt to tell your cousin to tell her best friend that I think Dylan's a prick."

Elsa giggled. "I'll do that." She took a drink then said, "I know for a fact that the other men respect the hell out of you. Everyone, except for maybe Ron, heard about the sheet incident."

I stopped chewing, swallowed and said, "Did everyone know at the luncheon Friday?"

She nodded. "It spread like wildfire."

"I shouldn't have done that, but something came over me. I don't understand why people won't stand up to him. Where's everyone's balls? Ron seems like he'd be open to at least a conversation if someone had a legitimate complaint. I can't believe that he'd be happy with things in the embalming room if he knew. Also, Dylan is fearful for his job. He isn't as tough as he seems. He's just got the other men buffaloed. His so-called status is a facade."

She said, "Paul used to come up and tell us all the rude things Dylan would say. He didn't know how to keep him out of the embalming room. They gave up a long time ago trying to keep the bodies covered. It's like

Dylan got off somehow looking at them. You know, some people like that kind of stuff."

My throat closed as I nodded.

She continued. "It's not like they're hurting anyone, but still, it isn't right."

Again, I nodded. She leaned forward and whispered, "When they dress them, especially the young women, their hands are all over them, and well, I'd think it'd be hard not to be somewhat turned on. I can easily understand how that whole thing could get started. Fondle a breast, touch a nipple, pinch an ass. It could begin very innocently."

"You act as if you don't think there's anything wrong with it, Elsa."

"I'm just saying it doesn't hurt the dead person. I could see how it'd be a temptation."

I wanted the subject changed. "Does Ron ever do embalming anymore?"

"No. He used to be totally involved in the funeral home. Now he runs things from afar. Probably feels as if he did his time. He doesn't want to do the dirty work anymore. No more calls at night."

"I can understand that. My husband was…" I immediately stopped. I didn't want to share anything about my marriage.

She tilted her head. "Your husband what?"

I didn't want to continue but finally said, "My husband got called out all hours of the night. It gets old after a while."

Elsa's eyes opened wide as the pieces fell into place for her. It was like watching her work a jigsaw puzzle and find a piece she was searching for.

"Your husband's a funeral director?"

I nodded. She opened her mouth to ask more questions, but I laid my hand on her arm. "Elsa, I can't really talk about this right now. I'm still trying to work through a lot of things."

She nodded, but I could see all the questions in her eyes. We needed to return to work, and I needed to get the hell out of there.

Back at the apartment, after working almost ten hours, I had a major head-ache, and my head was swirling with all the crap from my conversations with John and then Elsa. Was I the only one who thought this was wrong?

I worked the rest of the week without incident. Friday, I went to lunch with Elsa and Glenna. Glenna had learned that my husband was in the funeral business, but thankfully, she didn't ask any questions. Once we returned to the funeral home, she invited me over for supper. She wanted me to meet her husband, but I thought it was probably because she was curious about my previous life. I sort of wanted to meet the short, little, bald man myself. She didn't give me an actual date—just a general invitation. I'd had these before. The ones that never materialize. I said, "Sure, anytime."

Saturday morning, I unpacked the makeup shipment that had arrived. It kept my mind occupied for a while, but when I was finished, my thoughts returned to John. I couldn't quit replaying our conversation. Everything about it haunted me. That he'd seen his father. That the incident was never discussed. That he thought his father knew, when in fact he didn't. All the family secrets. And poor Charlie. Stuck in the middle of everything. Plus, he still didn't know the truth about his father. Not that I thought he should. But it was just another family secret.

With the whole afternoon before me and with time on my hands, I Googled "necrophilia." Wikipedia didn't even refer to it as a sickness or disorder. Just stated the motivation—as if it was OK. If you had a tendency for it, if you leaned that way, then this could be why. What the hell? I mean really. What the hell!

The site gave percentages—categories for the reason a person would turn to necrophilia:

- Sixty-eight percent were motivated by a desire for an unresisting and unrejecting partner (I never resisted or rejected John.)

- Twenty-one percent by a want for reunion with a lost partner (That made me sad. Did he still want to be, long to be, with Fiona?)
- Fifteen percent by sexual attraction to dead people (That was sickening.)
- Fifteen percent by a desire for comfort or need to overcome feelings of isolation (I gave him comfort, or at least I felt I did.)
- Eleven percent by a desire to remedy low self-esteem by expressing power over a corpse (OK, that was just wrong. Talk about the ultimate bully.)

I then stumbled across this little tidbit: as of May 2006, there was no federal legislation specifically barring sex with a corpse. States had their own laws. The Georgia state law: "A person convicted of the offense of necrophilia shall be punished by imprisonment for not less than one nor more than ten years."

I wanted to call John and inform him of the Georgia law. His ass could end up in jail, so he couldn't tell me it wasn't illegal. Also, I wanted to ask him which category he considered himself to be in. For some reason, I could accept three of the explanations. I understood how some men liked tying women up. They didn't like to be told no when they wanted sex. I could also understand the second one. If he still wanted to be with Fiona, then that seemed reasonable to me. I'd never lost someone, never had a lover die, so I didn't know how that would feel. I also understood the fourth one: needing comfort. Men needed comfort. Robin never gave him what he needed; she only wanted his money. Maybe when I became pregnant, I didn't give him what he needed either. The rest of the reasons were inconceivable to me. Desiring a dead person was wrong in my judgmental book, and the last one didn't fit. John didn't have low self-esteem. He just didn't.

I wondered how prevalent this "disorder" was in the funeral industry. I searched but couldn't find anything. When I really thought about it, though, I had to wonder, who would admit to it? I certainly wouldn't go online and blog about it. I wouldn't make a YouTube video about my husband's weird fetish. So there wasn't any way for me to know. But deep down I knew that it wasn't common. This wasn't something that people in the funeral business did on a daily basis.

There was one thing that I knew for certain, though, and that was the fact that I loved John. Even though I knew about his sick obsession, I realized that I was trying to make sense of it so I could find a way back to him. The way he looked at me, his desire for me, his love for me, was something I couldn't walk away from.

I poured myself a shot glass full of bourbon. As I drank, I couldn't let the Georgia law rest. Maybe I wanted to prove to him that not only did I think it was wrong but that the whole state of Georgia did too. I decided to text him.

"FYI: The Georgia law—'necrophilia shall be punished by imprisonment for not less than one nor more than ten years.' When you're at work, you might want to keep your pecker in your pants."

After I pressed Send, the realization of what I'd just done hit me. Talk about incriminating evidence. If he was ever caught and his phone was confiscated, then that text could be recovered. Since I'd sent it, I'd placed myself in the hot seat. I wouldn't be able to say I didn't know. Was there a law for withholding evidence of a crime? I wanted to call him and plead for his forgiveness. John. John. I simply didn't think about what I was doing. I wanted to protect him. Also, I didn't need to be so hateful, so crude with my words.

CHAPTER 19

Sunday morning, Lucy called. She wanted to come see me. This was a huge surprise, and I couldn't wait for her to arrive. I needed a friend that day.

I fixed a light lunch, but she only ate a few bites and was so nervous that I knew something was wrong. Finally, I said, "Lucy, just tell me."

She looked down, swallowed as if she had a lump in her throat, and said, "I'm losing the salon. I have to file for bankruptcy. I can't pay the bills and can't continue borrowing money from my family. I thought I could do this. You made it look so easy."

"Oh, I'm sorry. I really am. The difference was I had money to start with. You had to borrow everything. Also, when I bought the land, it was cheap. When you bought, the price had escalated because the business was so successful."

She sighed. "I never told you this, but the night before we signed the papers, I wanted to call you and cancel. I had a feeling, an intuition, that I couldn't do this."

"Why didn't you? I didn't want to sell, Lucy. I didn't want to renege on my agreement with you, so I went through with the deal."

We looked at each other, wishing we'd been honest with one another.

"The reason I'm here—well, I saw your grandmother the other day. In passing, she mentioned that you were trying to buy a place here to start over. I wondered if you'd be interested in paying off my bank loan. That's all I'd ask. At least my credit wouldn't be ruined. I'm going to work in my cousin's nail salon."

I was surprised by this; she hated doing nails.

We talked money, and she told me the dire shape the salon was in.

"You'll have to rebuild the business. I've ruined it. No one wants to work there. Customers are finding other places to go. I've just really messed it up, Macie."

"I'll come back next Saturday. Give me time to think about this. You haven't signed any papers, have you?"

"No."

"OK. Don't until I've had a chance to weigh the pros and cons of returning."

After she left, I thought about how my selling the salon had turned out to be the worst decision for the both of us. I felt the same way about the salon as John did about the night he went down to sit with Fiona. That one choice, that one decision, had made a mess of my life. If I'd kept the salon, I wouldn't have been working for John. I couldn't have done both jobs, so the salon would've been my top priority. I wouldn't have known about John's sick obsession because I wouldn't have been checking the bodies in the caskets. I wouldn't have lost Jordan. I wouldn't have moved away. And I'd still be with John, although ignorant of his desire for dead sex.

If I bought the salon back, I could return home and be with my family and friends again. I could either return to John or move on with the divorce. One thing I knew for sure: I was done with the funeral business. I wasn't cut out for the day-to-day heartache of dealing with death. It was a calling, and I realized I hadn't been called. I'd keep my promise to Grande and the bunco women; I'd do their makeup when the time came. But other than that, I was officially done.

I wanted my own business. I hated working for someone else. I'd prided myself on being a business owner. Having a career of my own. I wanted that back again—that sense of accomplishment. Working with John, at first, had given me that. I'd felt I was using my expertise, but that had quickly faded. His name was on the funeral home. He owned the business. I had been no more than an employee for him and certainly for SafeHaven. Clock in. Clock out. I needed more than that.

Just when I thought I couldn't take any more of SafeHaven, things got better. The embalming room's atmosphere seemed tranquil instead of sleazy. Everyone was friendlier and more talkative. It seemed the whole sheet episode had changed my coworkers' attitudes for the better.

It was a typical Monday. I worked late and was exhausted by the time I arrived back at the apartment. Collapsing on the couch with a tub of cottage cheese, I wondered how mad John was at me. He'd never texted me back or called. My foolishness was inexcusable. He probably wanted to rip the skin off my ass with his teeth.

The next day, I stepped into Glenna's office to chat with her before my lunch break was over. As I sat down, I noticed a small casket on her desk. Taken aback by its tiny size, I couldn't even form words to ask a question. I ran my finger over the walnut top.

Glenna said, "That's sad, isn't it? I had a couple in here earlier this morning. She had a late-term miscarriage over the weekend. They were wanting to bury their baby."

"Is that done?"

"Yes, more than you'd think. Some parents just have a memorial service, but others want a burial."

Moved by that, I didn't know what to say. I'd wished countless times that we'd done something for Jordan. Some little something to say goodbye. But I had been so distraught with everything that had happened, I couldn't even think afterward. And after I lost Jordan, I hadn't wanted to be anywhere near John.

I touched the small coffin again. When I raised my eyes to Glenna's, my pain and loss must've been written on my face. Her face clouded over, and she said, "Oh my, my, Macie, I'm sorry. I'm so sorry."

I didn't say a word. Didn't admit or deny anything. I stood up. I needed to return to work.

She said, "If you ever need to talk, Macie, I'm a good listener."

I nodded and returned to the embalming room.

That night, I lay awake thinking about Jordan. What exactly had happened to him? I couldn't bear the thought of him being tossed out like a piece of trash. Dumped into the hazardous waste like a diseased organ or a lump of flesh.

The next day, my stomach was unsettled—churning and queasy. Working on the cadavers was almost my undoing. I couldn't wait to get home; I was in a state of mourning, as if I'd lost Jordan all over again. That evening, I was unable to shut off my mind, to stop the ugly, twisted images that kept haunting me. At midnight, I had to talk with someone. John was the only one who'd truly understand my pain. I called his phone. I didn't really expect him to answer, so when he did, I started to cry.

He was instantly alarmed. "What's happened? Are you OK?"

I nodded and then realized that he couldn't see me. I squeaked out a yes. He started firing off questions. I finally said, "I'm sad about Jordan. I just needed to talk to you about him."

"Ah, Macie, let me come to you. I can be there in a little over an hour."

"No, I only want to talk to you."

"Please, just tell me where you live. I'll come to you."

"John, I don't want to wait for you to drive here. Talk to me over the phone. Just tell me what you remember about that night. About him."

"I don't want to do this over the phone."

I gave up. "OK. I should've known you wouldn't help me." I ended the call and turned my phone off. The rest of the night, I dozed off and on. The next morning John had left five text messages and one voice mail.

"Sorry. Plz call me back."

"I'll talk with you over the phone."

"I handled that wrong. Plz call me."

"Sorry sorry sorry I'm an idiot."

"Macie."

The last one made me cry. He always said my name. If he was happy with me, if he was sad with me, if he was making love to me, or if he knew he'd hurt me. I listened to his voice mail.

"Macie, I'm sorry. I just wanted to be with you the first time we talked about Jordan. I never wanted to do that over the phone. I think about him every day. I think about how you held him in your hands. When I think about him…you…us, it breaks me. It hurts so much that I can't even breathe at times. I know I've hurt you. I keep hurting you. I want us to be together. I just want to be with you." He sobbed and finally said, "Jordan was beautiful. Our son was simply beautiful. I thought he had your nose. He was just so tiny. Just so small. Our son."

I wanted to call in sick, but they were counting on me. I dressed and went into work.

That evening, Valley called. I wondered why she hadn't told me about the severity of Lucy's problems, but she'd probably thought I had enough of my own.

She said, "I wanted you to know that I'm not going to work for Lucy anymore. I think she's going under. She won't talk to me, but it's obvious that she can't hang on much longer."

"Where are you going to work?"

"I don't know; I just know I'm not staying here. I'm really pissed right now. She should've known she couldn't pull off buying your place. You had your makeup income, and you just have more money skills than she does. She raised the booth rent again, so much that it's ridiculous. Only me and one other stylist are still there now. No one wants to come in. Like today. I had one client. Why bother coming in for that?"

"I'm sorry, Valley. I never should've sold the place to her."

"She's let the place run down. The building's a dive. I wasn't going to tell you this, but I'm so furious about it that I need to spew. Today, I heard her bad-mouth you to someone over the phone. Said she paid too much for the place. You overinflated the price of the business. Fudged the profit margin. That it wasn't worth it, and no one could've made a profit. Hearing her talk like that…well, I made my decision to leave."

It hurt my feelings, broke my heart, that Lucy felt that way. I knew I should tell Valley my plans, but I needed to see the salon first before I got everyone else involved.

"Valley, I'm coming home this weekend. Let's plan on getting together. I need some girl time with you."

"Gosh, that sounds like fun. I can't wait to see you again."

"I'll call when I get into town."

The next day, as I was collecting my purse to leave SafeHaven, I heard a man out front asking for me. The voice was familiar, but I couldn't place it. I got a surprise when I stepped out and saw Skylar standing with Elsa. She raised her eyebrows at me. I knew she assumed he was my husband. I introduced them and made sure she knew that he was only a friend.

In the parking lot, he said, "I told Valley I wanted to come check on you. See how you were managing in the big city by yourself."

I laughed. "Let's go get something to eat. I'll fill you in on what's been going on."

As we were waiting for our food, I said, "I'm going this weekend to visit everyone."

"Are you seeing him?"

"I don't know."

"It's been a while now, and you've made no effort to go back to him."

"It's complicated, Skylar. I'm still reeling from losing the baby."

He squeezed my hand. "Does he blame you?"

"I don't know. We've never talked about it. But I blame myself."

"Lots of women lose babies. It's not like you're the only one it's happened to."

"I know, but it's more than that. I...well, it's difficult to talk about. It's very—"

"Let's change the subject, Macie. Tell me about your job here."

"Heavens no. Let's not talk about that. Tell me about your job."

Thankfully, he talked about his management job for the next several minutes. I relaxed somewhat. As I listened to him and looked at his pretty boy face, I couldn't help but think how nice it would be to have a normal relationship. A normal man. Why couldn't I have found a normal, uncomplicated man like Skylar? He had a great job, he was good looking in a boyish kind of way, and we liked the same things. I was crazy about his sister, and my parents liked him immensely. For a fleeting moment, I thought of taking him back to my apartment and stripping him bare. It had been so long since I'd been with a man that the very thought filled me with desire.

After we ate, I invited him to my place. Once settled on the couch, we talked about Valley and Charlie.

"I like Charlie. They're good together. I'll admit, though, at first, I was a little concerned about him working in the funeral business. That gave me the willies. It still does when I think about it."

I laughed. "When I first met John, I felt the same way."

"I can't believe that you do their makeup. You know, the dead people."

I smiled. "Me either."

He leaned over and kissed me on the cheek. It was nice to have a man that close again. A man who was so uncomplicated. Skylar and I had chemistry—I couldn't deny that. But I didn't want to be a cheater. And I wouldn't be.

He must've felt my resolve, because he moved away from me. Neither of us wanted to make a big deal out of it. I didn't want to make him feel as if I was rejecting him, but he made it easy on me by not kissing me again. Maybe he knew I wasn't ready. When he left several hours later, we were friends and nothing more. He asked me to call him if John and I called it quits. But I knew Skylar would only be a substitute. John was the one I really wanted to be with.

CHAPTER 20

Saturday morning, I left early and drove straight to the salon. Upon entering, I was appalled. The last time I was there, I'd been disappointed with how the place looked, but three months later, it was a dump. Not only was it dirty, but it had an abandoned atmosphere. I'd already decided to buy it, after talking with Valley, but now I really needed to rethink that decision. The place would have to be closed down and totally remodeled. Clients would need to see that new management had taken over and that it was an entirely different place.

I wondered if any of the former hairdressers would even return. I understood why Valley was mad. I was mad. In fact, I was furious. Lucy hadn't changed the name when she took over. I wondered if I should change it now. As she looked at me, I wanted to confront her for blaming me for her failure, and I would have, if Valley hadn't told me her little eavesdropping story in confidence. My ass still burned with rage, but I bit my tongue. I had the money in the bank to pay off her loan but wasn't sure I had enough to revamp the place. I'd have to rebuild the business. I wasn't sure how long that would take. Once people had a bad opinion of an establishment, it was hard to reclaim their business.

"So what do you think?"

My dismay and disappointment were both working overtime. "Honestly, Lucy, it's worse than I thought."

I saw defeat, possibly fear, in her eyes. I was being truthful but also, maybe, a bit spiteful as well. I didn't want her to think I was just going to fork over the money without giving it a lot of thought. But I already knew I wanted to buy it back. Wanted to rebuild my life. Wanted to start over—a do-over. I wanted to start back at the beginning, when it was just me, my business, my own life.

I needed it…for myself.

I'd made arrangements to stay at Grande's house. Mom seemed a little disappointed, but she knew how much I missed my grandmother. Since Grande and I were eating at my parents' that night, she wanted to leave early to help Mom cook. As I drove her new car, I aired my doubts and concerns about the salon. She listened without comment and finally said, "Talk to Valley. See what her outlook is."

I dropped her off at my parents' and headed to Valley's. John's mortuary was on the way. The closer I got, the more guilt ridden I became. I needed to apologize for the awful text message I'd sent him about the Georgia law. It was midafternoon, so he could have been anywhere. If he wasn't at the mortuary, then I'd swing by the mansion.

As I was waiting on the light at Covet and Hyde, I saw his vehicle in the lot. Just as the light changed, he and Kelly came out of the building. He walked her to his Ferrari and helped her in. I certainly knew what that meant. I drove on by unnoticed in Grande's car.

On my way to Valley's, I decided if she gave me any indication that I shouldn't pursue this, then I'd drop the whole notion. She'd always been a straight shooter with me, so I knew I could trust her advice. I actually thought she might tell me my idea was insane, but she only gave me the inspiration I needed to move forward.

Grinning with excitement, she said, "This will be like old times, working together again. I can't wait."

"Well, Lucy won't be there."

Charlie was there, and he had listened to my plans. He said, "I don't want Valley working with Lucy anymore, so that's good."

Shocked by his rather bitter attitude, I looked at Valley.

She said, "That might be a blessing. She's alienated a lot of people. She started spending money on the wrong things. She says that she paid too much for the place, but instead of putting her money back into the business, she bought a new car and went on several trips with her boyfriend. Also, she ruined our friendship. I hope you don't let her come back."

Valley's attitude upset me, but I wasn't even sure how I felt about Lucy. She'd hurt my feelings, but I understood what an embarrassing situation she was in. I also understood her wild spending. Lucy's cousin, the one she was going to work for, was wealthy. When Lucy bought the salon, she'd borrowed half the amount from the bank and the other half from her cousin. I was sure there were a lot of hard feelings in the family now.

Valley said, "I'm not even going to look for another place to work. I'll wait until you come back. When the salon reopens, I'll send a flyer to my customers. Give them a free haircut if they return." She looked at Charlie and grinned. "You can support me for a couple of months, can't you?"

He nodded and in all seriousness said, "Yes. Yes, of course."

Valley and I avoided looking at each other as I tried to hide the smirk on my face. Then we discussed ideas for the salon. New looks. New layouts. My mind was spinning as I stood to leave.

On my way out, she said, "We heard you had a visitor yesterday."

Shocked, I said, "Wow, news travels fast."

"Skylar stopped by for coffee this morning."

"Oh, well. We had a nice time together. He's nice, Valley. Nice company. I've always liked him."

Charlie said, "He's sweet on you." He shifted uncomfortably on his feet but didn't say anything more. If he had, I'd have said that I'd just seen John and Kelly together. We were both moving on.

With Valley's stamp of approval, I drove to my overjoyed parents. Mom's first words were, "When are you moving back?"

"*Might* be moving back. I've got a lot of stuff to figure out first."

Dad said, "We can help you move."

"Dad, I'm not sure about the building. It needs a lot of work."

"Let's get someone over there and see what needs done."

Mom asked, "Does John know you're thinking of moving back?"

"No. Anyway, he's moved on. I'm on my own now."

She grabbed my hand and squeezed. I squeezed back.

"Divorce isn't the end of the world, Macie. It might feel like it, but we're all still here for you."

"I know, Mom."

That night back at Grande's, she and I discussed the pros and cons of the salon. She knew how hard it was to build a clientele. She strongly believed that the majority of my clients would return, but it was the gap in between that'd be the killer.

"If Lucy had borrowed all the money from the bank, I wouldn't even consider paying off her loan and buying it back. Honestly, her loan isn't that much; it's the fact that she's run the place into the ground. I'll need to spend money making it look completely different."

"You can move in with me. That'd save you rent money."

I didn't want to do that, but it certainly would help me out. Seeing the conflict in my eyes, she said, "It'd only be for a few months. Six at the most. Just until you get on your feet."

I nodded but didn't think I'd ever be on my feet again.

She looked slightly ill at ease when she said, "If you decide to move in, you need to know that I have someone who stays over sometimes. Actually, quite a bit."

This didn't surprise me as much as it probably should've, but I said, "Bloody hell, Grande. Do I know him?"

She smiled sheepishly. "It's Bruce."

"Bruce?"

"Bruce, the pharmacist."

Well, that made me rethink moving in with her. Bruce had a potbelly. I didn't relish seeing him sitting at the kitchen table in his pajamas (or worse, his underwear).

"When did this start?"

"I went in to fill a prescription. He came over to the consultation window to instruct me on the side effects. He patted my hand and said to call him if I had any questions." She just smiled as if that was all that needed to be disclosed.

I said, "That must've been some consultation, or those drugs had some serious side effects."

"I went into the store a couple of days later. He saw me and asked how I was doing. I invited him over for supper that night."

"Well, that just explains everything."

"I know what you're thinking, Macie."

"What's that?"

"At our age, we can't do much."

That's exactly what I had been thinking, but I didn't want to admit it, so I said, "I wasn't thinking that."

"He makes me quite happy."

"OK, Grande. I don't really need to know the details."

"You told me all about Shane Franklin."

"Yes, I did. But you were eager to hear all about him. I'm not so eager to hear about Bruce."

She laughed. "You might be surprised at what I'd tell you."

I smiled but thought I'd had enough sex surprises to last me a lifetime.

The next day, I called Lucy and told her I'd buy the salon. I'd need to ask Ron if Ricky could work for me again, but I went ahead and made tentative plans to meet her the following Friday afternoon at her bank. I wanted to leave for home, but Mom had invited Grandpa and Marabeth to lunch. She immediately spilled the news about the salon. Marabeth looked at me with a newfound hope.

Grandpa took me aside. "I'll loan you the start-up cash if you're short."

"I wouldn't feel comfortable doing that, Grandpa. People shouldn't borrow money from relatives." I punched him on the shoulder. "And you shouldn't loan money to relatives."

He grinned. "I could simply give you the money, then, hon. No loan."

I shook my head no.

After lunch, I drove back to my apartment. I'd be moving in a few weeks. I'd have to give Ron my notice. I was actually dreading it, instead of looking forward to it. Only a few months ago, I couldn't wait to leave. I certainly didn't love my job now. No, not at all. I still hated it, but the people...well, I'd grown very fond of them. Elsa and Glenna had become friends. Nothing like Valley and Lucy, but I considered them girlfriends. Paul had loosened up with me, and two of the other funeral directors had become quite chatty. They made a special effort to stop and talk with me. Dylan had settled down and rarely came into the embalming room. Now that all the bodies were covered with sheets, he probably had no reason to linger. No ogling for him anymore.

Back at my apartment, I fixed a cup of tea. I wanted to quit the shot-glass drinking—at least slow down, anyway. I sat down at the kitchen table and started making a list of the things I'd need to handle.

As I was writing, John called. "Are you ignoring me?"

"No. What gave you that idea?"

"You were in town and never stopped by or called."

"I did. Well, I guess that's not true. I drove to the funeral home to talk with you, but you were leaving with Kelly. I didn't want to interrupt your date."

"We didn't have a date. I was dropping her off at the mechanic shop. Her car was in for repairs."

"That's nice of you. You used to dislike her, and now you're her personal chauffeur."

He sighed. "I would've liked to have seen you. I still want to talk with you. You know, about the night you called. I didn't handle that right."

"That's OK. I'm over it now."

"You're over what now?"

"My hope of ever getting any kind of support from you concerning Jordan."

"That's a cruel thing to say."

"The truth hurts, doesn't it, John?"

He didn't say anything for a moment, and I really wanted off the phone. I told him I was hanging up, and I did.

Monday, I wanted to give my notice to Ron but decided to wait until all the paperwork was done and I'd paid off Lucy's loan. I couldn't believe how much hope I had that it would work out. Now that I'd decided to do it, I was ready to move back home. Ready to work my tail off to re-build the salon. I couldn't wait to see Valley every day and be with my family again.

Tuesday, I was totally worn out as I cleaned my makeup brushes. I'd had two of the busiest days I'd ever had at SafeHaven. Over the weekend there'd been an abundance of deaths. It seemed to me that every person over the age of ninety had died that weekend. Someone was being em-balmed every single minute I was in the room. I worked ten hours the day before and came in early that day.

Paul told me, "You're earning your money, aren't you?"

Before I could answer him, Elsa knocked on the door. She had never actually come inside, which tickled me, because I used to be the same way. I went to the door. Her eyes were huge as she said, "You have another visi-tor. He's the most gorgeous man I've ever seen."

"Did he give his name?"

"No."

"OK. I'll be up in about fifteen minutes. Can you keep him enter-tained for me?"

She nodded as if words had failed her.

It was either John or Charlie, but I was leaning toward Charlie. John didn't know where I worked. Charlie probably wanted to talk to me pri-vately about Skylar or possibly Kelly. I finished with the brushes and looked one last time at the bodies in the coffins. Everything passed my final inspection.

I walked to the front of the funeral home where I imagined Elsa had seat-ed my visitor. I was sure he'd been offered coffee and was having his ear bent by either her or Glenna, but I was surprised when I saw Ron talking to John.

When John saw me, he stopped in midsentence, his blue eyes watching me as I walked toward him. My name floated into my ears from his beautiful mouth. The moment I was close enough, he hugged me hard.

Ron said, "I'd no idea John was your husband. We met a few years ago at a conference."

I didn't say anything. Since I'd kept my maiden name, "Harnon" wasn't on any of my personal information. I hadn't mentioned him at my job interview because Tim Carton and Mr. Bower, Ron's brother-in-law, had given me glowing endorsements. Ron had never asked, so I'd never volunteered the information.

When I introduced John to Elsa and Glenna, both were speechless. As they looked from me to John and back again, it was plain that they thought I was an idiot for not trying to work things out with him. He did his smiley, friendly, you're-my-wife's-girlfriends thing until I wanted to kick him in the shins.

Standing in the parking lot, I leaned against Sunny, waiting for an explanation.

"Charlie told me where you worked. I can't believe you got a job doing makeup at a funeral home."

"I needed a paycheck."

"I know, but I just assumed you were cutting hair."

"I needed a decent wage immediately. The hair business takes time to build."

This fact seemed to register, and he slowly nodded. He raked his eyes over me, probably surprised at how I was dressed. I didn't give him a chance to question me—to ask why I wore such a short skirt.

"I don't meet with the families. I stay in the embalming room all day and do makeup and hair."

His face just seemed to fill with misery. Of course, he knew how much I hated the embalming room, knew what that would be like for me every day. He started to reach for me but then dropped his hand. "Macie, you don't need to work here. I'll give you money."

I didn't even acknowledge that. "What's up? Why'd you come here?"

"I learned from Charlie that you had a visitor last week. Valley's brother. I decided if he could come here, then so could I."

"Boy, Charlie's been quite a source of information for you all of a sudden. I guess I need to visit Valley alone."

"Now, Macie."

"Well, since you're here, do you want to come back to the apartment? See how the poor people live."

"No, I don't want you to go underground. You always said if I knew where you lived, you'd move away. I'm not giving you the opportunity to use me for an excuse to do that. We can go eat, though."

At the mention of food, my stomach growled. My lunch was long gone. We drove separately to a restaurant down the road. Once seated, we talked of nothing important. A public place wasn't the setting for the kind of conversation we needed to have. He didn't mention anything about my moving back, so I wondered if Charlie had told him or if he'd kept that tidbit to himself.

When we were done with the meal and were merely killing time before he returned home, he said, "I wanted to see you today because I wanted to tell you that there's nothing between Kelly and me. I don't really want her working there, but I don't want to do the makeup myself. Charlie doesn't want to do it, and I don't want Mom to do it. Kelly's work isn't bad, but I don't like her attitude. I never did and still don't."

I just shrugged.

"I don't want you going out with other people, Macie. I don't want you dating."

"I'm not dating."

He raised an eyebrow.

"I'm not dating, John. And anyway, if I want to, I will. You're not going to tell me what to do. If you're so worried about it, then let's sign the papers and end this thing."

"I don't want to do that."

"Then don't tell me what I can and can't do. You're really kind of an ass, coming here and telling me not to see other people when your infidelity is the main reason I left to begin with. You're a hypocrite."

He stared at me, probably trying to decide if we should have this conversation in a restaurant. Since he didn't say anything, I presumed that he thought it wasn't the best venue. Our waitress came with the bill. I reached for it, but he snatched it out of my hand, almost giving me a paper cut. One thing he'd never allow: me paying for anything. Always the alpha.

He paid, and we rose to leave. I didn't offer any other suggestions of places we could go. In the parking lot, it was obvious that his plan was to return home. I thought it was the strangest thing that he'd driven all the way there just to tell me not to date.

He walked me to Sunny and said, "I'd really like to kiss you."

"Here in the parking lot?"

"Yes. What's so wrong with that?"

"I guess nothing."

I moved closer to him, put my hands on his face, and pulled him to me. Bloody hell, I missed kissing him. Really, all he needed to say to me was, "Where exactly is your apartment?" and I would've had him inside and naked before he could've said another word. But he only held me to him until we were both weak and needy. Then he climbed in his Ferrari and drove off.

At midnight, I woke from a sex dream. Hot, horny, and missing John so much, I was damn near out of my mind. I missed his arms around me. The smell of his skin. The very taste of him. I loved his mouth on me. The way we'd laugh at each other's excitement. If he felt any of the sexual need that I felt just then, I was certain that he was probably on top of some corpse at that very moment. Some dead woman was getting laid that night.

Jealousy filled me. I'd never considered myself a jealous person, but I guessed it was time to accept the fact that I was. I'd been jealous of Avery Power, and honestly, I still was, which when I thought about it was pure insanity. I simply didn't want him with someone else. Alive or dead. I always came back to John's quickies. From those encounters,

I knew he truly had no emotional connection with the women. It was just a weird sexual release for him. That realization alone made me want to make it work. But as a woman, as his wife, I simply wanted to be everything he needed.

I really understood why Charlie had gone off the deep end when he witnessed his father on top of Fiona. Why he'd burrowed down inside himself, simply lost himself, because I was almost there myself. The images swirling in my head, the visions of John with other women, were just too much for me.

The next day when I came out of the embalming room for lunch, Elsa and Glenna were waiting for me. They wanted to know all the details on my drop-dead-gorgeous husband. Before I could say too much, Ron stepped out to talk with me about John.

"How long have you two been separated?"

I didn't want to talk about it but didn't want to be rude either. "About eight months."

"He's one of the nicest morticians I've ever met. I was shocked when he walked in asking for you. I thought he was trying to hire you from me, only to learn I'd snagged you from him."

As he yapped on for a few more minutes, I realized that if everything went through on my purchasing the salon, Ron would accept my quitting without blinking an eye. From the way he talked, it was obvious that he thought I was wrong for leaving John.

Glenna and Elsa were bound and determined to go to lunch. I thought I might as well go with them and satisfy their curiosity. After we ordered our meals, they both stared at me, waiting. I merely hit the highlights. We'd met. Fallen in love. I sold my salon. Worked in his funeral home. One miscarriage. One stillbirth. I'd left to regroup.

Elsa sighed. "If you could've seen the look on his face when he asked if you worked there and I said you did; he was so relieved he'd found you. Then when he saw you, the look in his eyes…well, it was something to see a man looking at a woman that way. He loves you so much, Macie. My God. Go back to him."

Glenna agreed. "Men don't know how to help with grief. Even though John works in the funeral business, your mourning was probably too much for him to handle."

All this unasked-for advice was getting to me. I felt like the bad guy in the marriage. John came off as the victim, as the spouse who wanted to make everything right. I came across as the spiteful, grief-stricken bitch. As if I was punishing him for Jordan's death. Well, maybe a part of me was. But honestly, I blamed myself for becoming so upset that I'd basically aborted my baby. That's the thing that haunted me. That I hadn't protected Jordan.

The next morning, Dylan came down to the embalming room with a new hire. Arnie looked like a bouncer, and I couldn't help staring at his arms. They looked as if they could smack a person to hell and back.

Dylan said, "I'm going to start helping Arnie move the bodies to the viewing area."

I said, "OK." The thing was, I thought that was part of his current job duties. I showed them the two caskets that were ready to go. Dylan grabbed one side; Arnie took the other. I didn't think Arnie really needed help with the caskets, but I chose to keep that tidbit to myself.

Dylan said, "Man, your husband has some car."

"Yep."

"He owns a funeral business?"

"Yep."

"He's got to be loaded, then. Why don't you sock him for a settlement?"

"I don't want his money."

"You're the first woman I've ever heard say that."

I wasn't going to talk with him about it, so I turned my back and started laying out clean brushes for my next body. Thankfully, he and the bouncer took off with the casket. I began working on an eighty-year-old woman. She had lovely gray hair. After using tissue builder on her, I opened the folder and pulled out the pictures her family had left for me. I wanted to see how she normally wore her makeup and hair. There were three eight-by-ten pictures, all wedding portraits of when she was twenty years old. Her hair was jet black and piled on top of her head. I wanted to pull my hair out. These were absolutely useless to me. I began applying her makeup, and when I fixed her hair, I styled it the way I thought made her look as lovely as she had every right to be.

CHAPTER 21

Friday morning, I went into work early. I helped dress two overweight corpses and was totally worn out afterward. (Dressing dead weight was hard enough—dead overweight was a true workout.) As per my agreement with Ron, I again did the women and left the men for Ricky. When he arrived, we talked for a few minutes as I finished with my last woman. I really kind of liked the guy. He was friendly, and even though he did giggle a lot, he was entertaining.

I was able to leave earlier than I'd planned, which gave me time to stop at my bank before meeting Lucy at hers. I wanted to make sure the funds were there and everything was arranged for me to write a huge check. The bank teller's eyebrows raised at my apprehension. She pushed a paper at me showing my balance.

Disbelieving, I said, "There must be a problem…some mistake. I don't have this much money."

"A deposit was made into your account on Monday."

"By whom?"

"I don't know, but I can find out."

She left and returned with one of the bank officers. His smile was so wide that I wondered what the hell was going on. He shook my hand. "Mrs. Harnon, I'm Victor Wiley. You have a question about your account?"

"Mr. Wiley, I'm Macie Emerson. I'd like to know about this large deposit made on Monday."

He blinked at me, confused by my name, but said, "John Harnon made the deposit into your account. He specifically asked that it be available for you today."

I was speechless and then pissed. John was trying to buy me back. Trying to smooth things over with money. I didn't want his money or for him to have any part in my business. I didn't want him to feel that he was a partner—even a silent one. I wanted to do this on my own.

I didn't have time to straighten it out. My meeting with Lucy was supposed to start in thirty minutes. I thanked the teller and Mr. Wiley and then drove to Lucy's bank. Several people were in the meeting, and for one second, I thought maybe I should've retained a lawyer, but everything was on the up and up. I'd been through the process before, so I knew what to expect.

We signed a stack of papers; I paid off her loan. She cried uncontrollably, which seemed to embarrass everyone but me. I knew how she felt because that's how I'd felt when I sold it to her. The only difference was, I didn't cry at the bank. I went home and remained in a funk for several weeks afterward. I told Lucy I wanted to keep in touch. She said, "OK." But I had the distinct feeling she'd avoid me every chance she got. Her pride was wounded; I was the last person she wanted to see.

Leaving the bank, I drove to the mortuary—directly to the source to handle the bank-money situation. Anger boiled inside me as I stormed into his office. Kelly was sitting in front of his desk with her long legs crossed. John was perched on the corner, probably trying to look up her skirt, but I realized from his tone that he was talking down to her. Maybe a boss's reprimand or a lover's quarrel. I probably should've waited outside until he was finished, but it was too late.

He immediately stood and said, "Macie."

I smacked my hands against his chest with such force that he fell back on the perch that he'd left. I snarled, "Don't try to buy me off or win me over by throwing money into my checking account. I can buy the salon on my own without any help from you. Just because you're a rich son of a bitch doesn't mean that I want your money. Stay out of my business. Stay out of my life."

"Now, Macie."

I yelled, "Don't 'Macie' me."

As I turned to walk out, Kelly was wide eyed and openmouthed. I blurted out, "Shut your mouth, Kelly. A bug could fly in there."

I stomped out of the building and floored Sunny out of the parking lot. When I'd driven down that morning, I hadn't decided whether I was staying the weekend or not. After that confrontation, I only wanted to return to the apartment. I could start packing, notify the apartment manager, and maybe get in contact with Ron. I wanted to give him a heads-up as soon as possible. I knew how hard it was to find a makeup person.

Within moments of my leaving the mortuary parking lot, my phone started buzzing. I knew, without a doubt, that John was trying to reach me. He'd want to ream my ass. Skin me alive. I turned my radio up and drove on home with music blasting in my ears.

Arriving at the apartment, I finally looked at my phone. John had left a voice message. I knew it wouldn't be pretty, so I poured a shot glass of bourbon and sat down to listen.

"The next time you decide to bust my balls, would you at least do it in private? You didn't even give me a chance to explain. I did put the money in your account, but it was your money to start with—from the sale of your house. After we sold your house to Mom, I deposited the check into my account since we'd just bought the house—the house you now always refer to as the mansion instead of your home. You said I ruined everything for you. Said you wanted to start over. I was only giving you the money that was rightfully yours so you could."

Well, that made me sit back and feel like a schmuck. And if I was honest, it totally changed my plans for what I wanted to do with the salon. I wouldn't have to borrow any money; I could remodel the salon like I wanted to. I swallowed another shot and then picked up the phone to call John to tell him that I was sorry for my outburst, that I'd jumped to the wrong conclusion.

He gruffly answered, "What?"

"I'm sorry. I flew into you without first letting you explain. I appreciate the money, John. It'll make all the difference in the world for me. I can do everything I envisioned. Everything I wanted is now possible. Thank you."

I waited for his reply.

He hung up on me.

OK. I deserved that.

I located the apartment manager and gave my notice. Then I called my electric provider and my phone and Internet companies. After that, the only thing left was to tell Ron. I decided to wait until Monday. I couldn't have another confrontation that day. One was enough.

I'd already decided to use Franklin Construction again for my remodeling job. Bob Franklin was my former boyfriend's father. Even though he'd done a wonderful job the first time, and I trusted him totally, I wasn't sure how he'd feel about doing another job for me. I found his number and called his office. His secretary put me right through. I sat back for a long chat. Bob was a talker.

"Macie, sweetheart," he boomed, "how have you been?"

"OK. How about you, Bob?"

"Good. Me and the little lady just returned from a trip to the Caribbean. She likes it down there. Both boys are still working for me. Guess they think their old man's OK. How's that hot little mama of yours? Is she still down in the mouth?"

He laughed uncontrollably at his stupid hygienist joke. When he'd settled down, I said, "She's good, and so is my dad."

"Heard you were married."

"Yep."

"I told Shane he was stupid for letting you slip away. You two were so good together."

"What's he up to now?"

"He had a live-in, but he ended it. When she got pregnant, he was so excited about the baby. She had a little girl, but it was the wrong color. They broke up in the hospital."

"Bloody hell, Bob, that's awful."

"You're telling me. What can I do for you?"

"I don't know if you knew, but I sold my salon a few years ago. Today I bought it back. It totally needs redone now. I was hoping I could hire you to do it."

I heard papers shuffling, and then he said, "What's your time frame?"

"Bob, I'm like all your other customers; I want it done yesterday."

He roared with laughter. "Shane's almost finished with his project. His crew could start in about five weeks. Zack won't be available for probably ten weeks."

I swallowed. I wanted to start as soon as possible, but I wasn't sure I wanted to work with Shane. We'd been in love, but he'd become impatient with my working almost every weekend on the bride packages. I finally got tired of his constant complaining and his ultimatums and broke up with him. I'd thought at some point we'd reconcile, but since we were both young and stubborn, neither one of us would bend.

I wanted and needed the salon done as soon as possible, so I said, "I'll take Shane and his crew if he doesn't mind working with me."

"Now, Macie, sweetheart, he won't mind at all. You want to meet over there in about thirty minutes, and we'll go over what you have in mind?"

"I'm not in town right now. I could meet you there in about two hours."

"Where are you?"

I might as well tell him the truth. "I live in Atlanta now. My husband and I are separated. I moved here about six months ago. Can you meet me in two hours?"

I heard him breathing; then he said, "Yeah."

"OK, I'll head that way."

"Shane will definitely want this job."

I ate some food since I wasn't sure what the two shots of bourbon were doing in my stomach. Then I called Mom and asked if I could stay at their place that night.

"What's going on? First, you're staying, then you go back home, and now you're staying again."

"I'm meeting Bob Franklin at the salon. He's agreed to do the remodel. Shane and his crew will be doing the work."

She didn't say another word.

Bob Franklin was a big man with a big voice, a big laugh, and a big heart. He arrived with his clipboard, a tape measure, and a bear hug that almost broke my back.

"You're just as pretty as ever."

"Oh, stop it."

"Well, what have we got here, Macie? It looks like a mess." He scrutinized the situation with disgust.

"Lucy let the place run down. The salon needs a totally new look."

"I agree. This is a shame. People—"

I pointed to the wall of sinks in the back as I interrupted him. If I hadn't, we'd have been there all day. "Last time I had you put those sinks in the back because I didn't want to spend the money to do it the way I really wanted. I've always regretted it. This time I'm doing it right. I want each station to have a sink, so the customers won't have to move to be shampooed and rinsed."

"Macie, that's going to cost a lot. Plumbing isn't cheap; we'd need to pull tile up and cut into the cement." He glanced down. "Well, look at these tiles. Several are broken or cracked. They'd need redone anyway."

"Bob, I'm going to tell you everything I want. Don't cut any corners."

"OK." He clicked open his pen.

"I want this tile taken up and the concrete floors painted to look like tile. I want the shelves redone and a makeup station added. We can make the lobby smaller. It's wasted space anyway. The walls will be painted a soft gray, and everything else will be black and white."

We went over a few more things; then he said he'd call me with the bid. I didn't tell him that he was the only one I was considering. I didn't trust anyone else and didn't want to waste time looking for someone else.

I spent the night at my parents'. Never once did I try to contact John.

CHAPTER 22

Monday morning, I left a note on Ron's desk, saying that I needed to talk with him that day. I couldn't believe how much I was dreading it and how much I'd miss Elsa and Glenna. But I was on a mission to do what I really wanted to do.

As I was applying makeup on a seventy-five-year-old woman, Ron stepped into the embalming room. He talked a moment about some game he'd watched over the weekend. Paul had also watched it, so they exchanged accounts of different plays. Ron then asked Paul if he could give us a minute. I knew then that he'd realized what I wanted to tell him. After Paul stepped out, Ron looked at me, waiting.

"I'm giving my two-week notice. I'm going back home. This has been a great job. You've been the best boss, but this isn't my career choice. This isn't what I want to do with my life."

He smiled. "So you and John are getting back together."

I shook my head. "No, I meant my life before him. John's not in the picture."

Two deep wrinkles creased his forehead as he frowned at me.

"I know it's hard to understand, but John and I aren't well suited. He and I disagree on some very fundamental issues. Another woman would be better for him; another man would be better for me."

"So you're not going to work for him?"

"No, I bought my old salon back."

"But, Macie, you're so good at this job. You have such a respect for the dead. It shows in your work. I'm not trying to talk you into staying, because it's obvious you've made up your mind, but I just think it's sad you're quitting the business."

"I never wanted to do this to begin with. When I met John, I sold my salon, so I could spend more time with him. Make my hours match his. Make our lives more compatible. But honestly, I've never been happy with it. I can't do it anymore. I simply can't."

"I'm going to miss you. You're a dedicated worker, so easy to get along with."

Obviously, Dylan had never told him about our run-ins.

"Can I ask a favor of you?"

I said, "Sure."

"Would you be open to teaching my sister the art of applying makeup?"

I didn't want to do it, but I agreed.

That evening, I started packing the things I could live without. There wasn't much because the apartment had been bare to begin with. As I was eating a limp carrot, John called. I wanted to answer the same way he had, with a rude "What?" but instead I said very pleasantly, "Hi, John."

"Hi."

We breathed into our phones for a few seconds, until he said, "I've cooled off since our last phone conversation."

"That's good. I'm really sorry that I burst into your office. Also, I shouldn't have talked to Kelly like that. She didn't deserve my wrath."

He laughed. "I guess you could say she was having a bad day. I was chewing her out for giving the impression that I'd taken her out. Charlie heard some shitty rumors floating around. I told her I'd never do it again. If she needed a ride somewhere, she'd have to find someone else. Then you bust in and rip me a new asshole."

"I was so mad at you. Why didn't you call and tell me you were doing that?"

"Because I didn't want you to know that Charlie had told me you were buying the salon back. You were already annoyed with him for telling me about Skylar and telling me where you worked."

"OK. Truce?"

He laughed. "Truce."

"I gave my notice today. It was harder than I thought it'd be."

"Ron's a nice guy. I've always liked him, although I only see him once a year, if that. Macie, can we start being civil to each other? There are things I'd like to ask you, but I don't want my nuts shot off."

I giggled. "I'll try."

"Where are you going to live when you come back?"

"With Grande. At least for a while, anyway."

"You could live here. There are four bedrooms. I could move upstairs."

"No, I wouldn't like that."

"OK. How about you live in the house, and I'll live in the guesthouse?"

"No. I was lost when I lived in the mansion all by myself."

"OK. You can live in the guesthouse."

"Would you stay away from me?" Before he could answer, I said, "No, if I decide to file for divorce, then I'd have to move away again. That'd kill me."

"Please don't talk about divorce. Please don't say that to me."

I didn't say anything to that because, honestly, that's what I had in mind. Ever since Mom had said her piece on divorce, it seemed the most logical solution. Even though I knew I loved him and I'd never love anyone else the way I loved him, I couldn't accept his fetish. His freakish obsession was simply too much for me.

We talked for a few more minutes. When we ended the call, we were at least back on cordial terms.

That weekend I invited Elsa and Glenna over to give them the first opportunity of some clothes I was giving away. Both were almost the same size as me. Elsa wasn't as busty, and Glenna was shorter, but I thought my funeral suits would fit them. I hadn't worn them since leaving John's funeral home. I knew I'd never wear them again.

When Elsa and Glenna arrived, I fed them a light brunch and told them about my new business venture. They immediately assumed that I was reconciling with John, but I assured them that wasn't happening, at least not at that time. As they gave me their unwelcome advice, I wanted to shout at them the real problem. See their shock. Witness the horror on their faces when they knew the truth. But like always, I kept the secret tucked inside me.

I laid out the suits and dresses—all forty-eight of them. Bloody hell, I couldn't believe I'd bought so many. They squealed with delight, stripped down to their undies, and began trying everything on as I watched with amusement. I knew I'd miss both of them. And really, if it hadn't been for them, I never would've made it through the past six months.

The next two weeks flew by. I taught Ron's sister (Dylan's wife) the art of applying makeup. Sierra was a solid, well-built girl. Her arms were well defined, and her thighs looked strong, but I couldn't have been more shocked by her small bustline. For some reason I'd pictured Dylan married to a petite woman with a boob job.

She was all thumbs at first, dropping the makeup brushes and hot rollers, but after she got over the initial awfulness of death, Sierra became a very teachable student. I knew Ron wouldn't be 100 percent pleased with her work, but over time, she'd become more proficient.

The problem I saw with her, and also with Kelly, was that she couldn't see or didn't care about the finer details. They both left long hairs hanging from the men's ears and noses, and on the women, they didn't seem to understand the importance of matching the correct shades of makeup with certain hair colors. What looked good on blondes didn't look good on brunettes, and redheads were in a class of their own. And did I even need to explain about gray hair?

Kelly liked green eye shadow and used it almost exclusively. Sierra favored bright teal, which was popular just then for the living sector but was a little too stylish for the dead. I tried to explain that people didn't want to be shocked when they looked into the caskets and saw their loved ones (especially if the casket contained their eighty-year-old grandmother).

On my last day of work, Ron had a luncheon for me. Everyone seemed genuinely sad that I was leaving. Dylan was probably the only one who was glad to see me go...clicking his heels in private. For one thing, he was sick of my mouth. For another, his wife had snagged my job. One thing made me truly happy about her working at SafeHaven: I was certain he wouldn't be in the embalming room viewing the naked bodies.

At the luncheon, he did personally thank me. "Sierra talks about you all the time. 'Macie this. Macie that. Macie said.' In fact, the other night I told her I'd heard enough about you."

I laughed. He said, "Thank you for your patience with her."

I wanted to say a myriad of things, but it was my last day. I wanted to leave on a good note. And really, you couldn't change men like Dylan. You really couldn't.

CHAPTER 23

Saturday morning, I had everything packed and was waiting for Dad to arrive with his truck. Boxes were stacked by the door, and Sunny's small trunk was stuffed with as many of my clothes as would fit inside. The manager stopped by to check on the condition of the apartment and determine whether I was entitled to my rental-deposit refund. He left only to return a few minutes later with his brother who was interested in the apartment. He seemed to like everything...even the kitchen chairs.

As he looked around, he asked, "Where's your TV?"

"I don't have one. I watched everything on my computer—Netflix streaming."

He looked at me in disbelief, as if I wasn't human. "I don't know anyone who doesn't have a big-screen TV."

I laughed. As we entered the bedroom, I asked if he wanted the mattress. He looked me up and down, as if to determine how sleazy I was, trying to imagine my bedfellows. I started to say that it had never been screwed on but didn't want to admit how pitiful my sex life was. I must've passed his inspection, because he reached for his wallet.

"How much?"

"It's free. You'd be saving me the hassle of moving it. I don't need it where I'm going."

He grinned at his good fortune. The manager handed me my deposit refund; I turned over my key.

Dad arrived moments later...with John. I didn't think he was trying to be a matchmaker—probably just thought we'd need help with the lifting.

Still, I wasn't sure how I felt about the unexpected turn of events. A phone call would've been nice—a little heads-up to prepare myself. A part of me wanted to be pissed, but John immediately grabbed boxes, so how could I be upset with his help? And because of John, it took less than thirty minutes. There wasn't any furniture, no TV, and I was leaving the unsexed mattress.

Once loaded, Dad said, "I'm heading out."

Obviously, the plan had already been discussed; John would ride back with me. I was upset—mad at both of them. I started to tell John that I thought it was pretty shitty of him to use my dad in his scheme, but before I could ream him, he said, "Were you happy here?"

His hands gripped the counter as if to brace himself for my answer.

"Bloody hell, no. Look at these kitchen chairs. Who could be happy waking up to these every day?"

He grinned as a huge sigh escaped him. His eyes looked into mine, almost pleading, as he said, "I wanted this time with you to talk. I've missed you. Please don't be mad at your dad."

I didn't say anything.

"I want to hear about your girlfriends at SafeHaven. About your plans for the salon. I just want to talk with you."

"OK."

I toured the apartment one last time. It had served me well, but I wasn't going to miss it, that's for sure. In the car we snapped on seatbelts, and I headed to I-75. We hadn't driven far when I pulled over. John said, "What's going on?"

"I'm letting you drive. You can't grip the dash the whole way back home."

We changed places. Back on the road, he said, "I can't believe what a good driver Charlie is, with you as his teacher. He looks both ways and doesn't wait until the last minute to use the brakes. He's quite safe."

I reached over and pinched his stomach. He gave me that slow grin that always melted me. For the first time, I thought we could actually be like we used to be.

For the next hour, we talked as friends. Something about being in a car together relaxed me. I told him my plans for the salon and my goal date to open the doors for business.

"How did Lucy screw things up so badly?"

"Gosh, John, I don't know. Valley said she just mismanaged her money from the start. The salon was very profitable for me, and I guess she just thought the money would pour in for her. It doesn't work that way."

"I quit going there. Lucy and Valley both seemed so nervous around me. Like they had to watch every word that came out of their mouths. Afraid they'd tell me some pertinent fact about you. I'll admit, at first, I wanted to pump them for information, but I knew that I couldn't go to your apartment, so what was the point of finding out where you lived? I hate the way this new girl cuts my hair. She can't do shit with my cowlick. I feel butchered when I leave there."

I laughed and reached over to smooth it down.

"Your dad said you were moving in with your grandmother. The offer still stands on either the house or the guesthouse."

"I've really been thinking about that. Grande has a boyfriend...you know, a sleepover buddy. I'm not sure I want to be a witness to that right now."

John laughed hard. "Who is this guy?"

"The pharmacist at Target, where she goes all the time. He has dickey-do disease."

His head cocked quizzically.

"You know, his stomach hangs out further than his dickey do."

He laughed even harder.

"It's rather weird to think of Grande doing the horizontal dance, but she's a hottie. He's a few years younger than her. Mom likes him and says he's really sweet to Grande. I'm not sure I want to break up their little love nest. If I moved in with her, I think Bruce might be uncomfortable."

"Like I said, you can have the guesthouse if the house is too intimidating. I repainted it and had the wood floors redone just in case you changed your mind."

I turned to him. He glanced at me out of the corner of his eye—probably trying to gauge my reaction to the news.

"What color did you paint it?"

He laughed. "The color that you had picked out. Horse Hay."

"How did you know that?"

"You'd written on the back, 'Ask John—guesthouse?' I just figured you must've liked that color."

Before Charlie moved in, I'd wanted to repaint, but he hadn't wanted to wait...so anxious to finally have his own place. I couldn't believe John had found that sample. I stared at his profile. This was the guy I'd fallen in love with.

He said, "I promise I'll be as involved or as uninvolved as you want. I want to be involved in your life, but I'll leave you alone if that's what you want."

"OK. Let's try it."

John pulled in front of Dad's truck. I motioned for him to follow us. He undoubtedly knew John's intentions and was already prepared to drop my boxes off at the mansion. By the time we pulled into the drive, John and I had somehow been able to reconnect.

We carried my boxes into the guesthouse. I kissed Dad and thanked him for his help. He left immediately. Probably couldn't wait to get home and tell Mom that things were looking promising for their little Macie.

The guesthouse looked amazing. The new paint warmed the place up. The wood floors were buffed to perfection. He'd redecorated, or else my mother had. The place was designed for me. I could live there; but instead of unboxing anything, I turned to John. "You got a beer in that mansion of yours?"

He grinned. "I do."

As we walked through the backyard, I couldn't help but look around. The property really was amazing, with the stone walks, the pool area, the outdoor kitchen. And to think... it used to be mine.

Inside, I plopped down on John's sofa as he grabbed a couple of beers. After spending time in the car, I guess I was ready to talk. Maybe, too,

I was ready to listen with an open mind and an understanding heart. Whatever it was, I was ready.

He must've felt the same way. He said, "Our separation has given me time to think, time to understand how my actions hurt you. Even though I didn't see it as infidelity, the fact that you did opened my eyes. That you think I've been unfaithful is something I can't stomach.

"Macie, I never thought it would hurt you the way it has. If I'm honest, I knew that you wouldn't want me doing it, but I just thought I could satisfy this need until we'd completed our family. We both like rough sex. You seem to like it as much as me, but when I used to get off on you—you know, when I'd have a quickie—I know sometimes I got a little too wild, too forceful.

"You never acted as if you minded. You never asked me to stop or not to be so rough, but after the first miscarriage, I knew I couldn't treat you that way while you were pregnant. It was so hard to control myself with you. I felt the best thing to do was avoid sex with you as much as possible."

"Shit, John, pregnant women have sex all the time. You act as if a baby can be knocked loose. The miscarriage was just an act of God. It had nothing to do with you."

"I don't believe that. I'll never believe that."

I reached over and rubbed the back of his head. He wouldn't look at me, so I knew he was about to cry. I said, "Well, I'm the reason we lost Jordan. I let myself become so distraught that I aborted him."

He jerked his head around to me. "That's not what happened. You can't blame yourself for him."

"I do."

"I've relived that night a thousand times. When Charlie called and told me you were bleeding, that he'd taken you to the hospital, I died a million deaths. I should've been the one to take you. I should've been the one you ran to."

I swallowed the lump in my throat and said, "I'm done having babies. I won't get pregnant again. If that's something you want, then you need to know I'm not the woman for you."

He didn't say anything. I figured he was trying to think of something to say to sway me, so I said, "I won't change my mind, John. Don't even ask me to. Don't even talk to me about it. I mean it. It won't happen. I can't go through that again. I won't. Two was enough."

He placed his hand on my leg. "I feel exactly the same way. Exactly."

A calmness settled over me. He said, "Can we try again…you and me? I'll do whatever it takes. You name the terms; I'll do it."

"How many women have you been with since I left?"

"I told you. None."

"No. I mean dated."

He looked at me as if I'd lost my mind. "None, Macie. We're married. Did you forget that when you went out with Skylar?"

"It was nothing."

"He gave Charlie the impression that it was more."

"Well, it wasn't."

A huge sigh of relief escaped him.

I said, "I have questions I still want answered. When I ask, I want your honest answer no matter how painful it will be for me. If I ask, then I want to know the answer, so just tell me."

"I'll answer any questions you have. I'll do anything you need. If you want to go to marriage counseling, I'll go."

That shocked me. I couldn't help but look at him in disbelief.

"I will, Macie. I'll do whatever it takes to get you back."

"If you screw a dead woman again, I will leave. I won't come back. No questions. No discussion. No looking back. I will leave you and never return."

"OK. I promise. I won't do it again. I haven't, and I won't."

I finished my beer and stood up. He must've thought I was going to leave, because he started to walk toward the back door. I grabbed his hand. He turned to me, and I wrapped my arms around his neck. I kissed him with such hunger that we were naked on the bed in no time.

I'd longed for that, craved it for so many nights that I could hardly catch my breath. He tried to take his time like he used to, but my need for him made me dig my hands into his firm butt and pull him into me. He, obviously, was as sex deprived as I was; he couldn't resist. I might not have totally returned emotionally, but I'd definitely returned sexually.

Afterward, I called Grande to tell her I was moving into the guesthouse.

"Macie, I hope you aren't doing this because of Bruce."

"No, John and I are going to work on our marriage. I want to be with him."

Hearing this, John leaned over and kissed the back of my neck.

I never made it to the guesthouse that night.

CHAPTER 24

Bob called with his bid—high, but everything I wanted. For the next three weeks, while waiting on Shane and his crew, I made good use of my time. I sent letters to all my former hairdressers. I hoped that I could recoup a few of them. I'd kept the same number of booths (ten), which I hoped to have rented within the first three months of opening. I raised the booth rent from when I'd left, but it was still less than what Lucy had been charging. Within the first week of sending the letters, I received replies from four who wanted to come back. With Valley, me, and the four of them, I only needed to find four more hairdressers.

I was agonizing over whether or not to change the name of the salon. Gut instinct told me changing the name would be the best business decision—totally separating myself from Lucy's salon. But coming up with a catchy name was harder than it seemed. That's probably why I was so opposed to changing it. I thought of several different names. Macie Emerson Salon was one that I quite liked, but I nixed the idea. Perhaps it showed a lack of faith in myself, but if the salon bombed, I didn't want my name declared a failure. Finally, I decided on A New Direction. I wasn't really crazy about it, but I needed to order the sign and couldn't pussyfoot around any longer.

The following day I was sitting through a red light, waiting to turn onto the salon road. I'd seen the road sign hundreds of times, but that day it caught my attention. Ridgecrest. I knew then that I wanted to name the salon Ridgecrest Hair Salon. It had a nice sound, and customers would immediately know where it was located. I ordered the sign without a second thought.

Every evening when John came home, I was full of ideas for the salon. I knew that at some point we needed to have another conversation about our past, but just then, I honestly didn't want to deal with it. I didn't have the time or energy to work on the marriage. But I'd be the first to admit that I couldn't wait to see John each and every morning. When I woke up next to him, even during the night, I couldn't wait to touch him. Press my face against his back. Run my hands across his chest. I loved him and wanted our relationship to work, but my mind was totally focused on my business venture. When I'd say to him, "Do you have a moment to talk?" his shoulders would stiffen, and he'd look anxious, but my questions were always about the salon. He finally relaxed around me and seemed to accept that I wasn't going to dig up the past.

He'd done one thing, though, that had stunned me: he'd cleaned out Jordan's room. The crib and changing table were disassembled and all the baby paraphernalia boxed up. I only discovered it by chance when the cleaning ladies left the door open by mistake. Shocked by the bare room, I looked in the walk-in closet to find everything shoved against the wall.

I wondered when he'd done it. Maybe after our conversation about remaining childless. How hard had it been for him? Had he cried while he did it, or had he dealt with the loss already? Was it all just stuff to him? Just useless stuff no longer needed? Where were the yellow booties?

Shane contacted me right at the three-week mark. His crew would be ready to start on Wednesday. He said, "I can't wait to see you, Macie. I really can't. This brings back wonderful memories."

I laughed. "Well, Shane, it's just like before. I'm starting all over again. I'll be working my ass off."

"Still. It was our beginning. I'll see you Wednesday."

He was right about that. We'd met when I'd hired Franklin Construction to build the salon for me. Shane and his brother, Zack, were both working for their dad. Shane and I were instantly attracted to each other, and we immediately began a relationship. We were good together, but he simply wanted more, needed more, from me than I could give at that time. My priorities probably had been skewed back then, but I had been trying to get my salon up and running. I was looking forward to seeing him again… but not to renew our relationship. I already had a messed-up relationship to work on; I certainly didn't need another one.

On Wednesday, I arrived early to unlock the door and give Shane a key. As he walked toward me, I couldn't help but admire his body. His construction job kept him in amazing shape—rock hard and tan from the outdoors. I'd always liked his looks. Tall, with green eyes and sandy hair. Now, as he stood in front of me, we eyed each other.

He leaned down, kissed my cheek, and said, "Dad was right; you're just as cute as ever."

I was only human, and I grinned at his compliment. He said, "Come on. I'll introduce you to the crew."

I knew a couple of the guys from the last time, but the rest were new. We took a tour through the building as Shane outlined their jobs. He asked questions as we went along, but for the most part, his dad had it all written down the way I envisioned.

For the next week, I stopped in every day to check on their progress. Tearing up the floor tiles and redoing the plumbing bored me, so I didn't spend much time hanging around. Once that was completed, I spent several hours a day there. Shane and I had lunch together almost every day.

Wednesday at lunch, Valley stopped by to check on the progress. When she saw Shane, her face broke into a grin. They'd always liked each other. Her face registered awareness as she looked from him to me. Before leaving, she whispered to me, "I won't tell Charlie a thing."

Thursday afternoon, his crew left early. Since John wouldn't be home for another few hours, Shane and I stayed. He told me about his relationship with his live-in that'd ended badly.

"What's strange about the whole thing is that I can't really say I was crazy in love with her. Nothing like I was with you. But when she got pregnant, I was really happy. I was stupid about the whole thing because I always used a condom. I just thought it'd leaked or something. It never entered my mind that she was messing around." He looked at me and touched my leg. "You and I never cheated on each other. I wish back then I had the patience I do now. I was young, bullheaded, and just wanted to be with you, Macie. I'm sorry how I treated you—that I was so demanding with you. I wish I'd been more supportive of your dreams."

"Oh, Shane, my schedule was nuts. I was so gung ho on the salon. I wanted to make sure it was a success, and I'd just started the makeup line. I'm sorry I made you feel second best. You were everything to me, but I didn't treat you as if you were."

"I guess we've both grown up since then."

"Have you seen this old girlfriend since she had the baby?"

"Only when she came and got her stuff out of my garage."

"You never had a clue she was with someone else?"

"Never. Not once. I think everyone else might've suspected. They said so afterward, but that's easy to say after the fact. Mom and Dad didn't like her, but that's because they still wanted you and me to get back together. At the hospital, when the doctor held the baby up for us to see, you could hear a pin drop. Amber burst into tears. She'd probably been worried about that all along but had hoped it wouldn't happen." He stopped talking for a moment and looked at me. "You can't imagine what it feels like to realize that you've been cheated on. To find out that way. It was the cruelest joke."

I swallowed. I knew exactly what it felt like. He wanted to hear my story. I told him as little as possible, although he was the first person, other than my mother, whom I felt like sharing my horrible experience with.

He'd understand how hurt I was to learn that my husband was a cheater. Shane and I had always trusted each other; we never would've ruined that trust. He must've sensed something in me, because he leaned over and kissed me on the mouth.

I didn't kiss him back or pull him close, but I realized that we'd formed some emotional connection. We were two people who understood the heartache of unfaithfulness. The truth—if it weren't for my vows, I would've gone home with Shane. I wanted something normal. I was tired of secrets. I wanted a man I could trust.

When he walked me to my car, he said, "I'd do anything to have you back, Macie. I've never really gotten over you."

I didn't say anything because my throat wouldn't work.

The next day Shane and I had lunch together again. As we were eating, I asked him, "Do you remember that time at your grandparents' beach house?"

He laughed. "How could I forget?" Then he said, "I remember all the times. Every one of them."

"You couldn't possibly. There were at least a thousand."

He poked me and said, "A thousand and three. I remember every one of them."

At the end of work that day, as we were standing by our vehicles, John pulled up in his Ferrari.

Shane clamped a hand on my shoulder as if to protect me. "Who's this rich bastard?"

I didn't say anything, but when John got out of the car, my heart beat faster at the sight of him. My eyes devoured his face. I couldn't wait for him to see the salon. I introduced them. "John, this is Shane. Shane, this is my husband."

They shook hands.

At home that night, John said, "Shane seems overly protective of you."

"He does?"

"Don't act like you didn't notice. What's with him?"

I took a deep breath. "We used to be together. I met him when I hired his dad's construction company to build my salon. We dated for over a year and a half."

John's mouth set into a firm line. "You're just now telling me this."

I didn't answer.

"Who broke up with whom?"

"I broke up with him."

"Did you love him?"

"Yes, very much. I wanted to marry him, but he was always on my case about the salon. The salon has always been an issue for me and my relationships with men. He's the one who hurt me the most, though. He broke my heart."

"Are you two together now?"

"Bloody hell, John, of course not."

"I wish I could believe that."

"We merely share some history; he had a similar situation as I had with you. His girlfriend cheated on him, so we have that in common."

Hurt etched his face. "I'd like to tell you not to see him again, but I know you'd simply leave and I'd lose you anyway." He stomped off to the basement. I heard sounds from the TV.

I was emotionally conflicted. John and I hadn't really had another significant conversation since my first day back, but somehow we'd reconciled enough to live together in harmony. Our libidos were well matched, and we were making up for lost time. I hadn't spent one night in the guesthouse yet, but I guess I still hadn't moved into the mansion—not in my heart, anyway. Almost as if I was there on a trial basis.

Now that I'd reconnected with Shane, I wondered if I shouldn't move on. I saw in him what I could have. But the salon had been a major issue between Shane and me. What made me think that it wouldn't be an issue for him anymore? I was starting over again, so my hours would be crazy. Shane said he had patience now, but did he really?

For the first time, I realized that was why I'd sold the salon to Lucy. I didn't want John and me to argue about it. Although he'd never told me to sell it, there was an unspoken expectation from him that I'd be the one to change careers, not him. Maybe, unconsciously, I'd felt I'd already lost one man over it, and I wasn't going to lose another.

When he finally came to bed, I was waiting for him. I rolled over to him and said, "I haven't been unfaithful to you, John. You can either believe me or not, but I'm trying to make this work. All your shit takes time to get over, to work through. I'd think you'd be a little more understanding of that."

He rolled me over and climbed on top of me. Sex would never be a problem for us.

The next day I wanted to talk to Shane, but since John didn't work Saturdays, I knew he'd want to go with me. Thankfully, Charlie called, and the two of them went off together. I immediately drove to the salon. I didn't know exactly what I was going to say to him, but I'd think of something.

Shane was working in the back, and he looked up when I approached. He was friendly, but our chemistry was off. Probably meeting my husband had made my marriage real to him. He said, "Macie, let's not talk any more other than work. I've accepted that you're with him. The way you looked at him last night said it all. You might not want to admit it, but you're in love with him."

He turned from me and went back to work.

During the salon remodel, my parents' hair became quite shaggy. Valley had been their hairdresser during my stint in Atlanta. While she and I were waiting for the salon to reopen, they seemed at a loss as to where to go. I told them I'd call one of the former hairdressers that I knew, but Mom refused, saying she didn't feel it was right to use them only one time. Finally, both looking rather scruffy, she made an appointment at a local salon known for walk-in business only. I knew they shouldn't patronize the place, but I couldn't convince her. I told her I'd cut their hair at their house or at John's, but she just thought that was beneath her—leaning over the sink and not having a proper barber chair.

John and I were in the car returning from Christmas shopping when Mom called.

"Macie, you won't believe what happened. Marty and I had hair appointments at the same time. My girl took me back first and was in the process of blow-drying my hair when I heard your father yell, 'Son of a bitch,' at the top of his lungs. Startled, my girl hit me in the head with the dryer. I jumped up from my chair and ran to Marty. I expected him to be bleeding, his ear half cut off. When I got to him, he was standing, rubbing his eyebrow, and using the *f* word. Seeing me, he said, 'Pay these fucking people, and let's get the hell out of here.'"

I laughed so hard that John started laughing—and he didn't even know what'd happened. I said, "Dad said the *f* word in public?"

"Macie, not only did he say it; he yelled it. *F* this and *f* that. My hands were trembling when I went to grab my purse. My girl told me to leave, just leave. I didn't even pay. My hair was still wet and looked like shit."

Barely able to talk since I was laughing so hard, I managed to say, "I told you not to go there."

She ignored the comment but said, "In the car he was so furious, he'd hardly talk. Finally, I found out that instead of trimming his eyebrows, she'd tried to pluck them."

I laughed hysterically. Dad's eyebrows, like those of most men, had become bushy with age. He had four hairs on one eye and three on the other that were more than bushy; they were like boulders—thick tree stumps sprouting from his brows. I'd always kept them maintained by clipping them with scissors. That this girl had been brave enough to wrangle them with tweezers impressed me.

Mom started to cry.

"Now, Mom, it wasn't that bad. I'm sure those people have heard the *f* word before."

"It's not that; it's my hair. It looks like a rat chewed on it. I can't go to work like this. You've got to come over here and fix it."

"OK."

Mom had never had a bad hair day in her life. Since Grande was a hairdresser, she had been raised with her own stylist just down the hall. Her hair was always perfect and didn't even misbehave during the night. She prided herself on her looks, and her hair was one of her prize possessions, along with her slender body and amazing boobs.

I looked at John. "I need you to drop me off at my parents'. They're having hair issues."

"I'll tag along."

"OK, but you've never seen my mother when she's having a meltdown."

Mom was hiding in the bathroom. She didn't want John to see her. When I entered, she said, "It's bad enough that Marty saw me this way."

I wanted to say that John had seen women at their very worst and he still desired them, but my attention was focused on her hair, which had no style. It was flat and looked like a serving bowl. I had no idea what to do with that mess of shit, but I sat her down and started to work. There were so many things I could've said, such as "If you would've let me do your hair to begin with, this never would've happened," but I honestly needed to focus on her hair, so I kept my mouth shut. When I handed her the mirror so she could look at her new do, she perked up and became her bubbly, happy self. As she freshened her makeup, I went to find my dad.

His hair was even worse, uneven and chopped to hell. My only option was to try to straighten what was left. As I worked on him in their mudroom, Mom went out to the kitchen to talk with John. He whistled when he saw her, which melted my heart. He knew just what she needed.

I ignored their chatter until I heard Mom say, "I always liked Shane and was disappointed when she broke up with him. He'd bought her a ring but hadn't given it to her yet."

John said, "Did you see the ring?"

"No, but I'm sure it was something. He was so nervous when he asked Marty for her hand. It was kind of sweet."

I looked at Dad and whispered, "I didn't know he'd bought me a ring."

Dad nodded but didn't say anything else. I told him to lean his head back. Those last six eyebrow hairs were waiting for me.

They wanted to take us out to eat since I'd saved Mom from disaster. At their favorite restaurant, John was rather quiet, but he laughed at the appropriate times. When we finally arrived back home and unloaded the car, he was so subdued that I knew he was stewing over Shane again. I took him into the bedroom and made sure he knew he was the only one for me.

CHAPTER 25

January 9 was the grand opening. I was pleased with the finished look. The place had the elegant, chic look that I'd been striving for. I had a few customers booked but was hoping for walk-ins. Valley and the other hairdressers had more clientele than me since I'd taken a sabbatical from the hair business. I was the only one who was totally starting over.

John was one of my first customers. He couldn't wait for his annoying cowlick to become unnoticeable again. When I removed his apron, he said, "I have reservations for tonight. We'll celebrate your grand opening."

"OK."

He seemed genuinely excited for me. I wasn't sure how he felt about my purchasing the salon. We'd never talked about it, probably because I'd already made the decision without asking his advice. My working at the funeral home was never brought up. He never asked me to fill in for Kelly. In fact, we hardly ever talked about his work. He'd hired two more funeral directors; therefore, he was never on call at night. He never left me alone in bed to wonder if he was backsliding into his old desires.

Closing the shop, I was pleased with the first day. In the shower as I washed off the customers' loose hairs, I couldn't help feeling optimistic that my former customers would return and give me another chance. Also, John's acceptance of my career gave another boost to my optimism, and his restaurant choice wasn't lost on me. (He'd taken me to the same one on our first date.) He wanted to start over—a new beginning for us.

Later that night as we held our wineglasses, he toasted me. "To my beautiful, successful..." He stopped, probably trying to decide what to call me. I was still his wife, but maybe he didn't feel that I was. Then he said, "Macie."

I touched my glass to his. After the meal, as we were splitting a dessert, he pulled my wedding ring from his pocket. I'd never worn my ring since the day I took it off, whereas he'd never taken his band off. I knew how much he wanted it, and I didn't want to disappoint him, so I slipped it on. It would never mean the same to me. He seemed to sense that, as he grabbed my hands, leaned across the table, and whispered, "I won't let you down this time. I'll be everything you need because you're everything I need."

I wanted to believe him. I really did.

About a week later, I stopped at the meat market. The normal parking was roped off because an addition was being built on to the strip mall. The only place to park was by a dump truck. When I came out of the store fifteen minutes later, the air was full of chaos—lots of shouting and cussing. The commotion was by my car, which was smashed underneath the truck.

The supervisor took my information and helped me retrieve everything from the glove box. I wasn't even that upset. I still had the yellow Audi, which I'd hardly driven, in the garage. I hated that Sunny was totaled, but after all the shit I'd been though, it seemed rather minor.

I needed a ride home. There were several people I could call, several people who'd come to my rescue, but I considered no one and simply called a cab. Living by myself and alone in Atlanta for six months had taught me to be self-sufficient.

When John arrived home to find me there, without my car, he immediately started with the questions. Thinking he'd be entertained, I laughed as I told him my story. To my surprise he blasted me with words of anger and hurt.

"Why didn't you call me? I would've come and picked you up."

"I didn't even think about it."

"You didn't think to call me, your husband."

I swallowed and knew to tread lightly. "You were at work."

He crossed his arms and stared in disbelief. Finally, he said, "We're not going to get past this, are we?"

I didn't know what to say because I simply didn't know.

Grande—having heard about my car and probably wanting to see for herself that I was OK—came over and stayed most of the evening. She brought Bruce with her, and I had to admit, I liked the man. His potbelly wasn't as large as I remembered. All his exercise with Grande must have been whittling him down. Later in bed, John and I gossiped about them instead of talking about us, avoiding our own problems.

After the car incident, I realized that I needed to either work on the marriage or end it. I was like a boomerang. I'd reconnect with John, mostly through sex, and then something would happen, and I'd disconnect from him. When we made love, he did and said everything right, but then I'd shower, and it was as if I washed him from me…my bond with him. I'd step out of the shower, and the truth would be there waiting for me. The ugliness of it all. The details I needed to face but wasn't sure I could.

He tried everything to regain a foothold with me, and at times, it worked. But most of the time, I couldn't stop the visions in my head. Couldn't stop the movie that continuously repeated itself. Him with Avery. Him on top of Avery. Him inside Avery.

For me to go forward, I needed to know some facts. I had questions. I wanted answers.

But could I handle the truth?

Friday night, after we settled ourselves on the couch, I said, "Tell me about Avery."

As if hit upside the head with a two-by-four, his body tensed for another ambush. He was in for a night of soul baring.

"What about her?"

"Tell me about it."

"God, Macie, I mean really. I thought we were through with this."

"I told you I had questions I wanted answered."

"That was months ago. When you never asked, I just assumed it was over. That we were good."

"I've been busy with the salon. Now I want to work on me...on us. I need to deal with your cheating and your strange fetish."

"That's all behind us."

"Maybe for you, but not for me."

He sighed. I started again. "Tell me about Avery."

"I don't want to do this."

That was it for me. I got up and started to walk out of the room. He immediately jumped up. "What will it change? Talking about it? All you need to know is that I quit doing it."

"Forget it. Just forget it."

I stormed into the bedroom, and really, I wanted to pack everything and leave, but I just grabbed a top, some blue jeans, my purse and keys. I drove to my parents' house. Thankfully, they didn't ask any questions, and I went to my old room for the night.

In the morning as Mom and Dad ate some kind of gruel, I opened the fridge for bread and eggs. As I scrambled eggs, Dad asked, "How's John?"

"He's an ass, Dad. I think I might be done with him."

Focusing on perfecting my eggs, I didn't have to witness their making eyes at each other. Neither one said another word about him.

Mom and I ended up spending all day together. Again, I wanted to tell her everything, but I simply couldn't. I knew that at one time she had been hurt that I wouldn't confide in her, but I think by that point she was actually glad I didn't ask for marital advice.

The only thing she said was, "It's so obvious you love each other, but this back and forth isn't healthy."

Back at her house, I asked if I could spend the night again. She nodded.

As we were eating supper, John texted me. "Where are you?"

I didn't answer him, so it wasn't but a few minutes later that he texted again. "When are you coming home?"

I knew I might as well end it then, or he'd bug me all night. "I'm not."

His name popped up as an incoming call. I let him leave a voice message.

"You never give me a second chance on anything. I wasn't ready for the onslaught of questions. Please come home, and let's talk. I'll answer every question you throw at me. I'll tell you everything."

I texted back. "Maybe some other time." I shut my phone off.

I probably should've gone home, but I was mad at him. And when angry, I didn't have an open mind; I only wanted to argue. The night before, I had been ready to listen—this night I wasn't. Maybe I shouldn't have sprung it on him. I should've given him fair warning that I was going to want a conversation. Our problem was that John believed our marriage… our lives…were back to normal. I didn't. That was the difference between us. That was our obstacle.

After I returned home the following evening, we regarded each other like wary animals—each expecting the other to attack at any minute. I didn't want to start drinking again, but a shot or two sure would have helped take the edge off my frazzled nerves.

The next evening, we talked politely to each other but didn't say anything of importance. Wednesday night, I went to bed early, but when he came to bed, I rolled on top of him and had sex with him. He just satisfied me like no other man ever had, and there were moments when I simply didn't want to fight my need for him. John was like a drug, an addiction that I was lost in—dependent on.

The next morning, he pinched my butt when he came into the kitchen. For John, making love meant forgiveness and reconciliation, whereas for me, at that time, it meant sex. (Probably just the opposite from most other couples.) I needed that connection with him because on every other level, I was so disconnected from him.

He pulled me to him and said, "I love you, Macie."

"I love you too."

Before I could say more, he said, "Friday night I'll grab takeout. Then we'll spend the evening talking. I actually have some questions for you as well. A few things are haunting me; I'd finally like to know the answers."

"Friday night it is, then."

Once we had a date, I felt anticipation for his answers, relief that I'd finally have them, and also fear as to what might happen with the knowledge.

Friday after work, I stopped at the bank to drop off a deposit and then went home and showered. We ate and then moved into the living room. My stomach was amazingly calm for what was about to happen. My body was telling me it was time to have it over and done with.

He started before I could even say anything. "Before I met you, I did it as often as I could. If there was a somewhat attractive woman, then I screwed her. As you know by now, there aren't very many young women who die. It's usually an accident or something. If they'd had cancer or had been extremely sick, then I wasn't at all interested. Like I've already told you, when I met you, I controlled myself. You'd come to bed cold, and it seemed to satisfy this need in me. The second time you became pregnant, I was afraid of hurting you.

"Then there was a woman. A runner. It brought it all back for me— Fiona and my dad. So...I screwed her. Once I got home and saw you in bed, I broke down. You lay there so trusting of me and with Jordan growing in your stomach. I begged you not to leave me. You misunderstood and thought I was talking about dying."

I remembered the night vividly. Mistaking his guilt for grief.

"That was the first time I really thought what I was doing was wrong."

"Why's that?"

"Because I knew how disappointed you'd be with me if you knew."

He looked at the floor as if he didn't want to talk about that part. I waited him out.

"I can't really say what it is. Something just comes over me. It doesn't happen every time, but it does happen more with younger bodies, of course. Obviously, I liked younger bodies better than older ones."

"What's the youngest woman you've ever done?"

"I'd never do anyone under eighteen."

That almost made me laugh. He had morals about it.

"Did you screw Mrs. Grover?"

"Who's Mrs. Grover?"

"The woman at the funeral where we first met."

"I don't remember her, Macie."

"She was late fifties, quite a hottie."

"Then yes, I probably did."

Maybe that explained her eyebrows. He then volunteered this tidbit: "I probably was with four, maybe five, women after we were married."

"Weren't you ever worried that one of the morticians would find you? Catch you?"

He shook his head. "If it isn't their night to be on call, they have no reason to come back. They never concern themselves with the place."

I swallowed. "Tell me about Avery." I held my breath. If he said that she was the best, or that she…well, that was just it. What could he say that wouldn't break my heart? That would satisfy me?

He ran his hands over his face. "The only thing special about Avery, the only thing memorable about her, is that she's the one you caught me with."

That answer was the one I needed to hear. She wasn't exceptional to him in any way.

"I wasn't any more attracted to her than anyone else, but I went back to her several times because she was available. You were so big and beautiful with Jordan. I know it sounds like I'm trying to excuse myself, and I guess in a way I am, but I was simply afraid of having sex with you." He swallowed. "I really loved you pregnant, Macie. But I did desire her. I won't lie about it."

"What was it like with her?"

"No different than any of the others."

"Did you kiss her?"

"No. I never did that. I undressed them and looked at them, but I never put my mouth on them anywhere. I'd enter them and have a quickie."

"I was and still am so jealous of her."

He looked shocked. "God, Macie. Why on earth would you be jealous of her?"

"Because you were with her. You laid her. You desired her when all along I was home thinking our love, our lives, were something special."

Pain shot across his face. He couldn't say that our love or our lives were special, because they certainly weren't. They were tainted by his actions, and he knew it. We sat for a moment, both trying to work through our emotions.

Finally, he said, "I need to know something. I think I already know the answer, but I need to hear it from you."

"OK."

"If you hadn't lost Jordan that night, if you would've carried him to term, would you have left me?"

I swallowed. A lie formed on my lips, but he'd told me the truth, so I answered with the truth. "Yes, I would've left. I would've left the very next day. I would've hidden so far in the Amazon that even I wouldn't have been able to find myself."

"Charlie said you were talking to Jordan on the way to the hospital. You were already planning your escape."

"I was."

His eyes filled with tears. "I would've never seen him…known him."

"No, John, you wouldn't have."

He knuckled at his eyes and asked his next question. "You said you couldn't go through another pregnancy, but is it because you don't want me to be the father of your children? That my deviance would be…could be passed on? Our children might inherit my bad seed?"

I nodded.

He said, "I don't want you to give up your dream of motherhood because of me. I'd be willing to let you use another man's sperm if you still want a child."

I shook my head. "I don't want to raise a child on my own. You say that you won't do it again, but for me, that's a gamble I'm not willing to take. Not with a child. If you did it again, if you had sex with another corpse, then I'd have to leave. Anyway, I can't lose another baby. I can't do it again."

We stared at each other, both totally worn out. I knew I'd hurt him deeply, damaged his very heart with my words, but I wouldn't have a baby with him, and I most certainly would've disappeared with Jordan had he lived.

He finally said, "Where are we now? Where does all this leave us?"

"I don't know. I need time to process everything. Honestly, I don't trust you. I'm not sure I ever will. Also, I have other issues I still can't talk about with you. I need time to deal with this before I can move on to the rest of the baggage."

That night as I lay in bed, I finally had some answers…finally knew about the other women. I wanted to make peace with his past. But the thing was, in my heart of hearts, I didn't believe that he could truly change for good. I knew if I went back to him, I'd have to settle for a way of life that appalled me. I wasn't sure I could even do that. Maybe there was a better woman out there, a woman who could turn her head and look the other way, but that woman wasn't me.

For the next few weeks, we didn't really talk to each other. Maybe we'd talked ourselves out, or perhaps we were both preparing for round two. I still wasn't sure I wanted to remain in the marriage. Maybe I was waiting for something to happen. Something to force my hand.

CHAPTER 26

After the salon had been open for two months, all the stations were full. My makeup line was doing well, and I was convinced I'd definitely made the right decision on buying the salon and moving back.

One day, I was cutting and coloring Marabeth's hair. I knew she wanted to befriend me, and honestly, I wanted to have a good relationship with my mother-in-law. We'd lost our closeness, and I harbored hard feelings toward her. She'd let her sons down—at least in my opinion she had. As she was preparing to leave, she asked if I'd meet her Saturday for brunch. She and I needed to have a sit-down. We both realized it. I wanted to hear her side of the story. Would she admit her shortcomings? Did she feel any guilt at all?

"I'd like that, Marabeth."

She sighed so loud that I realized how hard it had been for her to make the first move. I wondered if my grandpa had put her up to it or if it had been totally her idea. Grandpa desperately wanted us to get along. He'd told Mom he hated that Marabeth and I ignored each other. Avoided invitations if the other was going to be there. John, I'm sure, had noticed too, but he'd never said anything.

That evening, when I told him that I was going out with his mother, he didn't say too much. He probably was afraid for her. That I'd chew her ass out. Depending on what she said, I thought I might just do that.

Saturday morning, I swung by and picked her up. Then we went to a little tea shop that served a breakfast buffet. She and I ordered our tea and filled our plates. She seemed somewhat nervous, but after a little small talk, she relaxed. Even though I loved that place and appreciated her invitation, I didn't know how we were going to talk about the sensitive issues that were on our minds. She must've realized I was wondering about her plan, because she leaned over and whispered, "I thought we could drive to the botanical gardens afterward."

I nodded and then ate my quiche with great delight.

At the gardens I found a pretty area to park. She didn't mess around with starting the conversation. Maybe she was afraid she'd back out if she didn't jump right in.

"I've wanted to talk with you ever since you came back. I had no idea that you didn't know about John's sexual preference. He was wrong for not telling you. He should've told you. But then, I thought maybe he didn't do it anymore. Maybe he told you, and you said it was a deal breaker."

I was totally shocked. My mouth hung open as if my jaw muscles had gone soft.

Seeing my astonishment, she said, "A few months before I married Jake, he told me he had a problem. Said he was working on it, but if I couldn't accept it, then he'd totally understand. I respected him for telling me. He made me happy, and I was so in love with him that I was willing to overlook anything. I mean, they were dead. The women were dead. It wasn't as if they were meeting somewhere and having a fling."

She looked at me. I'd managed to close my mouth, but now it wouldn't open.

She said, "He thought it was a huge problem, but honestly, I never saw it that way. He and I had a great sex life; I just felt it was something he needed to do. You know, like looking at porn or something. All men have their needs, their whims, their weird sexual fantasies. I just never let it bother me. I merely looked past it. Never took it personally. In fact, I was glad his needs leaned toward necrophilia instead of paraphilia."

I couldn't speak, but my mind was whirling with things I wanted to say. The first was, "Well, fucking hurrah for you."

She took my silence as a green light to keep talking. "Jake was a good man. A gorgeous, gorgeous man...the best-looking man I'd ever seen in my life. I fell in love with him, and I fell hard."

She closed her eyes. When she opened them and looked at me, I saw the same thing in her eyes for Jake that I'm sure were once in my own for John. Total love. Total devotion. Maybe, too, I saw in hers total acceptance. That's the one I didn't have.

"Jake always thought his problem was deviant...perverted. He never wanted that for his sons. He prided himself that his sons were so healthy. Charlie had a few problems, but at the time, they were minor. He just needed a little special attention. We were such a happy family. Jake took the boys everywhere. They loved him. Loved being with him.

"When Fiona died, I never thought too much about it. I mean, I knew John had a crush on her. Puppy love or maybe something more. It's hard to tell when you're in high school. Every emotion is major. Every love is powerful. Don't get me wrong; I knew he was hurting. The night they caught their dad, I didn't know they'd seen him. I just thought John had found the casket moved and thought something had happened to the body. Years later, I learned the truth. That both witnessed their dad on top of her.

"When John came back to work at the mortuary, his dad never guessed that he had the same penchants. I suspected John had a problem. If I have guilt about anything, that's probably it. I should've told Jake what John was doing. The reason I suspected John was because he tried to cover his tracks. Jake never did. Jake knew that I knew, so he usually waited for me to help him move the body back into the casket. John was young and strong. He put the bodies back himself, but I could always tell they'd been moved."

I rubbed my temples. The damn conversation was giving me a headache.

"When a young female was called back to the coroner's for further investigation—that's when Jake first realized John was a necrophiliac. Jake

225

was so distraught. I couldn't reason with him. Couldn't get him to see it wasn't a big deal. Then when John told him that he and Charlie had seen him with Fiona, that was really the end for him. He blamed himself for both of his boys' failures—John's sexual kinkiness and Charlie's off-kilter world.

"I couldn't break through his pain, his blaming himself. He condemned himself. He left us both a note, John and me. I've never read John's. I don't even know if he still has it, but I've always kept mine. Jake knew enough about the human body to make it appear he'd suffered a heart attack. He didn't want any issue with his life-insurance money."

She took a deep breath as if worn out from all the talking. She wasn't the only one worn out. My nerves were flat out frayed. She looked at me. Wanted something from me. Some kind of comment that I understood the dynamics of her family. That her explanation was enough for me. I finally reached my hand out and touched hers.

"The thing is, Marabeth, I can't accept this kind of behavior. It's just something I feel is very wrong. Immoral. Criminal. Depraved. John told me that he's stopped. That he won't do it again. If he does, though, I'll leave, and I won't return. He knows that. I've made it crystal clear."

She nodded. I couldn't help but ask. I was afraid of her answer, but I had to know. "Have you told any of this to my grandpa?"

"I didn't, but he knows it's something bad. He was so upset with you when you left John, but I told him not to judge you. You had your reasons. He asked if John had cheated on you. I told him no, but John had broken your heart. From that point on, he's always taken your side. I never wanted you to lose the support of your family over this, Macie. I wanted you to have your grandfather's support."

For that I was eternally grateful to her. I needed and wanted my family's support and didn't want them to know about John, to think poorly of my husband—that he was a pervert. Also, I couldn't bear for them to look at me with pity. I couldn't help but think Marabeth was a better woman than me. She was so accepting. Maybe she had loved Jake more than I loved John. I simply wasn't a woman who could look the other way as John enjoyed himself at work.

I simply wasn't.

Back at the mansion, John was waiting for me. I told him it had gone well; his mom and I had settled some of our hard feelings toward each other. He looked at me with surprise.

"Mom never had hard feelings toward you."

"I felt like she did. When I left you, I felt like she blamed me for not trying harder."

"Well, you misread her, because she never felt that way. She blamed me for not being totally honest with you. I should've, you know. I should've told you, but deep down I knew that you'd run."

I didn't say anything.

"You would've, wouldn't you?"

"Yes. I wouldn't have seen you again."

"Are we good now? Do you feel like you know everything you need to know?"

That was a loaded question. I didn't know how I felt anymore. Honestly, my life had taken a path I'd never wanted to be on. Almost as if I had been tricked into this. He'd kept the truth from me, let me fall in love with him, and then wanted me to be OK with everything.

That evening I called Grandpa to let him know that Marabeth and I were good. I knew it bothered him; I didn't want him to stress about it anymore.

Once I was off the phone, John poked me and said, "How about a game of pool?"

We'd never resumed those games since I'd returned, and I didn't really want to, but I said, "OK."

In the basement we picked our favorite cue sticks. He chalked his stick and said, "Do you want to break?"

I shook my head, so he aimed, scattered the balls, and immediately entered his competitive mode, sinking ball after ball, but I couldn't get into it. Honestly, I didn't care if I hit a ball or not. I knocked a few around but never pocketed one. My thoughts weren't on pool but on Marabeth—how could she be so nonchalant about her husband's deviance?

When it was my turn again, I aimed and totally missed the cue ball, knocking the eight ball in the pocket. Hurt by my indifference, John took his cue stick, broke it over his leg, and threw it against the wall. Turning on his heel, he left the basement. His reaction shocked me, but then again, it didn't. John merely wanted our lives to return to the way they used to be. I did too, but things were different. I wasn't the same person, and he wasn't the person I'd thought he was.

I walked into the wine cellar, where I kept a bottle of bourbon, and poured myself a shot. After gulping it down, I settled myself on the couch and stuck a throw pillow under my head. I didn't even bother going to bed that night. What could I have said to him that would've made things better?

In the morning, I woke with a crick in my neck and a slightly foggy headache. The pillow was soggy, as if my mouth had dripped like a faucet. I was covered with a light blanket, and when I stood up, I noticed that he'd picked up the broken cue stick.

He was in the kitchen when I went upstairs, but I went into the bathroom and took a shower. As I entered the kitchen, he was drinking coffee. Hopefully, a couple of cups would clear my brain.

"Hi." I should have said something more, but what? When he turned to me, his desperation showed in his tired and weary blue eyes. His need broke me. I leaned over, kissed his mouth, and hugged him to me. Neither of us said anything. There was simply too much on our hearts that early in the morning.

For the next week, I couldn't quit thinking about Marabeth's confession. It rolled around in my head. I'd think of things I wished I'd asked and things I wished I'd said. I didn't need an excuse to go to Grandpa's house, but I made some bourbon balls—delightful little morsels. He and I adored those bite-size treats. Also, they gave me a pretext to see Marabeth.

Saturday midmorning, I called to make sure they'd be home. Before I was even out of my car, Grandpa skipped down the drive. I wasn't sure if he was excited to see me or the bourbon balls. Inside, Marabeth was making tea. The three of us sat down to have our little snack. Grandpa popped a bourbon ball in his mouth and closed his eyes. I did the same. The delicacies had pickled themselves into just the right liquored state— moist and rich in flavor. I ate three. Grandpa ate five; then he lost himself somewhere in his garage.

Grabbing a dishrag, I wiped up our crumbles. Marabeth remained seated and simply waited for me. I sat back down, studied my hands, and asked, "Did you ever ask your husband to quit?"

"No, Macie. I know it's hard for you to understand, but it simply didn't bother me. I really didn't have a problem with it."

"If you would've asked him to quit, would he have?"

She picked at her cuticle. "I'm not sure. I know he certainly would've tried, but I never asked him to. Also, I didn't mean to give the impression that this was a daily, or even weekly, thing. It came and went. I'm sure the urge would just hit, and since I didn't care, he simply relieved himself. It reminds me a lot of my craving for pork rinds. I don't think about them, and then I'll see a bag in the store, and I'll have to buy them…have to have them right now. That's how I imagine it was for him."

Well, shit. That was the craziest analogy I'd ever heard. I didn't even acknowledge it.

"Didn't it bother you that Fiona was so young?"

"She was dead, Macie."

I wished she'd stop saying that. She acted as if that made all the difference in the world, which I guess maybe it did, but not in my eyes.

She touched my hand. "You need to let this go. It was all in the past. John isn't Jake. John wants to do what pleases you. He'll do whatever it takes to keep you. He will. I know that for sure. He was nothing but miserable when you were gone. He won't take a chance on losing you again."

That gave me some peace of mind. It helped a lot.

As I drove back home, something kept stirring in the back of my mind, a nagging curiosity. I wanted to see what this Fiona girl had looked like. What was the appeal that had drawn the Harnon men to her?

I went to the basement and started digging through boxes. I knew John's old yearbooks were in one of them. When Marabeth moved, she'd given John and Charlie all their high-school memorabilia. I'd never gone through any of the boxes, and John didn't want to. He'd just shoved them all on shelves in the storage room.

I dug through four boxes before I found his senior yearbook. She was in several pictures, mainly the track ones. She wasn't beautiful by any means, but she had a cute little face. She was young, so her body hadn't matured to all it would have been, but she did have amazing legs. Runner's legs. Long and lithe.

Stuck toward the back of the annual, I found some loose pictures. One was of prom, and the others were of the couple sitting together outside. In all of these, she was perched on his lap. In one he was hugging her to him. In another she was kissing his neck, and his eyes were closed. The last one was of them looking in each other's eyes. They looked sweet together, so young and happy.

I shoved the yearbook back in the box. My new mental picture left me deflated. I'd known John had had a life before me just like I'd had a life before him. There was something to be said, though, about a person's first love. It was the one always remembered no matter how it ended. But when it ended like theirs did, well, it probably could never be competed with.

CHAPTER 27

John and I hadn't talked about the upcoming anniversary, but I knew it was on his mind the same way it was on mine. Jordan's birth and death date was Saturday. I was just glad I didn't have to work that day. I wanted to acknowledge the day in some way and wished we'd had a memorial or something—anything but this nothing that I had. I was still haunted by the fact that we'd left him at the hospital. Why it bothered me so much, I couldn't say. It just did.

Friday night I couldn't sleep. When I got up during the night to use the bathroom, I decided not to return to bed. He saw me leave the room and called for me. I walked over to him.

"I'm sorry I woke you. I can't sleep. I was going to the other room to call Grande. She's sometimes awake at this time of night."

"I'll talk with you."

"You don't need to. Go back to sleep."

"I can't sleep either. Come back to bed, Macie."

I slipped back in bed with him, my head on his chest, his arms around me—neither one of us saying what was on our hearts.

The next morning, John seemed ill at ease. He'd start to tell me something and then change his mind. I assumed he wanted to say something more about Avery, about that night, but I wanted and needed to talk about Jordan. He had never talked to me about him other than the one voice message he'd left on my phone. I'd never deleted that message and had listened to it numerous times. It comforted me. Hearing John talk about our baby was such a solace to me.

Around ten o'clock, Mom called. "Macie, I wanted you to know that your dad and I are thinking about you today. We know how much you're hurting."

"Oh, Mom. Thanks for remembering. Jordan was so tiny but so perfect."

"He was. He was beautiful. I lost my grandson that day."

After we hung up, John sat down beside me. I blurted out, "I have so much regret that we didn't do something for him. I hate that I left him at the hospital. That he was just thrown out...like his life didn't mean anything."

John did the strangest thing. He took me by the hands and pulled me to my feet.

"I'm not sitting here any longer, just moping. We're going on a little drive."

That's the last thing I wanted to do, but maybe I needed to get out of the mansion. Moping didn't suit me either. We climbed into the Ferrari. The farther we drove, the more confused I was by John. When we entered the cemetery, my heart began beating erratically. We came to an area I'd never seen before. "BabyLand" was engraved on the gate. He climbed out, came to my side of the car, opened the door, and pulled me out. Then he wrapped his arm around my shoulder and led me down a path to where the tiny tombstones were. Some had flowers. Some had stuffed animals. Finally, we stopped in front of a little grave. My eyes filled with tears as I read the stone: Jordan Emerson Harnon. At the top of the stone were two little entwined hearts. My name was etched on one; John's was on the other. At the bottom was the date. A small blue teddy bear was wedged in the grass.

Dropping to my knees, I sobbed. Big, ugly, gulping sobs. That he'd done this for our son—done this for me or himself—who knew which it was. It didn't matter. All my heartache over how I'd left things was gone. It was all gone.

I plucked up the teddy bear, rose to my feet, and turned to John. I loved him. I simply couldn't help that I loved the man. He took out his handkerchief and wiped the mess off my face from my ugly cry. Then our eyes met, and it seemed almost as if our souls were naked to each other.

"Thank you, John. Thank you."

"I wanted to tell you about this for so long but never knew how you'd feel about it. Some people think it's wrong. Way too much. But I needed this for myself. That he was here. That he existed. That we made him."

He pulled me to him, buried his face in my neck, and cried.

Back home, the strangest, lightest mood filled me. Although still sad, somehow I was unbelievably overjoyed at having this burden taken from me. A gift John would never understand. I needed to thank him, express my gratitude for this amazing thing he'd done.

"I love the stone. I love the entwined hearts, John. I couldn't have picked out anything better myself. It's so perfect. So amazingly perfect."

He confessed. "I had a small service two days later. Only your mom, Charlie, and me. I wanted you to be there, but your parents didn't think you'd be able to handle it. I honestly didn't think you could either. You didn't want to be around me, and I had to be with him. I know that's hard to understand, but I felt so god awful about everything—I had to do this last thing for him."

I nodded. Surprising enough, I wasn't upset I wasn't there that day. I'm not sure I could've handled seeing the tiny casket and knowing Jordan was in it. Knowing that Mom and Charlie had been there touched me. Poor Mom. That had to have been so hard for her.

"I wanted to wrap him in one of the little blankets, but all that wouldn't fit into the casket. Your mom told me she'd handle it. She came over, got one of the baby blankets, and then went home and reworked it. She came to the funeral home, and we wrapped him up."

He ran his hands over his face and then looked at me. "He was so perfect, wasn't he?"

"Yes," I said, "he was."

After a moment he said, "That night, I hadn't decided yet if I was going to do it again with her or not. But after everyone left the funeral home,

I decided I would. When the chime sounded in the embalming room, I'd just crawled off her. I was removing my condom and still had my pants down. I never imagined it would be you.

"When I walked out to the parking lot and saw you, I was stunned. Then, of course, you know the rest. After you left, I went back inside. She was still naked, and I needed to shower. It seemed to take forever to redress and reposition her in the casket. My hands were shaking so hard I could hardly handle things...the buttons and rearranging her hair. In the shower I debated if I should return home or what I should do. I knew I'd ruined everything but thought possibly we could work through this.

"I'd just stepped out of the shower when Charlie called. I knew...I knew it wouldn't be good. I saw how you were. How distraught you were. I considered whether or not I should go to the hospital. I knew you wouldn't want me there, but I couldn't stay away. Then..."

He broke down. I rubbed his back as he cried. Finally, he said, "I won't ever do it again. I won't. I promise."

We crossed over a wall of hurt that'd built up between us. I could breathe again.

My heart broke open. The hard shell was gone.

That night as I lay in bed, peace embraced me—something I hadn't felt in a long time. Just as I drifted off to sleep, it occurred to me—Mom had her own secret.

She'd kept Jordan a secret from me.

Monday, at the sporting-goods store, I bought the best cue stick I could find. That night when John arrived home, he did his normal routine: emptied his pockets in the mudroom; found me and kissed me; then went into the bedroom to hang up his suit coat and put his shoes in the closet.

I'd left the cue stick lying on the bed where he couldn't miss it. When he came back into the kitchen, where I was waiting patiently for his return, he didn't say a word but walked to me and buried his face in my neck.

I said, "You better hope you can beat me, or else you'll have blue balls tonight."

We ate a light meal, as both of us had one thing on our minds. We cleaned the kitchen and headed to the basement. Even though out of practice, I played for all I was worth. Whenever he missed a shot, I danced around with delight, but he wasn't about to let me win. When the game was over, he shed his clothes immediately and acted as if he wasn't sure what to do next. That maybe I wouldn't do the things I'd been willing to do in the past. I stood facing him and said, "I'm waiting for your instructions."

He didn't ask me to strip or to dance for him, which I would've done. He removed my clothes, lifted me up, and sat me on the edge of the table. He stood between my legs and grabbed a lock of my hair in each hand. I put my hands on his face.

"Please tell me we're OK, Macie."

"John, we're OK."

With that he climbed onto the table with me.

CHAPTER 28

The salon was a success. I'd like to say I wasn't at all surprised, but really, it could've gone either way. I totally enjoyed my reconnection with Valley. Being able to see her every day was such a pleasure. She was so happy with her life—so smack-dab in love with Charlie. Every time she opened her mouth, Charlie's name came out. "Charlie thinks. Charlie says. Charlie wants." I actually made fun of her.

Lucy was a different matter. She'd come in to have her hair trimmed— a ploy to check out the salon and investigate the possibility of returning. When I called to see how she was doing, I'd offhandedly mentioned to her that one of the hairdressers was moving in a couple of months. She'd asked me then about renting the booth. I had no problem with that. In fact, I liked the idea. It'd be like old times.

When she arrived, the four hairdressers who'd previously rented from her were not the least bit friendly. Even Valley gave her a rather cool welcome. I was totally shocked and disappointed. When I told John about the incident, he'd taken their side, which surprised me.

"Macie, you moved away. You weren't here to watch the place fall apart. Those women lost business, lost income, because of her poor management skills. You've always treated them well; she didn't. Charlie told me a lot of crap you don't even know about. Valley only stayed because of their friendship. If it hadn't been for that, she would've left months before."

"So you don't think I should let her rent a booth?"

"I'd let the women decide. Take it out of your hands. Anyway, you've never had trouble finding someone to rent from you."

"That's true. I guess I just want to help her out."

He was quiet for a bit. Then he said, "I've always wanted to tell you that I'm sorry I had you work for me. I just saw your talent and kind of lost my head. I shouldn't have messed up your career. I've regretted that so much."

That was one apology I'd never expected to hear from him. The "wow" that came out of my mouth must've told him that as well.

Taking his advice, I put Lucy's coming back to a vote. When I asked for a show of hands in favor of her return, I was the only person who raised one. I thought if I showed approval, others would follow, but I quickly learned there weren't any sheep in that herd. I immediately lowered my hand in fear of being bitch-slapped.

When I asked for a show of hands opposing her return, it was unanimous other than me. Women who didn't even know Lucy voted against her. The others had bad-mouthed her enough that the newcomers had already formed an opinion. Obviously, not a good one.

I almost said, "Piss on it. It's my salon." But I knew that wasn't the right attitude. Also, I wanted everyone to get along, and we all did. I hated catfights. Hated bitching and moaning. Hated backstabbing. Therefore, I put my big-girl pants on and called Lucy.

"This is hard for me to do, but I'm not going to rent the booth to you. I don't have a problem with you coming back, but honestly, the other hairdressers do. I can't have animosity in the salon."

"I expected this. I really did, Macie. It just hurts my feelings that you let them tell you what to do. You own the place. They'd accept your decision."

Actually, I agreed with her. I almost reneged and told her to come back, but I held strong. I kept John's advice in my head. A lot had gone on that I knew nothing about. As the salon owner, I needed to do the best thing for it and for the women who worked there. I stuck to my decision, and because of that, I lost a friend.

The following week, while Valley and I were eating lunch together, she said, "Don't you think Jackie's making too much of this baby shower for her sister?"

I laughed and said, "Bloody hell, yes."

For the last month, all the talk in the salon, at least from one of the hairdressers, had been about an upcoming baby shower. The last several days had been shower-preparation overload for all of us. Valley and I were both glad it would take place that weekend.

She leaned close and said, "Jackie told me last week that she felt horrible when she asked you your opinion on cupcakes over cake. She said she'd had a moment of forgetfulness…totally forgot about you losing a baby."

I tried to shrug it off. Valley and I had never really discussed my losing the baby. I was sure she would've talked to me about it if I'd wanted to, but she was leaving the decision to me. She'd never ask on her own. I'd never told her I wasn't planning on having more children. John might have told Charlie, and she could have learned it from him, but she'd never heard it from me.

I said, "I bet Jackie will be relieved when it's over."

"Won't we all." She sighed. It was that sigh that got me. Was she sighing because she'd never have a shower of her own?

"Will you and Charlie adopt?"

Her brow knotted. "Why would we do that?"

My mouth popped open. Didn't she know Charlie only shot blanks? Had he never told her? Before I could say anything, she said, "We're happy the way we are, Macie. I never wanted kids like you did. You know that. Charlie just made things easy for me."

"When did he tell you?"

"The first time we had sex. I think his parents were wrong, but then again, I totally understand why they did it." She paused. "There are things Charlie won't tell me about his childhood. He has secrets. In fact, he told me there are family secrets he won't share with me. I think at times he feels guilty. That he should be able to tell me anything." She looked at me and said, "You know what they are, don't you?"

I could hardly breathe. "I know some. But honestly, I wouldn't press him if I were you. They're in the past and over with."

"I don't pressure him about it because I don't want him lying to me. Making something up to pacify me."

I nodded. She said, "I can tell when he's lying."

Shocked, I asked, "Does he lie a lot?"

"Just sometimes, but only about stupid things. I asked him the other day if he'd bought my birthday present. He said yes, but I could tell he hadn't."

I laughed. "How could you tell?"

"He blinks, looks to the right, and blinks again. It's real subtle, but I can spot it every time. What about John?"

"He's a poor liar. He looks down at his hands. I can tell he's trying to come up with a half-truth or something."

She giggled. "They're so alike, yet different."

Boy, if she only knew.

She took another bite of her lunch. "You guys are the only couple that I like both, you and your husband. We should go on vacation together."

That night I asked John if he and Charlie could be gone at the same time. "Valley wants the four of us to vacation together."

"We could do that. Now that I'm never on call, the place can run with both of us gone."

"Do you want to go with them?"

"I'd love to, Macie. You and I haven't been somewhere together since… well, for a long time."

That was all the boost I needed to start planning a trip with Valley.

She and I found a beach where we could lie in the sun and swim in the ocean. She made the calls to locate a condo while I arranged our flights. We packed our bikinis and were gone within the month.

I couldn't remember the last time I'd laughed and had as much fun as I did with the three of them. We frolicked in the sun and swam in the ocean all day, every day. During one moment when John and I were alone in the water, he pulled me to him and said, "I'd love to move away to an island. Just the two of us, or even with Charlie and Valley."

I laughed, but actually, I would've loved to do the same thing.

The next day, John and Valley were swimming together as Charlie and I sat on the beach. He looked amazing—tan and buff. Out of the blue, he said, "I'm so glad you came back to Johnny. That you forgave him."

It took me by surprise, but I didn't know why, since Charlie and I had always been able to talk. I took the opportunity to tell him something I should've a long time ago.

"I never thanked you, Charlie, for helping me the night I had Jordan. I was an emotional mess, and you immediately took over. Thank you for doing that for me."

He reached out and patted my leg. "I'm just glad you taught me how to drive. That sure came in handy that night."

I smiled at him. "It sure did."

We watched John and Valley as they played in the ocean. She was beautiful with the sun on her red hair. Charlie must've noticed the same thing, because he said, "I love Valley. She's so pretty. Her hair. You know, I've never been with a redhead. It's red everywhere."

I laughed. "I knew that. We've been friends forever, so I've seen her naked as well."

He grinned. "Well, I really, really like that."

I couldn't help but laugh.

"I never thought I'd ever get married. You changed my life, Macie, when you became my friend."

"Oh, Charlie. You would've found your way. I was just there to push you along."

I turned to him so our faces were close. I wanted to see into his eyes as I asked him, "Does John still have sex at the funeral home?"

"Absolutely not."

I was so relieved by his answer that a puff of air blew out of my mouth. His bangs moved slightly from the force.

"Are you sure?"

"Yes. Positive."

"How would you know, Charlie?"

"I would know. I would know."

"Would you tell me if he started again?"

He blinked, looked to the right, blinked again, and said, "Yes."

His movements were very quick, but I caught them. I sighed and asked, "Do you think he's over it?" Again, I held my breath.

"I've seen no signs." He looked directly in my eyes. "He wouldn't take a chance on losing you again. I'm positive it's over. Positive."

He didn't blink or look away. My insides uncoiled. My doubts and the knot of fear were released. I then asked something I'd always wondered: "Is that why you didn't want to be a mortician when John wanted you to join him as a partner? Were you afraid you'd have the same desires?"

"Maybe. I didn't think I would, but I didn't want to gamble with what Valley and I have."

That touched me. That he loved her so much. Their life together was more important to him than anything else. Did John feel the same way? I could only hope he did.

CHAPTER 29

Life was sweet. It had been three years since I'd come back. Our marriage was solid. We loved each other—had an unbreakable connection. Both our businesses were successful. We had friends. We loved our home. We were happy.

But then life happened, as it always did.

Two funeral directors quit. One moved to Florida to be closer to aging parents. The other quit because he could. John was trying to hire their replacements, but until then, he was taking up the slack. He was on call two nights a week.

That simple thing changed everything for me.

From the outside looking in, it appeared nothing was different, and it wasn't—except for one teeny-tiny problem: I didn't trust John. I tried to, but I couldn't convince myself (he couldn't convince me either) that he wouldn't return to his old desires. He never gave me any reason to doubt him. Not one indication he'd reverted to his old ways.

When I was with him, I knew for certain I was the only one. At those times, I trusted him. I believed him. But when he was called out during the night, my trust would falter. My certainty in him walked out the door with him and left me with nothing but doubt. Nothing but suspicion and mistrust. I'd lie awake until his return, where he'd find me in a state of utter distress.

After one of his late nights, I'd be sleep deprived the next day. John would try to regain my trust. Try to convince me he wasn't doing that anymore. That it didn't even enter his head, which was bullshit. To me it was like an alcoholic working as a bartender. He only wanted to wrap his lips around the vodka bottle. John, well, he only wanted to climb aboard another stiff.

Because of my doubts in him, he no longer trusted me to stay. We were both miserable and unsure of each other. The only way I'd be totally free of those doubts was if he left the funeral business. He'd mentioned it. We'd talked about it. But it was what he knew. It was what he did. His and Charlie's livelihood.

At times, I could make myself believe there wasn't anything wrong with it. The women were dead. It wasn't as if they were wrapping their arms and legs around him. They weren't begging him—like I did—to push harder or to do it again. On the flip side, though, they had no voice to refuse, so why would he feel he was doing anything wrong? Why would he stop?

The other thing I hated to admit was the fact that John was everything to me. He satisfied me like no other man had—maybe because I loved him so much, or maybe because he was simply good at sex. He would try anything with me and knew instinctively what I needed, easily gratifying me.

So why couldn't I be everything for him? Why couldn't I satisfy all those quirky needs of his? He said I did. Why couldn't I believe him? I knew for a fact that if he reverted to his old ways, satisfied his old desires, then I'd be forced into a no-win situation.

I wouldn't be able to stay with him.

But the reality was…I couldn't live without him.

I was at the salon when I first heard about her: a beautiful young thing in her early twenties, killed instantly in a boating accident. Her body was somewhere in a funeral home. I just hoped it wasn't John's.

I obsessed about it all day. By the time I got home from the salon, I was in a state of torment. I broached the subject while we were cleaning up the kitchen.

"Are you doing the funeral for Hana Down?"

"Yes. God, that's sad, isn't it?"

I nodded but thought, "Yes, and in more ways than one."

He said, "I was thinking of a game of pool tonight."

Relief flooded me. In the past this would've been a night he would've climbed on top of me for a quickie. That he wanted to spend the evening making love was all I needed to hear.

By bedtime I'd put it all behind me. He'd changed. I had nothing to worry about. We went to sleep together, but I woke when I heard him leave the bed. I immediately sat up.

He said, "I've been called out. I'll be back shortly."

"OK. Drive careful."

I lay back down but couldn't sleep. It was his night to be on call—that fact was true. But still, I imagined the worst. It would happen that night. If he decided to regress, it would be then. I was at a pivotal moment. Standing on the edge of a cliff. I could be brave and jump off, controlling my fall, or I could be a chicken and simply stand on the ledge waiting to be knocked off by the blow that would surely come. Either John would come home and nothing would've happened, or he'd come home damp from a shower and…well, I couldn't live with that.

I dressed quickly and hurried to my car, numbing my brain for what I'd decided to do. Too much thought and I'd change my mind. As I drove, I focused on one belief: I was saving myself.

As I pulled into the parking lot, relief filled me. The hearse was gone; therefore, the corpse call was real. The fear in my stomach eased a notch. I entered the building, walked down the hall, and went immediately to the embalming room. The smell of formaldehyde filled my nostrils as the cold room surrounded me. Several bodies lay under white sheets. The first sheet I lifted covered an old man. The second, a black man.

The third was her.

I pulled the sheet down to view her in all her nakedness. Her hair was blond, but her pubic hair proved otherwise. Her tanned body was beautiful, with high, firm breasts, a small waist, and long legs. I was immediately jealous. John had embalmed her, gazed at her for several hours. I wondered how turned on he had been during the process. Earlier on the pool table, when he'd finally crawled on top of me, had he thought of her? Had he pretended I was her? That he was inside her instead of in me?

Then I saw it—the truth of my life. Even if he didn't screw her, even if he somehow controlled himself that night, there'd be other times, other opportunities, other women. Even after he hired two new funeral directors, in time, someone else would quit. I needed to accept that even if he wasn't still doing it right then, he would someday return to it. In the future, I'd be at this crossroad again. This was my life. This was my reality.

He'd be returning soon with a corpse. He'd embalm that person, and then...well...and then he would climb on top of her. She wouldn't stop him. She wouldn't care. In fact, she lay there in anticipation of him. She was ready. She was waiting. She wanted him. I could hear her beckoning him. Enticing him to have her. She knew she had something I couldn't give him and was more than happy to pleasure him the way he liked. I hated her. I hated her loveliness. I hated that she would please my husband. She thought I wouldn't find out. That it would be their secret. Well, she was wrong.

The door chime alerted me to John's arrival. Should I hide and witness what I believed might happen? No, I wouldn't be able to endure that. I stepped over to the embalming table and touched it with my finger. My hand jerked back from the marble's bitter cold. I swallowed the lump in my throat. It was either her or me; I was determined it would be me. She wasn't going to screw my husband.

Making a snap decision, I removed my clothes. My skin reacted instantly as the cold seeped into my every pore. Goose bumps covered my body. Both nipples immediately puckered hard. My lips were numb. Chilled to the bone, I lifted myself onto the embalming table. The marble was so damn cold that frostbite claimed my ass. Lying down, I draped the ice-cold sheet over me. I tried to warm myself, but that was impossible.

The icy sheet made me shiver even more. The cold soaked into my skin, numbing me.

I closed my eyes, stilled my body, deadened my mind, and waited for John.

ACKNOWLEDGMENTS

Diantha Grabinski, thanks for your friendship, your expertise, and your patience with all my questions. (The Applebee's waitstaff in Wichita are probably grateful that we've both moved.)

Thanks to my beta readers and friends: Mary Williamson, Ann Foley, Deanna Jones, Irene Dirks, Teresa Heilevang, Karen Eshelman, Cassandra Jones, and Lynette Kill. And Amber Howell (we really must meet sometime).

Debbie Gaskill: Thanks for my great website.

My husband, Robert Craig. You always tell me you aren't a reader. Well, you read this.

Any and all errors about the funeral business—applying makeup and any other duties and functions—are all mine. I have never worked in a funeral home. This book is entirely a work of fiction.

ABOUT THE AUTHOR

Linda Cookson received her dental hygiene degree from Wichita State University. She is a native Kansan residing in the beautiful Flint Hills with her husband. She is currently at work on her next psychological thriller. *The Mortician's Wife* is her debut novel.

Website: lindacooksonauthor.com

Made in the USA
Lexington, KY
07 November 2017